yearning, Butler captures the high...
boom' *Time Out*

'Debut coming-of-age novels are nothing new, but ones that
freshen the genre are. John Butler's *The Tenderloin*, about three
young Dublin twenty-somethings who head to San Francisco
during the dotcom explosion of 1995, updates a familiar story
without sacrificing those things we've come to expect – sexual
exploration and identity, loneliness, the ambiguities of adulthood.' *Independent*

'*The Tenderloin* is well-written and drops all the right cultural
references. Butler captures the flamboyant optimism of the
times.' *Sunday Herald*

'A bracingly honest, entertaining and sharply well-observed
coming of age story . . . *The Tenderloin* is a story which could
only have been written now, but whose themes, the loss of
innocence, the difficulties of embarking on adult life, are uni-
versal.' *Sunday Independent*

'San Francisco is the setting for this endearing, episodic coming-
of-age tale . . . John Butler has a terrific, eavesdropper's ear for
dialogue . . . but it's Butler's sketches of the city and its residents – from the Deadheads to the dealers to the blow-dried
MBA types – that is at the heart of this funny and unexpectedly
moving novel's appeal' *Daily Mail*

'John Butler's *The Tenderloin* is a charming and funny coming-
of-age story set against the backdrop of the dot.com bubble in
1990s San Francisco . . . Butler has an easy-going prose style
that brings warmth the tale' *Big Issue*

'Butler writes comedy well and there are plenty of laugh-out-loud passages.' *Sunday Times*

'John Butler's sharply written novel captures the excitement and madness of the city in its most recent heyday . . . There is punchy dialogue, clear description, humorous asides and a few well-appointed moments of lyricism . . . I read *The Tenderloin* over one weekend and was absorbed and entertained throughout – excited even. There's plenty of room on the shelf for his second novel which I'm already anticipating.' *Dubliner*

'A large-hearted innocents-abroad romp' *Guardian*

'I read this book over a weekend and was captivated by the lyricism and laughter of John Butler's wry prose. This book is sharp, intelligent and funny. Excruciating moments of early adulthood are rendered triumphant by a narrator whose heart longs to be opened to a world of love and purpose, and to the truth of sexual identity. But with the final chapter comes a revelation – brave and affecting – one that left me reeling and haunted by the sad inadequacy that can inhabit us all.'
Sarah Winman, author of *When God Was a Rabbit*

'It all came rushing back, reading John Butler's *The Tenderloin*: the awkwardness, the uncertainty, the nervousness of being that age: the age when they tell you you've got the world at your feet, but all you know how to do is to trip over it. Funny, sharp-eyed and deeply atmospheric, this is a novel which plunges the reader fully into a time, a place and a wonderfully conflicted inner life.' **Belinda McKeon, author of *Solace***

'*The Tenderloin* bleeds its raw honesty onto every page – it is a truly felt and moving book – but also it's terrifically paced and extremely sharp-witted. The author has a talent that's fresh, zingy, and original.' **Kevin Barry, author of *City of Bohane***

THE TENDERLOIN

John Butler directed the award-winning
TV sketch show *Your Bad Self*, and his writing has
been published in the *Irish Times*, the *Dublin Review*,
NPR and the *San Francisco Chronicle*.

JOHN BUTLER

THE TENDERLOIN

PICADOR

First published 2011 in paperback by Picador

This edition published 2012 by Picador
an imprint of Pan Macmillan, a division of Macmillan Publishers Limited
Pan Macmillan, 20 New Wharf Road, London N1 9RR
Basingstoke and Oxford
Associated companies throughout the world
www.panmacmillan.com

ISBN 978-0-330-51989-2

3 5 7 9 8 6 4 2

A CIP catalogue record for this book is available from
the British Library.

Printed and bound by CPI Group (UK) Ltd, Croydon, CR0 4YY

Visit **www.picador.com** to read more about all our books
and to buy them. You will also find features, author interviews and
news of any author events, and you can sign up for e-newsletters
so that you're always first to hear about our new releases.

FOR RICKY

THE TENDERLOIN

DECEMBER 1995

When I woke up in the trunk of Sam Couples' latest Land Rover the damn thing was already moving, presumably being driven by the man himself. Using the corner of a picnic blanket I wiped encrusted spit from my chin and cheek. At least the cops on a stakeout have the electro-prod of coffee and donuts, and guns to tool around with, and a good many of them are sober too. I am no cop, nor have I ever been. Earlier, at a celebratory barbecue in a technology start-up based at the foot of Telegraph Hill, the CEO, CFO and COO flipped meat for the minions and announced the news of our imminent IPO on the NASDAQ – you could not move in this town for acronyms. The cute inversion of hierarchy represented by bosses flipping burgers for their employees was more than a gesture for our benefit. In San Francisco, the meek were about to inherit the earth.

How long had I been sleeping? Just then an electric gate opened and a car window buzzed back up. Ahh. Not long at all. We were just leaving the underground parking

structure and now, finally, were on our way. At the beginning of the year, thanks to the man whose languid brown
eyes could now be glimpsed in the rear-view and whose
tanned right hand allowed the wheel to pass through it in
a smooth and frictionless action, I had joined a team of
desk-builders for minimum wage and had been induced
to do so with a hypothetical bundle of stock – were we
ever to go public. And even though I was just the runner,
assembler of flat-pack furniture, fetcher of latte, sceptic,
Luddite and rube, I too had been swept along in the gold
rush. ForwardSlash was now 'bleeding edge', staff numbers quickly swelling from twenty when I joined to four
hundred and still counting; HTML coders, designers and
ad sales men boarding our ship at a rate of fifty a week,
and now that we had gone public, our ship had come in.
Everyone's ship had come in, it seemed. The harbour was
jammed.

The party had all the signifiers of vigour and success
that you could have imagined: spirited foosball tourna-
ments between ad sales men in chinos and twenty-
one-year-old HTML waifs from France, blonde sales reps
in corporate-slutty miniskirts, woollen tights and brogue-
ish shoes, Pakistani Unix guys wearing ForwardSlash
baseball caps, drinking Odwalla and plunging chips into
salsa. I had chosen Sam to serve me because it had been
quite some time since I had seen him on account of one
thing and another, and we needed to talk. Standing outside in line for my burger I clocked a ForwardSlash apron
cinched around his waist. If a company's success could be

measured by the sheer breadth of their merchandising reach, with our aprons, Nerf balls and java jackets we were crushing them on this one. As I focused on the flames licking around the grate, Sam flipped a patty then saw it was for me.

— There he is! Where have you been hiding?

He held a burger out towards me with a warm, languorous smile that said, 'Chill, brother. There's no hierarchy in the end, because there's no need – we have enough for everyone.'

Right. I let him keep holding onto the sandwich while with one eye closed for accuracy I streaked mustard across the patty. Then, with the burger in both hands, I bowed deeply and backed away from him like a Japanese dignitary with a trophy, a priest with a host.

Back indoors, leaning against an I-beam on the edge of the studio floor and watching as all around me cheeks flushed with alcohol, happiness and wealth, I was an auditor, able to see it for what it was and no more than that. They say money makes money, and apparently in a while our stock could split and without doing anything to earn it we would be rendered richer once again, and everyone appeared to believe this meant we were governed by free will. But that was nonsense. In the space of a year I had contrived to lose everything I held dear, and money couldn't help me now. As euphoria spread across these faces, this city and the country itself, the wheat in my stomach fermented, and I felt ill. Money couldn't get near the heart of the matter. Sam joined me, digging his arm into the cold icy depths of a bucket, his sleeve rolled up beyond the elbow like a farmhand's.

— Hey, why the long face?

Right at that moment Hardy Townsend jumped onto a desk, holding the largest bottle of champagne I had ever seen, it too emblazoned with our company logo. Man, those branders didn't miss a trick. I welcomed the interruption because even if I could have spoken it was clearly far too late for talking. Sam didn't have a clue.

— Can I have your attention? Ladies and Gentlemen!! Before we get into this whole deal, some housekeeping.

Sam stopped digging, produced four beers, and whispered as he carried them away, his eyes on Hardy:

— Remember we have options, Evan. We all have options.

Easy for him to say.

Our pressed, silky-fringed CEO held his arms out, begging for calm. He really liked to speak in public and every time he did so, it reminded me of *Lord of the Flies* and of tyrannical, youth-led regimes from history.

— Okay, listen up everybody!! Dina, do we not have a mic? We don't? That's ridiculous. We need mics. I mean this is like a proper thing, so yeah, totally. Mics. Can you get on that? Okay. EVERYBODY!!!! Before I get started, if you see some guys in black suits around the building later, do not be alarmed. The President of the United States might be joining us for a drink. Yes, you heard me. Bill Clinton's coming on over to congratulate us. Or Al Gore at least. So, ignore the Secret Service. And simmer down!

Attempt to be cool! I do not want a feeding frenzy around
the President. Now, what else am I saying? Yes. As 1995
draws to a close, tonight is a celebration of us ooh . . .
how shall I put it . . . nailing the *hell* out of our targets.
So take a bow!

Over the course of a year, we had worked ourselves
into the ground, weeknights, weekend mornings and
national holidays, and many now actually bowing before
him had experienced first hand the volcanic temper of the
thirty-three-year-old wunderkind standing above. Now
though, emboldened by alcohol, the crowd was raucous,
and its interaction with Hardy telling. Someone tried to
interpret his perch high above us as a position of weakness and heckled from behind a hand, but either he didn't
hear, or managed to ignore it.

— Lemme bust out some facts here, peeps. Forward-
Slash has only been in *existence* for eighteen months and
today we have four hundred employees and a publicly
listed company. So yeah. Do the math! What a trip. And
I wanna thank you all, from the lowest of the low, the
people working in . . . I dunno, like, the mail room . . .
to the journalists, reviewers, coders, sales and marketing
people, research, TV and so on. Whatever. I promise I'll
stop talking soon and we can get back to the business of
partying!

A twerp whooped. Hardy dipped his head, steepled his
hands and pretended to think.

— We are in the future business. We look forward – it's
what we do, what we're paid for. But sometimes, in this

race into the future, people forget the importance of the past, and what the past can tell us. Now, as we approach 1996, I want you all to guard against complacency. An army general once said, 'There are no extraordinary men, just great challenges, which ordinary men out of necessity are forced to meet.' Okay, I'll 'fess up, that was my great granddaddy! But he was right goddamnit. And I can think of some competitors that might have benefited from cracking a history book. You know what I'm sayin'?

Hardy's feet were planted either side of an Apple, and lightly, he tapped it with a foot. The monitor rattled, to guffaws from the assembled. But the joke wasn't that funny. This was the pleased laughter of those who were delighted to get it, whatever 'it' was. Everyone here knew that Apple was being crushed mercilessly by Intel and Microsoft, consigned to the history books, an also-ran with so many similar versions of itself competing with other versions of itself that no one knew what it was any more, apart from slightly rubbish. PCs were the future and even I got the joke, but couldn't find it in myself to laugh because I felt sorry for that machine trembling on the wooden block beneath Hardy's stance, its disk drive a mouth agape and hopeless, its powered-down monitor a blank, defeated face. He might as well have been standing over me.

Hardy flashed a vulpine smile.

— Take this computer. Remember it. Remember where we are now. Because in what? Five years? In five years, using a machine like this will seem as ridiculous as Elliott wiring up a 'Speak and Spell' to get E.T. home. In ten years, this technology will be handheld. In twenty years . . . well, who knows? Forget about looking forward for a minute, forget Microsoft and Netscape and all the big kahunas, and think about what happened in the past. Even as it sinks, Apple's story is the most compelling, because we learn much more from failure than we do from success.

I slipped away towards the basement, and as I went down woozily, Hardy's voice echoed around the stairwell, at every step validating my decision to leave all this nonsense behind me. Enough already. How could technology set you free? You could see how it held the power to make you rich, certainly, but that was just money. How exactly would it set you free? How was that going to happen?

Back in the Land Rover, the initial panic subsided and I concentrated on being perfectly still and quiet. The way we were now roaring up then braking and plunging back down hills, we were clearly nearing the peak of Pacific Heights. Soon we'd be out on Lake Street and from there it was a straight shot to Seal Rock Drive, where rudimentary online research had told me Sam lived. The buzz of an epic hangover was beginning to sound in the back of my head. Breaking into someone else's car and waiting for them to drive home wasn't close to my kind of style. To be honest, I was only doing it because it was something Milo would've done. In January he and I came all the way over to this new city together and before that we went all the way back, but now that was over too and it was time for me to step up to the plate and behave like those I admired, instead of living my life through them. And I had to congratulate myself on the plan so far, because it seemed to be working pretty well. Hiding in someone's trunk was exactly the kind of wild and self-determining thing other people did.

We made a hard right and in my mind's map I put us on Divisadero and Broadway. A real intersection, that, the road dropping down from it into a distant speck, then rising again on the far side of the Fillmore valley, like its own true reflection. The faraway hills always shimmer here, unless they are dusted with fog, which only makes you sicker with desire for them. This is a city of beautiful reflections, one that infinitely mirrors itself from one peak all the way across to another, bouncing the same image across valleys and calling it another place entirely. Look over there. See? Maybe it's different over there, one single hill away! Maybe if you went over there everything would work out fine.

In the end though, all the hope could do was drive you mad. I put my head back on the picnic blanket and allowed myself to drift off. Life is a stakeout. Be on guard all you like, but at some point, you're going to fall asleep on the job. Close your eyes for what feels like a matter of seconds and within that brief moment you'll miss the vital event entirely, or come to and realize that you've been ambling across some dreamscape for the last couple of hours while the shit went down in the real world. And when you wake up you'll find yourself cast in a mould that is quite unbreakable.

JANUARY 1995

After the twelfth bing of the overhead bell and the twentieth sad-eyed rattle of ice in a triumvirate of plastic glasses, the air hostess with the beehive hair and flesh-coloured tights finally caved in and brought over an armful of tiny plastic bottles.

— You won't be happy 'til you've cleaned us out. Right?

— Yer darn tootin', nurse. Drop 'em there.

Milo smacked the seat-back table and smiled at her, then parcelled bottles out to me in the middle and Pauric on my left. He was wearing rings on both his thumbs and most fingers and always smelled of coconut bronzing oil, which he faithfully applied every day just in case it was sunny.

Milo's Mum had been an air hostess – Tom Moreland had met her on the Boston–Dublin flight when he was forty, and she a slip of a thing at twenty. Barely legal, that. We'd already devastated the complimentary champagne presented to us upon boarding and yet they kept acceding to the refill requests. Maybe Sheila Moreland had made a phone call on our behalf, or maybe this was transatlantic flying for you – I couldn't tell, it was my first time. An old man to Milo's right with a cruel, disappointed face was pretending to study a map of the California Redwoods, but had been earwigging all along, his wife tssking at our profanities over on the far side of the aisle. Now he pursed his lips in disapproval. Taking my bottles, I smiled over apologetically, but I wasn't remotely sorry. Who didn't want to get loaded on planes?

We broke the seals and poured. Milo opened a bottle of pills, took three then passed them over.

— Not exactly sure what they are, but if I know the old dear, they'll do the job.

When I shook my head he nodded at Pauric, like it was popcorn at the cinema. Pauric gave the label a cursory glance and ate one. He already lived in San Fran, had been home for Christmas, and was letting us sleep on his floor until we got sorted. He passed them back with a rattle.

— It's a ten-hour flight . . .

— You don't take Valium or whatever it is because you're bored, Pauric.

— I beg your pardon.

Milo was already nodding off, a hardback copy of *The Ginger Man* in his left hand, and in his right *Physical Graffiti* spun around a Discman. Leaving this scene behind I wandered down the aisle in stocking feet, and once wedged in the spare window seat way at the back in the smoking section, it became clear why it had been empty in the first place. Still, nothing much was going on up at Row 26, nor would be for a few hours. We were screaming across the Labrador Sea, enormous ice floes sitting on the blue water a mile below, white dandruff flecks on the shoulder of the planet.

The previous night had been a going-away party at Milo's house. Fifty years prior it would have been a wake, but now we were leaving not because we had to but because we kind of felt like it. He spent a summer in Santa Cruz the year before, and boy did you know it when you met him on a rainy day in February, scratching his jaw in his Chili Peppers T-shirt, the sleet whipping around. He'd greet you with this faraway look, John from the Book of Revelations, the one given a glimpse of heaven the better to understand hell, or Ireland.

— Wouldn't you love to be in Santa Cruz right about now, drinking a little whiskey and chewing on some LSD?

He knew I had never been there and I loved how he allowed me to forget that. In return I would agree with him. I mean, if you wanted to call him on the absurdity of what he was saying, most of the time he'd join you in laughing. He didn't take himself entirely seriously, but you didn't get the sense that he knew exactly what it was about himself that he was supposed to be finding funny.

I had a vague notion about finding work in television and knew for sure that America had more than two TV channels. That was as far as my planning went, but Milo's parents really despaired of him – his dad in particular.

— I mean, 'Theology'! Christ. What the hell is he going to do with a degree like that?

The way Tom said it to me at the party, it was as if I was older and in some way responsible, and not one year younger than his son. But some of us just aren't wired for self-preservation. Milo liked to think he was cursed with bad luck, whatever that is, but the truth was less romantic. In the course of the average day, Tom's son made about a hundred decisions that were either wrong, mostly wrong or just a fraction off being completely right, and it was for this reason that matters stacked up and occasionally he lost a shoe, got chased by slavering dogs or found himself having to steal his train ticket. It was pure cause and effect and had nothing at all to do with luck, but it was so much easier and more romantic to imagine that one was cursed by some invisible juju rather than accept you were lacking in smarts.

Loudly and often he cursed his luck, as on the night we were arrested for throwing wet balls of toilet paper at buses on the dual carriageway, from the flyover outside our university in Dublin. Even though (and perhaps because) it was a trivial misdemeanour by young idiots – a boozy prank – the cops brought us to the station and locked us up. For five hours we were kept in separate cells and any time a door slammed near our dank, freezing chambers, the heinous image of my impending cell-mate further germinated. I worked myself into such an advanced state of terror that after peeking through the spy hole, the guards on night duty took pity on me and let me off, hours before Milo. After, he put that down to his wretched luck. 'They've got it in for me, the total swines.' What he failed to understand was that throughout the night his continuous singing could be heard clearly, and when the guards peered into his cell you could imagine Milo wearing the pleased smirk of a man in dire need of a good lesson.

And when he was released finally in the cold dawn of the following morning and remembered he had left his jacket behind, he didn't just walk home cold and chalk it up to experience. Nah. He went back in and hounded the desk sergeant to let him have it back, and when the desk sergeant – who by now wanted Milo's head on a stick – finally snapped and told him to piss off, he didn't piss off as directed and instead went around the rear, broke into Pearse Street Garda station and nicked a police jacket, then walked home in it, along the very dual carriageway where the first incident had occurred. He didn't even take the side road.

Of course he was picked up by a squad car, and of course it was the same two guards who had arrested him the first time. And although I'm sure they had a giggle at his chutzpah after they had knocked off work, back then, at the distinctly unfunny working hour of 6 a.m., Milo was arrested a second time, this time for theft of police property. Of course this got him his day in court and of course, when addressed by the judge he responded by calling him 'your highness', leading to a fine of five hundred quid.

Naturally, Milo decided to leave Ireland rather than pay it, and this was the inciting incident behind his move to America, and therefore mine. Whenever he came back he'd consider the warrant and the escalating fine unlucky too. In this he never wavered: stubbornness in the face of overwhelming evidence – to be pure, all faith must be irrational.

The Morelands prayed devoutly for Milo, but clearly their religion returned little to them in the way of comfort. They should have been asking Róisín to keep an eye on him, because Milo's girlfriend was the most mature of us by some distance, but she was being left behind in Dublin. At the party, Tom watched her drifting into the living room. Róisín was a quick study, tall and willowy with long brown hair cut short into a fringe, and a cool detached air. She was almost fluent in French, rolled her own cigarettes, and had this slightly unnerving tendency to look at you for too long after she spoke, and the only way to get her to look elsewhere was to stare back, and that took longer than was comfortable, and could cause her to ask you what was wrong. Róisín could often be seen cycling around Dublin with a basket of flowers on her bike and I always thought of her when I heard 'Suzanne' by Leonard Cohen. I could see her subsisting on tea and oranges that came all the way from China – no bother.

She saw us and glided over, kissing Tom on the cheek, rubbing his shoulder then allowing her hand to glide down the arm of his shirt, her hand brushing absently against the raised veins on the back of his. She threw me a wan, jaded glance.

— What are you doing in here with the 'grown-ups'?

Tom threw an arm around me and gave me a manly whack.

— I've known this fine young man since he was a child.

— That's not what I meant.

— I'm trying to tell Milo's dad that his baby is going to be okay in San Francisco.

— Milo knows how to take care of himself, Tom. Take it from me.

Róisín raised a bottle of beer to her lips, slender fingers gripping it by the neck. Tom's eyes flickered to her low-cut Breton T-shirt and he coughed throatily, then Sheila Moreland appeared by her husband's side and flashed Róisín a set of teeth.

Much to his embarrassment, since we had been kids all of Milo's school friends fancied his mum – most of them chatting giddily about her in the dressing rooms, in the joking manner of boys who possibly just missed being breastfed, but some – the more developed ones – with impressively focused lust. Sheila knew all about the power she wielded over boys and men and she worked it. At school rugby games she spread out a leopard skin rug on the pitch side and when she patted it to the priests standing beside her, they would hunker down awkwardly just clear of the fabric, lest the decadent pattern contaminate them through the arse.

— Róisín, would you run inside like a good girl and get everyone in here to eat something? If you're planning to go to a disco then those kids are going to need a little . . . soakage.

Sheila linked her husband's arm and drew him into her. A kind of pressure hung in the air, then we watched Róisín walk out to the other room. Sheila must have loved how the addled priests sat on the grass, and in this respect she wasn't unlike Róisín. Maybe that's why Milo liked Róisín. Maybe that's why Sheila and Róisín didn't get along. The door burst open and the rest of the party piled in noisily – Milo up front. Sheila's eyes misted and she began to cry. As far as she was concerned, her boy was away on the famine ship. The way he attacked the food, you might have thought so too.

Hours later, climbing the stairs to the bathroom I saw Róisín filing a nail and trying to yawn a question to Milo, which technically is a very difficult thing to do.

— How *did* you put it?

— I never said 'you can't come'. I totally asked you to come. Remember?

— And you really meant that.

— What do you want me to say, and how do you want me to say it?

— I want you to say what you said, but I want you to mean it.

— I wouldn't have said it in the first place if I didn't mean it!

Linguistic trickery and jumping around, ambiguity, talking about feelings. This, for Milo, was special torture. I decided to give him a break and bounded up the last few steps, whistling. Róisín looked at Milo and then me.

— What are you doing up here?

— Downstairs was full. Sorry. I'll be out of your way in a second.

— Don't bother. We're done. Taking a piss.

Milo pushed by me into the toilet then slammed and locked the door, and immediately, Róisín linked my arm and dragged me into a room that I happened to know was Tom and Sheila's. Inside, two single beds were separated by a communal nightstand. Róisín saw me appraising the sleeping arrangements, and smiled.

— Been like that for years now. Poor Tom's at his wits' end.

She slammed the door with her foot, pushed me up against it and kissed me hard on the lips. Our teeth knocked off each other.

— Róisín, I'm not entirely comfortable here. With this.

— It's cool. Milo's still in the toilet.

She took my hand off the doorknob and we kissed once more but that wasn't what I had meant at all. As our tongues worked in neat, flickering circles, my gaze drifted to the beds, pondering the mystery of adult life. How did she know how Tom felt – had he spoken to her about it? Had Mr Moreland in fact slept with her? The image of Tom having sex with both Róisín and his wife at the same time wandered into my head and I tried to imagine the division of labour, Sheila lying on her back beside Róisín,

as Tom lay on top of them both? No, Tom lying on top
of Róisín, while Sheila did . . . something else, but what?
Something with Róisín? Something with Róisín and Tom?
Nothing? Over in a school friend's house I had seen a
worn-out VHS tape called 'Swedish Erotica' a few times,
but clearly I hadn't been concentrating.

After a few minutes Róisín discontinued kissing me,
went over to the panelled mirror on Milo's mother's side
and fixed her make-up. Clearly I had been supposed to
do something and once more had failed to do it. I sat on
Tom's bed and waited for her move, more virginal than
ever. This wasn't the first time I had tried and failed to get
that monkey off my back, and the monkey was growing
ever larger. My persistent virginity was becoming the dom-
inant story of my life and the main reason for the move
away – California girls would sort it out.

The bathroom door opened and we listened to Milo's
descending footfall, then Róisín left me with instructions
to wait a few minutes before rejoining the party. Was I
supposed to tell Milo what had happened with me and
her or not? She never asked me to keep it a secret. Maybe
it was nothing. What did she want me to do? And how
did she know so clearly what it was that she wanted? So
much information simply did not appear to be available
to me. In Sheila Moreland's three-panelled mirror I caught
my reflection sitting on Tom's single bed, found that sight
reflected in the other two panels, and then the four of us
stood up and left.

It was still night through the porthole and the plane had continued howling while I slept. I rolled my neck to release some of the stiffness, lit another cigarette, then saw the old man who had been sitting beside Milo being escorted down the far aisle towards the back of the plane by two hostesses, one of whom was holding a hand towel to his nose, stuffed with ice cubes. Blood stained his shirt front and his wife trailed behind, her face like thunder. Once they had gathered out of view in the galley area beside me, I slipped out of my smoking seat and went back up to Row 26. Milo and Pauric were fast asleep, but to Milo's right, the man's drink had clearly been spilled and his seat-back tray was streaked with a tiny trail of blood splashes. I looked around to see if anyone could tell me what had happened but like Pauric and Milo, the rest of the passengers sprawled under the dim lights were so far under it was hard to believe they had ever been awake. It was hard to believe they were alive. Walking back to the smoking section, the scene in the cabin was one of pure devastation, as if someone had tiptoed through the aftermath of a battle scene putting complimentary eye-masks on the dead.

The wounded man, his wife, some hostesses and another passenger (presumably a doctor) were now right beside my seat at the back. They had sourced a pack of frozen peas, but how? First class? What a perk it would be to order a side of peas with dinner.

— Excuse me. Is everything okay? What happened?

The wife was still shaking a little as she looked up and recognized me.

— Your friend with the book? He managed to break my husband's nose on the first day of our holiday. So thank you very much for that.

As was later explained to him, somewhere over Greenland Milo's cursed luck had caught up with him once more, as he came to with the kind of spasm you get when you dream you're falling out of the bed. His arms shot out to support himself, the dead weight of J. P. Donleavy's fiction catching the man square on the nose. Milo immediately resumed his narcotic slumber while all around, napkins were gathered to staunch the flow of blood. Now the old man was in the sick bay with a compress of peas and ice and in Row 26, Milo kept on snoring. I tried to apologize to the man and even the doctor and offered to hold something, but then I gave up, sat down and smoked, not three yards away. I had no idea why I was saying sorry, but it was perfectly in keeping with our friendship. Even though I had my own parents and family life, playing the son for a surrogate family is far more appealing, and really, I was apologizing for Tom and Sheila. When we landed, when he woke up and was told, would Milo accept the blame? No. Why? It wasn't his fault. It had nothing to do with whiskey, Valium and heavy books. It was bad luck.

My first view of the city came through the window of the shuttle bus. Sitting in the seat in front of Milo was the air hostess who had given us the Wild Turkey, the one who later tended to the man's broken nose. I left it to her to explain what had happened and when she finished Milo rounded on me like I had done something wrong.

— You knew about this?! The fuck! Why didn't you tell me?! God. I'm so embarrassed!

Now that he had an air hostess to flirt with, and no chance of meeting the old boy with the busted nose and having to apologize, Milo totally wanted to go back and 'Just make amends, somehow, you know?' The lying toad was doing a terrific job. Soon the air hostess was smiling again and he was blaming her for giving us all that booze.

— I ought to sue you, Caitlin. You're a terrible woman.

After a long stretch of freeway, which to the right offered a brief glimpse of a football stadium called Candlestick Park, we spun down an off-ramp then began running up and down hills, slowing at intersections then splashing through slick January puddles across the foot of the next block. Names were strange and exotic.

– 'Polk Street!'

Ads on the side of buses for something called Rice-a-roni and a radio station called KROQ, then I saw a guy with plaited hair in corn-rows reading *Urb* magazine. We drove through a black neighbourhood and I heard 'Mister Dobalina'. Bars were mysterious – who was in there? Two massive women in towelling tracksuits smoked the thinnest cigarettes ever, and then two gaunt old men with tracheotomies walked by chewing fat stogies, their matching oxygen tanks wheeling beside them. We shot up and down some more hills with tram lines and quaint wooden houses and then the air hostess was out.

— You live on 'Nob Hill'. Seriously?!

Milo stepped out to hold the door for her, then lifted her tiny wheelie bag from the trunk, to the amusement of our driver, who looked a lot like David Crosby. Because Pauric wouldn't leave him alone, when he got back in Milo displayed her number to us on a scrap of paper. He could be shy like that; shy, courtly and strangely chauvinistic.

I don't know how, but I knew we were getting close when we swung right at a street called Masonic which unfurled wide and twinkling. We dropped down beneath a thin strip of park and rose again to a supermarket on the far side by the name of 'Plaza Foods'. A Chinese woman jay-walked in front of the van, dragging behind her a huge bag made of deckchair material. The driver leaned on the horn, yelling out the window as we whizzed by.

— Fucking 9-iron!

The woman spat at the car and David Crosby cackled, then swung a hard right. He screeched into an empty bay and turned to face us, smoothing his handlebars with a paw.

— 1469 Fulton. Thirty bucks.

I unzipped my bum bag and parsed the money from the traveller's cheques my parents had given me, and thought of Mum's tearful smile at Dublin airport. The night before, she had told me that she loved me more than was good for her, and now her baby had gone and left her. But nobody sings songs from a mother's point of view.

The hooverish engine sound decayed into the night and for a minute we just stood there on the wet sidewalk. That damp, mossy smell and a kick drum thudding from a car nearby. A TV on commercial break through a window and two girls shouting, then a white guy in a Primus T-shirt bouncing a basketball while skateboarding down the street while checking a pager, his pants nearly around his ankles. He trundled on into the night, then Milo and I just couldn't do it any more and we hugged each other deliriously, jumping up and down.

We carried the bags up a small pathway of overgrown bushes above which three storeys of ornately painted wooden bay windows were clustered as in a fairy tale. From above an angry buzz let us in and climbing the stairs I thought of *Tales of the City* and of the drama being conducted behind these doors – all the men and women engaged in unfolding narratives: laughing, fucking, fighting, dancing, bouncing off each other and creating energy, in the performance of their lives. The night air was electric. In front of us a curtain was twitching and just about to rise.

They like to say that fog descends and shrouds but not here, no. Here it prefers to cross the road and confront you directly, or slink right around a corner, accosting you like an old school friend. Very early on, we climbed a hilly park called Buena Vista. It was hot and sunny in the foothills, the sprinklers leaking spits out the back onto my calves. We walked through drying puddles around the woodchip playground, winding our way towards the top, where furtive lonely men wandered with darting eyes and the city grid began to peek at intervals through tree trunks.

All the mornings spent down there, figuring out how to order eggs in the diner, the afternoons meandering along pathways of Golden Gate Park, watching the hypnotic sway of rollerbladers; the place was always shifting. Maybe jet-lag was still leaving prints on the windows, but I was woozy nearly all the time. In the morning wind chimes tinkled on balconies below and cats slunk around, scratching at dirty deep-pile carpets. A damp pine-y smell flowed along the breeze, holding in it salt from the ocean. Luminous plastic lizards clung to our bathtub on rubber suckers. When we went out, it was to the humming, vivid bazaar of Upper Haight, where young ravers floated in and out of clothing stores, their corduroy flares flapping dirtily. Buses rattled past, wired from overhead, second-hand clothes stores were cavernous and taquerias festooned with garish religious iconography, police cruisers rolling up and down.

Noc Noc, Kooky Ricard's, Don's Different Ducks: during the night there were the luridly named bars of the Lower Haight, and throughout it all I could feel my consciousness opening to its widest aperture, greedily sucking in the gaudy exotica. But it was making me sick. It seemed nothing was on the level here, all perception skewed and off-kilter. You were either above or below the thing you perceived, or else it was dead ahead but set at an angle; the falling rows of multicoloured houses drawn straight from the pages of a children's horror story, the streets you could nearly lean against, rising diagonal and vertiginous, buses wheezing up them like a climber with a rope. Sometimes you'd scale a hill and see that the summit was the width of a single intersection, plummeting away on all sides. The town was a board game, a fairground attraction.

At the top of the park, we caught our breath on a tree stump and at last I saw the city as a carpet, on the level, flattened to a single dimension. I needed this view. But within a minute the fog appeared from over the west side of the hill, approaching like dust from a slo-mo blast, its borders sharply defined. We could only watch and count from five to one before that moving wall boldly wrapped itself around us. Now there was no more bird song, no distant engines and rumbling jets. Now there was nothing to hear but the breathing of two stunned men panting on a log and smiling dumbly at the quiet force of nature and the lack of any view in Buena Vista Park.

A twig snapped and a man with a staff and long grey beard materialized in front of us. When he saw him, Milo smiled at me as if he had arranged it for our viewing pleasure. The man nodded gravely and from beneath the filthy blanket wrapped around his shoulders produced a small painted whistle, and began to play a shrill melody, his eyes unblinking. Beyond a single tree, nothing at all was visible behind him. It felt like we were on a set with a painted grey cyc, the city now closed and hollow, and I looked at Milo to see if he was laughing but he was wide-eyed and encouraging, dying to consider this lepre-chaunish pastiche an important moment of self-expression.

The man stopped playing and put out a hand, and Milo immediately dug in his pocket and came out with a twenty-dollar note. When I didn't move or offer any money, he gave him the twenty and the bearded man bowed and passed on by, on his way somewhere else, just walking through the fog with his whistle. Milo shook his head in awe.

— Wasn't that amazing?

— Yeah, but not twenty dollars' worth.

— But the whole thing. The setting, the fog . . .

— He didn't bring the fog. You didn't have to pay anyone for that.

The pitying way in which he looked at me made me feel like a pathetic Shylock, and he the more artistic and interesting person by far. Climbing downhill behind him in silence, I couldn't think of something to say to make it feel better. I hated bearing the weight of Milo's disap-pointment, but twenty dollars was a lot of money. As abruptly as it had come, the fog now lifted, the city sounds swelled and we were restored to the present, the man with his staff and flute nowhere to be seen. And walking past the rattling buses full of commuters, I felt vindicated by the elements and hoped Milo was beginning to regret his moment of weakness.

Inside a Victorian-style diner with impossibly high ceilings, I studied the menu. In a dish on the table butter was unsalted and came in individual rectangular servings pressed between two waxy paper rectangles. Tabasco was a condiment and impossibly hot, but what were grits and sourdough and steel-cut oatmeal? What was endive?

— I'll have the 'eggs any style'. Can you spot me 'til later?

Milo dropped his menu, the restaurant door binged, and out there amidst the shuffling jetsam, the Ewoks with filthy, baggy cords and dogs on ropes, the only incongruous detail in his presentation was an antique Rolex glinting in the sun – a gift from his dad.

Heroes are whispered about long before they're encountered, and maybe that's what makes them heroic. Milo was a year ahead of me in our school, a preparatory college of side-parted boys aged 7–12, governed by priests with wire-brush eyebrows. I had seen him stalk the playground wearing desert boots and a Fred Perry with the school tie cinched around it, a mod at age eleven, neither bully nor bullied, but comfortably occupying that sweet spot of school life, respected and un-harassed. On corridors and in assemblies he had nodded at me once or twice, knowing that my parents knew his. But long before I heard his voice there was all sorts of gossip about him, particularly in connection with Father Browne.

Playground gossip. Like Chinese whispers, even at the time you know what you're hearing is more than the truth, an original truth pulled and stretched out of shape, then stood on end and shown only from a distance, all for the sake of the story. But looking beyond the nonsense of exaggeration, the whispers of the schoolyard and where they end up say a lot about the people who pass them along. It suggests what the whisperers want to be true and what they think you might believe. That's not to say there aren't liars – in school, outright lies are bought and sold all the time. And maybe that's how it was with the story of Milo and Father Browne. Maybe their story was a total lie instead of a whisper passed along. But it doesn't matter. What's more important – what's so much more revealing about the story of Milo and Father Browne – is that we had no trouble believing it, none at all.

Father Browne, liker of Jesus, lover of Latin and hopelessly devoted to the stained glass window in the school chapel. Every day at lunch time, before our class, he'd carry a bucket of soapy water from the staff room down to the chapel, stiff-armed, splashily. Inside, he'd climb a ladder kept to one side of the altar and set about cleaning the panes piece by piece, using a minute corner of an old rugby shirt wrapped over the top of his huge forefinger. And in our Latin class after, he'd break off from declension to discuss the intricacies of his favourite work of art, pacing left and right, hands folded behind his stooping back.

— Amamus . . . fenestra. Who can translate?

— We love windows, father?

— Excellent.

You didn't need much in the way of Latin to get in his good books.

Around our classroom and school in general, Milo's year – one ahead of us – was freely and often referred to by teachers as being quite beyond redemption, composed of bad pennies, rotten apples and criminals-in-waiting. Local shops had taken to barring en masse the class in question, bus conductors knew the worst of them by name and kept photos, and teachers would march down the corridor disciplining one of them by the ear, unaware that revenge was being exacted at the same time in the form of greenish spittle, looped adroitly from the bunched fingertips of their class mates onto the teachers' long black robes. There was nothing heroic about that and none of it was spoken about in hushed terms by us, because our class was just the opposite, a room of shocked, cherubic sopranos watching a prison riot.

Milo wasn't a spitter but more than held his own among them, sharing a smoke with another older kid in the bushes, or bunking off school and setting two pees on the rail tracks down by the sea and letting the wheels of the train crush them into tiny brown discs of the flattest copper. These were the trophies of a life lived on the margins and we always heard about the trouble he found himself in thanks to these transgressions; another warning, a week's suspension, the biffer. I heard someone say that at the age of eleven he didn't know how to read – not the consequence of bunking off, surely, but the cause of it – all we knew for sure was that the guy still couldn't read.

Teachers know an outsider when they see one, so who knows whether it was a charitable impulse on the part of Fr. Browne when he insisted on extra tuition for Milo, but that's just what happened. It didn't go well. Within a week, from within the classroom we could see Tom Moreland parking the Merc in the middle of the playground with a screech and charging into the building, and moments later a boy with a note was presenting himself in Browner's class, and Browner himself sweeping out of the room like Darth Vader, crimson of face and leaving in his wake a rising swell of chatter.

The whispers had it that in one of his after-class tutorials, Fr. Browne suggested that Milo receive the extra knowledge on offer from a sitting position astride his knee. Apparently Fr. Browne insisted that this was the only way to learn Latin after hours, and once upon his knee he then felt him up, and Milo responded with an elbow to the priest's ribs before bolting from the room. When Milo was permanently excused from Latin, even though it was compulsory, it only added fuel to the fire. Sometimes the truth is less important than our willingness to believe it, and this time I found it hard to dispute the collective wisdom of that single, whispering organism. We couldn't all be wrong.

Given all that, how I came to meet Milo was the strangest thing of all, because he should have avoided it – he should have run a mile. Here's the deal: Neil Bunbury was given a Black Widow by his uncle over in Leeds and brought it into school, proudly retrieving the impressively black catapult from the brown paper bag. As I mentioned, we were good boys but that doesn't mean that we weren't stupid, and though the seagull whose life we had decided to sacrifice that lunch time was a good fifty yards away from the chapel window, it was a straight line from the taut elastic band the colour of pasta to the stained glass, behind which Fr. Browne was at that exact point getting busy with the soap and the wet rugby shirt.

As the boys before me took their turn, I couldn't for the life of me understand why they were firing their ball bearings high into the air, missing by miles. But my need was greater. In a class of one hundred in a school of five, I'd have done anything for recognition, anything to escape the brutal food chain of eat or be eaten. The dumb bird was right there, and with my right eye closed and the pouch drawn back towards me it all seemed so easy, and it was, until the bird happened to jump, vacating the very space I had aimed for and allowing a fizzing silver ball bearing to pierce the air and drill straight through the beige glass bum cheek of the naked baby Jesus, mere inches from Fr. Browne's buffing forearm.

There was a moment of silence, before any of us could think to run, and in that moment no one spoke or moved or giggled. Browner could have been killed. We saw the chapel door fling open and he marched out, white with essence of hatred. From nowhere Milo appeared, snatching the catapult from my quivering hand and pushing me behind him in one move. Already I was holding back the tears, but he smiled.

— I broke the window. Okay?

Had he been watching all this? Fr. Browne was steaming towards us, and before Milo turned back to face him, we all saw his nemesis clock him and slow his charge to a walk, doubt entering his mind about exactly how to proceed. It was then that I realized gossip was all well and good, but the story about Milo and Fr. Browne had been true the first time it was whispered.

Fr. Browne stopped in front of Milo and bellowed over him, to us. He must have known.

— Which of you boys did that?

— It was me.

None of us spoke before Milo did.

— It was not you. Go about your day.

Milo held up the catapult, shaking it lightly like a maraca and even smiling a little, but Browner never even looked at him.

— Again. Which of you boys . . .

We stood our ground as Browner's gaze raked us, he trembling with rage. Then Milo held out the catapult towards the priest. You didn't have to be book smart to be clever. With this contraband he was offering Fr. Browne an escape without losing face. Fr. Browne looked at the catapult and then at Milo, then realizing he had nowhere else to go, snatched it and shook it at us.

— The owner won't EVER be getting this back. You understand?

When he was gone, Milo turned to me and pointed, with a smile, before walking off.

— Evan, right? Behave yourself now.

He went on to the senior school that summer, where I would join him one year later. In the meantime the story was whispered about by all of our year and those below us, and from my central role in it I managed to acquire a modicum of respect, and this got me high. It wasn't long after that I began smoking. Much later, when we got to know each other, Milo told that story as if I had smashed the window on purpose, and I always let him cast me as a hero. Maybe he thought I was exacting revenge on Browner for him, but he couldn't have given me all that credit, could he? It wasn't nearly true and he knew it. And you could call him generous and brave, but looking back I think he wanted the confrontation at least as much as he feared it; in fact, he might have sought it out more from the thrill of attacking a priest than the responsibility of defending me, a stranger, from him, the dreaded Browner. Was that bravery?

— What can I getcha?

Back in the diner, the wallet in the waitress's corduroy trousers was connected to her waistband by a long chain.

— Four eggs any style. Two for him, two for me.

— Okay, but what style?

I thought 'any style' was a style of egg. Ordering breakfast still bordered on traumatic and Milo was still outside, talking to a stringy, shirtless tanned man with bright green eyes, a blue bandana wrapped around lank matted brown hair and five cats restrained by a web of taut, filthy twine tied to his belt. He was unrolling a large piece of cloth, laying it on the ground, and onto the cloth began to place tiny objects. Milo was crouching over them and peering. I watched him frowning, picking a thread of tobacco from his tongue. I knew this affectation well. You only needed to do that when you smoked roll-ups and he was smoking Marlboro Mediums because you couldn't get them at home. He knocked on the window and beckoned me out. I slid out of the booth.

Outside, the skinny man offered me a small hand-carved pipe. It was the size of a box of matches and the shape of a falling drop of water, utterly smooth to the touch, a stratum of tan wood ringing smoothly across the width of it. A hole had been expertly hollowed on the top, and a pristine golden gauze screen inlaid. Unlike the man's yellow, curling toenails and his furtive glance, I had to admit that this little object was beautiful.

— It's manzanita wood. I carved it myself, up on the bus. Ten bucks.

Milo dug in his pockets which I knew were empty. The man's eyes darted to his watch.

— Hey, I'll give you that pipe for free if you smoke me out.

Milo stopped digging.

— I don't have any weed.

The man cast a furtive glance around.

— I can prolly sell you some. Follow.

He was already walking off and Milo following him. In a half-handshake half-high-five the man exchanged something with another guy, then slipped down Ashbury in the direction of a long strip of park called the Panhandle, past kids on skateboards clinging to the back of removal vans, past those selling acid and pot, a ubiquitous code whispered out the corner of their mouths.

– Buds? Doses?

Abruptly, he ducked into a sloping garage entrance beneath a front stoop. The sickly smell of waffles and maple syrup drifted downhill from Ben and Jerry's, and I remembered that once upon a time I had been hungry. Not any more. I was spinning on tiny wheels and holding onto something much bigger, my nerves jangling in a way that was not altogether unpleasant.

The man began expertly stuffing a tiny green bud into the pipe, glancing around. When he handed it over to me I held the lighter to the bud and pulled hard, and once the smoke jumped from the chamber it tasted like sweet burning basil. I could only keep it in my gob for seconds before being overcome by a fierce coughing jag. The man smiled with mossy teeth.

— This is California Kind Green Bud. You only need one hit and then you're good, man. But hacking like that gets you real high.

Milo took his hit and then the dime bag the man held out, and I gave him a twenty. He slapped me on the back to stop my coughing jag, his eyes already glassy, and within a minute I was laughing uncontrollably at the cats. Nobody told me they were so funny.

The burning sun had vanquished the fog and on the stubbly grass of the Panhandle, we were now planted in the arid California of childhood TV, bleached, hot and exciting. The man's name was Dave and he was a Dead-head, one of a tribe who followed the Grateful Dead around from show to show, who were for the most part homeless, and who had created a sub-society with its own economic forces driven by acid, T-shirts and very long guitar solos. When the band paused their never-ending tour and recharged their batteries in Marin County mansions, the local chapter of the Deadheads took to the streets of the Haight to beg and busk for tourists and borrow money, food and shelter from residents. And when the music stopped for longer, Dead Dave beat a retreat up the coast to Mendocino county, where he lived in an abandoned school bus stationed on breeze blocks deep in the woods, and collected unemployment benefit from the state. He picked a nit from one cat's fur.

— You gotta check out 'Reggae on the River', dude. You guys can stay with me on the bus. We swim and lay out, smoke a little weed. Everyone's naked . . .

— That sounds not altogether terrible, doesn't it not, Evan?

All the negatives made me snigger then laugh for what must have been an hour, and when I noticed no one else was laughing I tried to catch my breath and talk about real things. But a fatal molecule had been displaced and my saliva must have floated away because my mouth was utterly parched. The trees began a slow revolution and the cats glared, reading my mind, their hackles rising. The spiky grass blades beneath me whispered something to the sun, something about me that I couldn't quite catch, and mistrusting gravity, I searched for something to hold onto.

— I'm . . . Jesus . . .

I had never been high before. In Dublin, it was dung-like chunks of hash burnt into Rizla and tempered with a Rothman's, the commerce conducted under a dull sky. Dave produced a can of pear juice and a butterfly knife, flicked the knife open with sleight of hand and plunged it into the side of the can, then passed it over.

— The sugar will bring you down.

I'm nearly positive we did go back and eat, because an egg stain on my T-shirt kept catching my eye. We wandered back up Haight, into a vast city of music called Amoeba Records. Reared within the limits of the buyers' imagination at Golden Discs, the amount of rarities on sale here was astounding. The Frames and Paul Weller were all well and good, but among the thousands of CDs in the section marked 'experimental', I didn't recognize one artist's name. And who were Redd Kross? What was baroque pop? Did I like Silver Apples? Each CD case was locked in a plastic frame with a hole you could fit an arm through, and I looped them onto my arm, my bracelet of ephemera rattling as I continued flicking. Our new friend followed cautiously, his eyes darting around, reminding me of a stray dog. Wire and Maceo Parker, Olivia Tremor Control. All of this choice. It was thrillingly, hideously American. How would I ever tire of it?

Drunks and the blind, rapping delinquents – the Haight 7 bus was a Petri dish. A man with a parakeet on his shoulders carried a large nettle in a plant pot, and two nurses in front were holding urine samples and talking about their daughter.

— We can let her watch *Xena: Warrior Princess*. She's a positive female role model.

I tried to study the addresses in my notebook but as we rattled past the projects the thrumming rain on the roof was a lullaby. We trundled across Van Ness Avenue and I was jolted awake. Market Street was the carotid artery of this strange new city, and it was ugly down here in the muck and bullets. People begging and sleeping and arguing; so many homeless, woven so naturally into the fabric of the town. We passed the Warfield – Ice Cube was playing with Da Brat – and then the strip clubs clustered around 6th – '$tock$ and Blondes'. Over here you got off buses by the rear door but there was some trick to it that I still hadn't mastered, something to do with how you stepped down, how you pulled the doors towards you. I had been shouted at before.

— Step down, sir!

— What?

— Step down, sir.

— I have stepped down.

Then passengers began repeating the command as I yanked frantically at the doors.

— Nigger, step down!

— Step down, bitch!

Even though I still didn't know the trick, I had learned my lesson. Now, even if my stop was approaching, I waited until someone else needed to get off, then jumped off after them and walked back.

From behind a ludicrously outsize wood and leather desk, tiny Bettina Ho bade me sit. She had a bob haircut and dull flint in her eyes that told me she would kill a man and possibly already had done. Placement Pros, Student Source or Talent Tree – there were hundreds of agencies in this town, all with horribly alliterative names. To Bettina placing temps was fishing and I was being sized up as bait. She examined my typing test and CV, snorted with derision, and when she spoke it was with the hang-dog resignation of a transplanted Brummie.

— Sweetie, there are Ivy League graduates literally KILLING for the job you want.

— Literally?

I arched an eyebrow but it wasn't funny to her.

— No boss is going to want to hear about your Robert Alton essay.

— Altman. It's a mini-thesis, on Robert Altman. Five thousand words.

— I could give a shit, Kevin.

This was going great. I decided not to correct her on my name, and as she read on, chuckling at my work experience, I daydreamed about Mr Ho, the lies he told to get her into bed, the horribly over-sold reality she discovered on their honeymoon.

Hook me, Bettina, I'm an open-mouthed minnow. Sling me into the fresh waters of short-term labour on your behalf, and watch me bag a shark. Couldn't I file at Andersen Consulting, Wells Fargo or a law firm? Couldn't she employ me without rights, insurance, benefits or any kind of decent salary, to cover maternity leave, or to perform the kind of job a permanent member of staff wouldn't contemplate?

— I'll keep you on file and if anyone calls and asks for someone like you, I'll give you a buzz.

— I really want to work, Bettina. I don't need my dream job – any job will do for now.

She checked her pager. I thought only doctors and drug dealers had them.

— You know what? Let's take a view on that later. You can't type, you can't drive, your voice is too . . . for answering phones.

— Too . . . ?

— The brogue, Evan. And between you and me, law firms only really like girls or gay men.

— Isn't that discrimination?

— Positive, kiddo. That's the good kind. And as a straight white man in this town, you need to go ahead and just suck that one up. Mm-kay?

Later, I was granted a seat in reception at Channel 5

because I had a name – Bryce Brynner. An Irish girl called Siobhan that Milo and I had met in a bar this one time knew this guy who met this one other guy who used to date the sister of the head of the Channel 5 graphics department. This was not a job interview, but a flop-sweat stained the back of my shirt nonetheless. If temping was a welcome trading post on the way out west, a tour around a television company was the first glimpse of that impossibly blue Pacific Ocean. A man with long blond hair and a goatee framing chiselled Nordic features bounded down the stairs. Bryce resembled a Bee Gee (Robin) and his handshake was bone crunching.

— Let's do this thing!

He bounded back up the steps three at a time. I knew that bounding wouldn't help the wet shirt situation but not bounding would convey a lack of enthusiasm and grati-tude towards Bryce. I bounded after him.

A security pass was swiped and doors glided open noiselessly – I was inside! I was inside, and the inside of an American television company resembled the inside of . . . an insurance company. We walked by some people with jobs and desks and stopped by a glass-fronted office. Bryce took receipt of a bunch of flowers, smiling at the note.

— We had a fight. Stupid boyfriend stuff. Throw your jacket there and we'll cruise round the studio floor.

— Nah, I'm cool. I'll hold onto it.

— It's hella humid in here, like eighty-some per cent.

— I'm grand. It's the best way to carry it anyway.

— But you don't have to carry it! Just throw it on the sofa there!

— Ah yeah, totally. But it's got my wallet in it.

— Dude, there are no thieves in here!

— I know! God! Yeah. It's just, my bus transfer . . .

— We'll be on studio floors with 2K lamps. Hot as hell. You should really take it off.

— I want to wear it, Bryce.

— You can just throw it there.

Do murder victims know their attackers? Of course they do – they just don't know what the murderers are thinking immediately before they get to murdering. I removed my jacket, Bryce fired it onto a chair and bounded out and this time I walked behind him, stripped down to my altogether, drenched and enraged.

We were speeding past the news graphics room when Bryce remembered something.

— Ho. You know what? 'The six' is looking for a production assistant. Do you know Chyron 5 or like another cap-gen program?

Chyron 5 could have been a planet, a car or a progressive house DJ, but lying was definitely how to get on the ladder here. Wasn't it enshrined in the constitution?

— I do. I mean, I'm not amazing at it, but I do know it. The answer to your question is yes.

Bryce placed a palm on the drenched fabric of my back and actually jumped.

— Whoa! You're all wet! What's up with that?

Another surge of impotent rage overcame me, but

before I could attack him and smash his Bee Gee face to mush, Bryce thrust me ahead of him into the graphics room where I stood before a 'team'. Like all of his team-mates, the mouth of the head of this department had been encircled with a goatee. He pumped my hand and gave me an application to fill out and goatee-d minions offered peace signs, yo's and what's up's.

— You wanna take the Chyron test?

— Right now?

— Why not?

My scalp began to itch furiously, and fresh sweat broke across my brow.

— Well . . . Carpal Tunnel Syndrome.

I flexed my wrist and grimaced. I had read about this new computer-related illness in a discarded newspaper that morning, and was about as familiar with it as I was with Chyron 5. But it worked. The rest of the tour was forced, with plenty of glancing at clocks on his part and mute nodding on mine, and after, as Bryce watched me tramp up Battery under a freshly epic rainstorm, he knew as well as I did that we would never meet again, because to him I was charity. That tour had been the work of the Make-a-wish foundation, karmic restoration to Bryce for all the mean things he had yelled at his partner the night before.

Five blocks down, at the far end of the media gulch, the now-familiar layout of Channel 4 hove into view. Mecca had revolving doors, a palm tree in a bucket of peanut-like stones and rogue cigarette butts scattered atop. Thankfully no one inside this building knew anything about me and as I saw it, that gave me an amazing advantage. The last nineteen times I climbed these steps, a guard called 'Karl' stopped me, took my CV and assured me they would get in touch. This time the amiable Pacific Islander grabbed an envelope from behind the desk and beetled across the reception floor and through the revolving doors to meet me outside, his truncheon bouncing off muscular thighs.

He beamed and held out the envelope.

— I told you they get in touch!

A job interview? A job offer? I glanced behind me, imagining the local press gathering for the photo-op. A bum shuffled past, swiping at the air with a callused, wind-burned fist.

— I tell them all about you, and they tell me to give you that. They say, 'Give him that.'

I took the letter, ripped it open and Karl studied the face of the rain-sodden rube for clues as to the contents. All the blood drained from my face. It was not just a rejection, because I had already received one of those weeks ago. In fact, the legal term for a letter of this nature was 'cease-and-desist'. I fixed a rictus of a smile.

— Yup. It's an interview date!

There was no point in upsetting two people here. I lingered on the steps talking for a few minutes because that's what you would do had the letter contained a call to interview. Karl talked about the Oakland A's, and how his nephew may make it as a pitcher, which would mean that Karl's brother could retire, even though he was only forty-one, but all of that was little more than buzzing in my ears as I concentrated on not crying in front of the nice man.

Milo and I stood beneath a slender glassy strip perched on top of Nob Hill. Mason and California was the apex of San Francisco wealth and it took a lot to get all the way up there – unless you were in the service industry. Milo had been on three dates with the air hostess, dates which he described as 'equally terrifying and amazing'. When Caitlin heard about our penury and my almost-two-month struggle to find work, she put our names forward to a friend of a friend who was having a drinks party and needed a couple of bartenders. Milo didn't want this job, but I insisted. I very badly needed the money and didn't want to know why he didn't, but I couldn't do it on my own.

On their first date, Caitlin had hosted a dinner party in her place. All her friends were her age or older, and Milo considerably younger. One of them worked in a restaurant called 'Chez Panisse' which was supposedly a big deal. Apparently he drank all the white wine and kept on referring to Milo as a toy boy and a 'piece of tail', even after Caitlin told him to stop, so Milo pulled him aside at one point and asked him why he thought it was okay.

— And you know what he said? 'Because, sweetie, you are very, very young, and very, very handsome. Deal with it.'

Milo had affected a fairly ridiculous lisping voice, and I laughed.

On the second date, on a picnic blanket on her rooftop, Milo tried to let Caitlin know that he wasn't comfortable with the idea of being referred to – by a man! – as a toy boy, and at that exact moment she decided to introduce him to the concept of champagne blowjobs. We adjusted our borrowed ties in the elevator on the way up and Milo went over it again in detail, as he always liked to do, and in retelling the event I could scarcely believe the decadence. Apparently, just prior to ejaculating, Milo had noticed a man in an overlooking building watching them through a pair of binoculars, his spare hand concealed beneath the folds of his bathrobe.

— Just the feeling of your cock in her mouth for one thing, but then the feeling of these bubbles all around your cock, and then like the whole voyeurism-thing of this one fella watching? I swear to God, Evan, she's lucky I didn't blow her head clean off.

The elevator doors opened and the hostess met us with a smile. She winked when she shook Milo's hand, and her smile diminished only fractionally upon shaking mine.

— You're the friend? Right. Hi.

Caitlin had told her that Milo had a friend, and clearly she had gotten her hopes up, and having appraised me she was now disappointed, but it was okay. I understood. I knew I wasn't Milo, I'd known that for years. And it wasn't just his looks that separated us, it was that ineffable vibe he projected, for which I searched in vain even to name. I knew I was at best a puzzling fellow. If my growing-up days could have been defined by one word it would undoubtedly have been fear, but all of the disguising, parrying and evasion was such a success that I didn't know if I'd ever figure out what was scaring me. To be innately laid back, to feel that easy in one's skin – that was the Holy Grail, and if I couldn't feel it within myself, it was something worth approximating at least, perhaps in the hope that it could be learned, or assumed of me by those in apprehension.

The hostess was petite and bird-like, constantly fingering a string of pearls around her neck as she toured us around the penthouse. Floor-to-ceiling sliding doors separated us from a balcony with Astroturf flooring, and the most devastating view of San Francisco, across Presidio and to the wild Pacific beyond. As far as the work went, Milo and I had this one well covered. The bar was stocked with spirits, and when the guests arrived, we began slinging drinks for women in men's Ralph Lauren shirts and light blue denims, and beside them, for the most part, were tanned men with feathered, layered hair, blue blazers with gold buttons and penny loafers. Each of the men was James Spader in *Pretty in Pink*, courting their dates with this comical old-world chivalry that began to erode with booze. Here, for the first time since I landed in America, there were no tattoos and no trainers, no hair-dye or vintage clothing, and no discernible ethnicity other than white and Asian. There was no music either. I could tell that this situation made Milo tense.

— What kind of a fucken' party is this?

— A rich one.

The men were Stanford MBAs that pushed money around for Oracle, Airtouch and Robertson Stephens. The women were Art History graduates from horse-breeding families in Kentucky, direct descendants of civil war admirals. The only time I had encountered another upper class was with the Anglo-Irish aristocracy at home, and unlike this bunch, they were down-at-heel in their way, fond of horses and heroin and clothes with holes in them. They had all of the old money and none of the new; castles in the country but nothing they could use to stand a round of drinks, and at the end of the party they would disappear to their estates to recover for a week, hanging upside-down from rafters while the rest of us took the bus to the office.

Was there a gilded upper-upper class in America, safely ensconced beyond yet another secret door? I didn't think there could be. It seemed that this was about as tony as it got. Every white American sounded the same to me, and in this room there was no shabby chic and no confusingly contradictory signals about status and aspiration. People here were who they were, and had precisely what they earned. Of course there was old money, but here old money had the same value as new money, for which you worked and got paid like the rest of them. I liked the honesty of it all. This is what I had been searching for each day, tramping around the city with a dwindling sheaf of CVs, with my hunt-and-peck clumsiness flunking typing tests at temp agencies, failing to secure a job answering phones ahead of the twenty beautiful, female Ivy League graduates whose accents a client could comprehend.

A similarly impassable set of barriers had been presented with 'man's work', such as it was. With the exception of a night like this, regular bartending was about the most closed shop of all, the domain of friends of the owner – just the way I'd want it if I ran a bar. As for construction, well, the Mexicans knew where to stand for the morning pick-up, when a flatbed truck would materialize out of the mist at the building supply store on Army, in the heart of their neighbourhood, not mine, and a Mexican foreman would select the young and fit of his own caste for digging and lifting. Standing there, waiting, being selected for how they looked. I heard someone call them hardware hookers.

When it came to finding work, no one cared what you thought about the tricky modernist opening of *The Sound and the Fury* or the Punic Wars. But pouring these sea breezes alongside Milo, moving in time and ducking around each other, feeling the heft of the lowball glass snug in my palm and the coldness of ice cube diffusing through it, everything fitted briefly. I might not have been the hostess's vision of a piece of ass but I was a decent barman. For the first time in ages I was useful, my heart pumping blood because it had just cause.

A heaving scrum of people waited for drinks. You couldn't fail to notice that most of the young women were down the far end where Milo was frowning and pouring like a depiction of artists in bad films, doing his Jesus-as-a-barman thing. He was a star and as a unique selling point, his reluctant handsomeness was quite a draw. The women were throwing fives at him, and quite a few blow-dried men too, stuffing them in his waistband when they could get close enough, and loving his pained response to all the attention. Milo could open bottles with his teeth, and had done perhaps a hundred times down the years, and now he did it for someone and they actually screamed.

The man at my end of the counter was waving a twenty even though this was an open bar, but I could tell that he knew that too, if not from the smile then from when I had served him not twenty minutes before. This party had a very specific age range and I could tell that he was older than the rest of the guests by about ten years – about forty, I'd have said – with brown hair that was slightly long, but not long in the manner of someone old trying to look young; long in the manner of some men in their forties who are able to have that hair – some, but not many. His eyes were dark brown, and heavy-lidded; languid, I thought. As I approached, he presented the bill between thumbs and forefingers and smiled at the absurdity of the gesture.

— I need – and it is need – a sea breeze.

He dropped the twenty in the plastic cup.

— Nah. You didn't have to do that.

— Sure did. Truth in advertising.

I poured, watching him for a 'when' sign. We both

watched the clear spirit stream from the tapered gold neck of the Stoli bottle and I had to quit before he ever indicated, and when I did, there was a barely perceptible lift of eyebrow to make it clear that despite the immutable physics, in this particular game of chicken, he considered it my defeat. I added a desultory floe of ice and set the drink on a napkin, whereupon it splashed everywhere, and he smirked.

— Are you a real barman?

— I'm good in bars, but usually from where you're standing. What is it that you do?

He smiled, twirling the straw, and the way he confided his response in me made me laugh.

— I am an 'evangelist'. But not religious. I am an evangelist for the Net.

I had seen the Internet recently, in a café on Haight and Steiner that had a grey coin-operated computer terminal in the corner. One guy was using it to read what another guy was saying about some computer thing. And another Irish friend of a friend had it in their apartment when Milo and I called over one night, and he tried to show it to us, but it seemed he was using it to talk to a guy just like him about some computer game and I couldn't understand why he didn't just pick up the phone. But at least I knew about it.

— Do people need to be convinced that the Net exists?

— Convincing people that something exists is not evangelism. That's a matter of faith. Convincing people that it can be their salvation – that's what I get paid for.

— Okay, then. How can the Net save my life?

— Not your life – not yet anyway. Maybe in the future. But your business, totally, if you have one. The World Wide Web is going to become the tool for commerce. Right now you and I are cursed to live at a point in time where we have to stand in line and write checks. In future, we'll do shopping for clothes and food on the Web. We'll book holidays, buy and sell property, bank online. Goods and services will be bought and sold there far more than in the real world because it will be easier. We're at the gateway to the future and for that we must be grateful.

I clinked my tip jar with his cocktail and searched his eyes for a sign, but he really believed it.

— To the future.

— Beats the past.

It was ridiculous to think people would prefer to buy things online without first holding them in their hand. How could such a fundamental value be disregarded? And how would we meet people in the future? But we all had to earn a living and he had tipped me a twenty. Besides . . . the faintest trace of a lisp, his eyes. Something about him reminded me of something.

— Will we live on the Net in the future?

— Actually, for the most part, we will . . .

He smiled.

— . . . not in the way that I think you're imagining, though. There are parts of us that will always need human interaction. I'm sure you know what I mean.

He took a sip and grimaced.

— Yow. At last. A New York pour on the West Coast.

— Told you I was good in bars.

He glided away and for the briefest moment as I watched him go the rest of the room was humming and distant. When he reached the doorway and was perfectly framed by twinkling lights on the far side of the city he turned back, saw me looking over and raised his glass. A single, swirling inchoate thought crept into my mind but before I could pin it down it was chased away by another part of me. I couldn't quite grasp just what it was about this man, beyond a vague sense that he had taken something with him, something precious which had belonged to me.

The drunker they get the more they tip and it wasn't my alcohol, so I could afford to be generous. News travels fast and pretty soon all the real drinkers were gathered down my end of the bar, waiting for the stiff pours. A good four hours before it had been expected, we were out of vodka, and I was making guests try a Maker's Mark and soda, then a neat brandy, and then the hostess was at the front of the queue, wall-eyed, swaying, pressing two hundred dollars in twenties into my mitt.

— Honey, I need you to run to the store and get more booze. You won't dash off, will you?

At the counter of a café recently I saw a sign on the tip jar reading 'support counter intelligence', but even without cute entreaties the patrons had dumped at least twice that in our tip jar already, thanks to our liberal pours. I was going nowhere. She grabbed my hand and led me out from behind the bar, half-dancing, half-walking.

— This is the greatest party ever. Am I right?

She led me through the partition doors and onto the balcony outside, bare feet skipping across the floor, woozy, rich and insane, Mia Farrow in *The Great Gatsby*. She clung to my arm as we reached the railing, and we leaned over into the cool night. When I saw how high we were I stepped back and she had to pull me back to the edge, her laugh now a coy gurgle.

— You have to lean over. All the way over. Okay, see that corner down there? See the store? That is my corner store. If you go down there and ask for R.C. and tell him it's me (here she curtsied), he'll give you a couple of bags of ice for free. Then spend every damn cent of the two hundred on vodka. To hell with sodas. Do you think you can do that?

— Which vodka?

— *Cheap* vodka.

The Bay Bridge strung itself across the water. Maybe the future was all the way up here. The hostess spotted some new arrivals and tiptoed over towards them.

— Come on in! You can't tell because there's so many people here, but my place is actually really big!!

Even more than money, it is religion that gets the best real estate and the gift of altitude. Confidently straddling Nob Hill, the cathedral revealed her glory to the heathens below and reminded them immensely of the heavens above. My arms were strained from the twenty bottles of generic vodka and the four bags of ice, handles cutting across my fingers like cheese wire. I set them down and as I did I saw the Evangelist hailing a cab just at the very moment that he saw me, and wandered over, smiling drowsily.

— I thought we were done up there.

I kicked the bags at my feet.

— Not at all. Fresh supplies.

He took out a bottle, studied the label with a frown, then put it back.

— The wedding at Canaan. I'm Sam Couples.

Down the years, I liked spending time with teachers, friends of parents, bosses in my school jobs, but had yet to learn how to be sociable with them on their terms. The age difference and discomfort it caused me was still insurmountable. Without a bar between us or a drink to be poured, I couldn't gauge what natural behaviour was. How to figure it out. How to be.

— So let me guess. You're from . . . Dublin.

— You've been?

— At my age, I'm sad to confess it, but no.

— We have people your age.

— Are you sure? I'm *fifty-one*.

Again the whisper made me laugh.

— You don't look it.

— It's the lifestyle. This city.

— What's your lifestyle?

— It's a good one. Let's leave it at that.

We both glanced at the cathedral. Architecture did this – if not religion. It gave people pause and made them smaller, briefly. He looked at the road.

— How long have you been in town?

— About a month.

— You tending bar much?

— I'm embarrassed to say this, but I can't get a job.

— Never be embarrassed. Waste of time.

He fished out a business card from his back pocket and, with a slender gold pen, wrote something on the blank side. He handed it over. There it was, Sam Couples, 'Internet Evangelist'. On the other side he had scrawled the name of a woman, and the initials H.R. The woman's name was Tammy.

— What's this for?

A cab swerved to the kerb though, honestly, it seemed that he hadn't been hailing it. The definition of power, I suppose. He turned one more time, pointing at the card in my hand.

— You never know . . .

Back upstairs, the elevator doors binged open and I met Milo, holding a fistful of notes (I could tell he had left the coins for me), his arms around a young blonde girl in a pinstriped shirt with another string of pearls. She was extremely drunk. He saw the bags.

— What's all that?

— Vodka. Where are you going?

— I thought we were done.

— Nope.

— Emm, I took my half and I'm gonna split . . . we're going to split. This is Anna.

— We're not done yet.

— Evan, this isn't me. This whole deal. It's a pain in the hole.

He gestured around then shrugged and trousered the money.

— I have a problem with being indentured like this.

— Don't you mean 'working?'

He had whispered it so that Anna wouldn't hear, speaking out of the far side of his mouth. But Anna was jack-knifed forward, held up only by his arm. And who was indentured?

— I don't want to work for all these yuppies.

— You're actually using the word yuppie?

— What's wrong with 'yuppie'? See you tomorrow, yeah?

When the hostess saw that I had returned with supplies, she ran over, grabbed my arm for support, and climbed onto the bar counter, to a roar of approval.

— Attention! A round of applause for our terrific barmen. Hey, where's the other one? The hawt one . . .

She held my hand aloft and people cheered. Up on the table, looking over a sea of semi-familiar faces, I could see the lift doors closing and beyond, the spires of Grace Cathedral.

Something was pushing at my shoulder. I opened my eyes. I was in my sleeping bag on the floor of Pauric's apartment in Fulton. Milo was in his sleeping bag beside me. We'd been thus arranged for weeks but this morning, Dead Dave was huddled in a filthy white sheet on the far side. Above me, Pauric looked at Dave then me with enquiring eyes and a sad smile, before setting his foot back down.

— No.

— I know. It's bad. Apparently, he's getting parts for his bus tomorrow, then he's going back to Mendocino County.

— No.

— 'No'?

Pauric shook his head.

— No. Rory's freaking out. We need our living room back.

Pauric and his room-mate had jobs at the same company called Oracle. They car-pooled in Pauric's cobalt blue, pre-owned Honda Civic, and when they were gone during the day it was fine, but when they came home, after jogging around the Panhandle or maybe seeing a movie, they would come back to their place and want to relax and we would still be there. Pauric couldn't smoke pot because he was due to take a drug test at the company before they would make him permanent, so if we were there at night, he'd have to sit with his head out the window of his own apartment, while Milo and Dave got massively high and I worried about work.

Sometimes we'd clear out to give them space and I never minded that Dave didn't buy a drink, because I knew he couldn't. I couldn't have bought any either if my parents hadn't given me money, so I was just as much of a freeloader, in a way. To be fair Dave didn't really drink, preferring to get high on the walk between bars, which he did mostly with himself despite Milo's protestations. At the end of the night, we'd queue for pizza slices in 'Escape from New York', and in our condition it was churlish for us not to spend one extra dollar each on another slice for him, and the largesse made us feel fecklessly Irish, in a way. When we did that he'd demur at first, then take the slice shyly with a spindly hand and appear uninterested in it. And every time, Milo would take the bait. 'Dave, you have to eat. Look at you. You weigh half nothing!' But I knew that Dave was only waiting for it to cool down, and if you were surreptitious and gave him the space – perhaps going to fetch the jar of parmesan at the counter – you would catch a glimpse of him really wolfing it down, holding the crust in both hands, a woodland creature in a Jerry Garcia T-shirt. On the street afterwards, Dave would produce a vintage can of refried beans from the burlap sack of pipes he always carried around with him, and offer to cook us up a meal the next time, by way of repayment. That same can of beans, each and every time. He knew it was no offer at all and we knew it was generous, considering it was all he had.

In an English pub on the lower Haight, Californians wore Fred Perrys and called each other 'mate'. That weekend, a skinhead spun 'Ring the Alarm' at a backyard barbecue and when the dreadlocked barman came over

Milo offered him his fist, which he analysed wryly, then shrugged and did spuds with, as with a kid.

— Can I get you a drink?

— Gin and juice, homie.

— Okay, 'homie'. What kind of juice?

— Umm. I don't know.

Dave looked at Milo as if to say 'tell him now', then slid off the stool and went outside. Milo cleared his throat.

— So yeah. I'm off to the bus, man.

— No. Serious?

— As a heart attack.

— But don't you love this? The city? All of it?

— I do, but I just don't feel like I'm away. Or far enough away. All of this . . . I've already done it, man.

It took a single sweep of his hand to transform the exotica and now all I could see was raw flesh, an odd Opel soccer jersey, men who looked like Noel Gallagher and women like Tori Amos. I had thought we were intrepid, hanging off the edge of the world, but in perceiving the same skin and milk-fed features as mine, and the trainers I had only bought because I thought they were rare, I was being betrayed to the rest of the world. In that instant I saw the backyard barbecue at the Mad Dog in the Fog just as Milo did – more of the same, in another town. And I hated him for it.

— If I get into living in an apartment and paying rent, who's to say I wouldn't just freak out and split after like a month or whatever?

I pinched the bridge of my nose.

— Do what you gotta do, Milo. Just, the thing is, you need to be careful up there. Dave's great and all, but people are crazy.

— Come on, Ev. Why don't you do it for a few weeks. It'll be amazing!

— It's not for me.

— Which bit is not for you? Persistent nudity? Hanging out? Sunshine?

He looked genuinely sad I wasn't joining him. It was hard to argue with his sincerity, but I just didn't have any problem being 'indentured'. For weeks we had been held in suspended animation between childhood and adulthood. For us, there was the strange future and the distant past, and all he wanted was to live for ever within the thin sliver of transition. Not me, though. Staring up at Pauric during the week, seeing him all scrubbed and in his work clothes, and us within our sleeping bags but on his floor, and a sleeping Deadhead beside us, the penny had dropped. For me, that tramp who smelled of patchouli oil and lay foetally cocooned in a sheet with dubious stains signified the beginning of the end.

Dave was winding his way back into the bar, cat-like. I whispered quickly.

— Can I just say something? Everybody's after something. Even Dave.

— Do you mean money? Dave's not on a material trip, Evan.

— You mean he's not rich. That's not the same thing.

— Sorry, brudder. I just don't want to get tied into a situation.

— Don't do that. I'm not trying to persuade you to stay! I'm just saying be careful. You know your bad luck.

— Yeah, tell me about it!

I smiled and punched him lightly on the knee, the great pretender. And I was pretty sure he couldn't hear what I was mumbling along to the trailing verse 'police and thieves, on the street . . . '

— 'Oh no no no . . . '

MARCH 1995

Lost amidst the strutting pigeons of Union Square, the second half of the previous night's pizza was unsheathed from tinfoil and dispatched. After, I sat on my hands and looked at a billboard for a computer company, urging me to 'do stuff'. I'd been walking for hours. Lunch had barely registered going down, which, given that it was certain to be the best thing that would happen all day, was a little disappointing. It had been weeks since Milo's departure, and I didn't much feel like returning to Pauric and Rory's place and staring at their cassette collection or the *Achtung Baby* poster. Other Irish people of my acquaintance were either working, looking for work or living their lives their own way, and I didn't know any Americans.

Once, when Tom Moreland was drunk, I asked him why he liked playing golf on his own so much, and he told me that he liked feeling alone. He said that after a while, you could sink so deeply into it that it warmed you and became a kind of comfort of its own. Not me, though. I'm not an only child, but when I was thirteen my brother

died from what was first described to me as a platelet defi-
ciency, but which ended up being leukaemia in some
rampant and untreatable form. Danny was ten and my
closest sibling. I also had a sister, but Suzy was ten years
older than me and had by that point left the house for
college. My parents were considerably older than other
parents of kids my age, and if it's possible to have two
adorable mistakes in a row, me and Danny were surely
them, and Suzy the intended family. She had already left
for Edinburgh when Danny was diagnosed, and wanted
to defer for a year to come back, but she was getting on
so well that Mum and Dad insisted she keep going at her
studies.

I have some memories of life in the year after his diag-
nosis, before Danny died but after Suzy left, how Mum
and I would spend hours in waiting rooms at Harcourt
Street children's hospital while he was having some of the
bone marrow from his spine removed for examination. I
remember examining bones that the butcher gave Mum
for our dog, and prodding at that dark, spongy circle in
the middle with a Bic biro. After the operation, Danny
wasn't allowed to play football because his back was so
sore, and once, after a platelet test that must have been
really bad, I saw Dad crying over the sink. I had never
seen a grown man cry before and I left him alone – I was
far too scared. Even when they told him that they were
putting him on a course of steroids that might make his
head very large, I never once saw Danny cry. It was difficult to imagine what it must have been like to be told

that very soon your head was going to expand, but he never let it get to him – or if he did I never saw it. Either my memory has recast him as stoic or he really was that brave.

The Morelands were friends of my parents' and after Danny died they took to spending a lot of time in our house and, in due course, Milo became a friend of mine. In the years following Danny's death, while my parents were grieving, they absorbed me into their family life, even bringing me on holiday once. What these events left me with – apart from a close relationship with Milo and a pair of slightly neurotic parents that couldn't watch me play rugby – was a morbid fear of being alone. For as long as I could remember I sought out company, and didn't know how to enjoy solitude of any kind: a house at night, an empty train carriage, a walk. For Tom Moreland, marooned in aloneness, beyond the petty grievances of being present in the world, the mind settled down into itself and started to dream, of what I didn't know. When he told me that I nodded politely, but if there was a melancholy pleasure in examining the texture of being by yourself, I never felt it. To me it was always dangerous.

With the departure of Milo my daily life had begun to assume a familiar routine – the stations of the cross, but with a job as the goal and not redemption. At the end of these days I had taken to killing time in Union Square, and in the evenings I'd add sweetcorn to noodles in Pauric and Rory's kitchen, then take my food out to the front stoop, saying hi to people heading out or into other apartments in our building, some of them high-fiving me as if we weren't strangers. It would be a relief when the clock on Rory's boom box said 11 and I could get into my sleeping bag and lie there with my eyes open, waiting for another day gathering rejection letters from companies up and down Columbus Avenue, and right across North Beach.

I didn't have money I could use to entertain myself and the sun was dropping in the sky casting a warm orange glow. I wandered over to the corner of Stockton and Geary and studied the map at the bus stop. Geary to Mason, Mason to Eddy, Eddy all the way past Van Ness and then all the way home – an adventure. At the corner of Eddy and Hyde, the sun finally dipped beneath the rooftops and a man with no legs on a converted pallet with wheels emerged from a convenience store lighting a glass pipe. I began to take lefts and rights based on how the block ahead looked, and at Larkin, the corner store was run by a gimlet-eyed Vietnamese man, who narrowly avoided landing a mouthful of green spit on my toe as he watched me pass with a golden-toothed smile. On O'Farrell the women were hookers if they were women at all, pushing off walls and stepping forward into my path, black mostly, with huge bruised muscular thighs and hair extensions the colour of nicotine. Each had long, feline nails primed for the art of war and not seduction. Milo might have stopped and chatted with them, or plunged into one of the forbidding bars for a laugh, but I certainly couldn't do that.

You could get lost in a grid system after all. By a tiny park there was gold around the necks of cholos, because where there are hookers there are always dead-eyed pimps, and where there are sketchy addicts clustering around burnt foil in the needle-strewn park on the corner, there are dealers serving them. And those men were the scariest of all, because only they knew for sure that they were in no danger. Unlike me, say. To go back now would have been to walk past people who already knew that I was scared witless. The people up ahead didn't know about me yet, and I supposed that was the key. To hell with the past. I pulled the collar of my jacket around my neck and began to half-walk, half-run, muttering, with a limp for some reason. I don't think anyone was following me, but nonetheless, I outright ran the last two blocks to Van Ness, and as soon as I saw the reassuring brand of the Hard Rock Café I ducked inside.

The bartender wrapped a napkin around my Corona and jammed a slice of lime in the top before moving off to serve a couple at the far end. Thanks to this order, I would have to walk home, and improvise dinner from Rory's shelf in the fridge. Down the bar, a portly, ruddy-faced man in his forties smiled apologetically, trying to stop his young son from arrowing a French fry at me. I smiled back then stared at my drink, tuning into the comforting rhythms of family chatter, a play in which everyone knows their roles. The bottle was warm and empty by the time the group settled their bill and loudly exclaimed that they were going down to Fisherman's Wharf. When they left I surprised myself by following, out into the night and down the street behind them, away from home. They paused at intersections and I lingered behind, looking at store fronts. Occasionally I walked ahead of them to deter them from the notion that I was following them and almost together, we walked all the way down Van Ness to the waterfront, where they turned right, hit the tourist strip of the Wharf and stood outside a restaurant called O'Hoolihans frowning at the menu. When they went inside I sat on a bench, having only just begun to realize what must be obvious to everyone else in the world – that when you get married and have kids, your own Praetorian guard is assembled to walk with you and examine menus outside restaurants for the rest of your days. If you don't, you invite a future of contemplation, of pre-packed sandwiches chewed on municipal benches, among gangs of pitiless seagulls. I walked home alone.

The following evening I returned, picking up the trail of another family on Fisherman's Wharf. Friday was a cool night and I followed them for a while, speculating on the dynamic of their relationships, until I lost them at a T-shirt shop. I wandered around for a while, then found another family and trailed them as far as Fish Alley. I moved as close to them as I could without joining, and each time the point of pick-up and drop-off changed – Pier Market, the Alcatraz Bar and Grill – but the warm feeling from each group persisted. Without it I was spectral, a ghost with a frozen heart, but near them I thawed. And when they disappeared inside to order the Machine Gun Kelly burger, I would feel myself freezing and wander back up the Wharf to find another father with a sweater draped across his thick back, another mother proud and concerned for her little son and daughter, another dancing, giddy set of kids oblivious to the blanket that was wrapped around them and the coldness of the world without it.

On one of these peregrinations, the trail went cold in the bar section of a restaurant by the name of Scoma's, and as it was a weekend night and I could feel the girth of an envelope of dollars my mum had sent across in my pocket, I sat at the counter and ordered a drink, then another, and then I got a little drunk, and took out Mum's card and examined the front of it. She always sent these white embossed cards with photographs of Irish landmarks on the front. This one was of Kilmore Quay and the purple water in the picture began to swim before my eyes.

— Ohh. A nice spot, that. I been there a few years back.

It was the guy beside me, wearing a Chicago Cubs baseball cap. I bought him a drink. Our chat had the uniquely macho defensiveness of Irish American conversations, all punch, parry and counterpunch.

— It's raining then it's sunny then what. It's raining again?

— I take it you're from Chicago?

— Evanston. You Irish?

— I live here. You on holiday alone?

He wagged a meaty hand at me. His wedding band was wedged on a finger that seemed to grow around it.

— Wife, kids, bowling.

— You're not bowling?

He drained his shot, pounded the counter for another, gesturing one for me too.

— I'm not bowling. What's your sitch?

— Ah, you know.

We clinked and drank.

— Lemme see. You say you live here, and if that's true, then you're definitely on the Wharf for some reason. So okay . . . you work at one of the restaurants?

— Nope.

The barman had a go.

— Youuu . . . your girlfriend works here and you're waiting for her?

I shook my head and the customer waved his fingers around the possibilities.

— You're meeting your sister down here? Brother. Aunt!

— Naw.

It became a game and I wondered why I was enjoying it so much before it dawned on me that apart from a barman, some bus drivers and a teller at the bank, I hadn't spoken to another person in days.

— You're waiting for your parents to join you and buy you a seafood dinner?

— You cycle fat tourists up the hills on one of those bicycles?

— Okay, I give up.

— I'm just having a few drinks.

— Here? Really?

— Yup.

— On your own?

I thought about saying nothing, but why not?

— I like watching the families, you know. Walking around near them. Seeing them happy.

The barman began wiping down the far end of the counter, though it looked clean to me. We drank in silence for a few minutes, and I tried to buy him back another shot but he said no this time, and when his wife and children came by a few minutes later with a plastic trophy from the bowling alley, I wasn't introduced to them, and he seemed in a hurry to go.

— Hey, you won! Show me the trophy?

— Get your coats, kids. Come on. Let's go eat somewhere else.

I stayed for another hour or so and in that time I put away a Maker's Mark with every beer, just like the man had done. I probably had about five of each drink.

— Hey kid, you're far too young to be drinking alone, down here on a Friday night. Why don't you go to a bar with some young people in it, over in the Haight or somewhere.

I looked up at the barman.

— Thanks, but hey. Why don't you mind your own fucking business?

Six eights are forty-eight and for under fifty dollars before she took her cut, Bettina Ho finally came through, leaving a message on Rory and Pauric's shared telephone to say that she had found me a single day's work, cleaning out a storeroom at a company called Otremba, on New Montgomery. I had no idea what Otremba did but their storeroom was rank. The high window had bars on it but what a robber would have wanted with the paint tins, arcane stationery and oddly shaped pieces of wood was beyond me, let alone the banana skins and a used condom – the ghost of Christmas party past. I had been told to bag or bin everything that had no value but because the whole room wouldn't fit in a bag in its current shape, the job had to be broken down into tiny sections.

Whenever a bona fide Otremban stopped by for a new pen or a book of Post-its, they'd hold their nose and look at me as if I had authored the smell in here and by lunch time I wanted them all dead. I had already cased the staff fridge under the pretence of needing ice, and it was stuffed with labelled lunch boxes. I worked until I was worried that my stomach was trying to escape and at 3.04 made for the lunch box marked 'Sandy' in the fridge. Not only had this Sandy been the first to blank me while I cleaned her storeroom, holding a sleeve over her nose and spilling but not replacing a box of index cards, but she had marked her Tupperware with a Sharpie'd note, a keep-out in all caps indicating some very real aggression at work. 'THIS IS SANDY'S LUNCH. IF YOUR NAME ISN'T SANDY GEIGER, STAY AWAY!!!' 'Geiger.' I loved the way she didn't even allow for the faint possibility of another Sandy taking her stupid food.

Having cased the kitchen and found assurance that everyone was now back at their desks, I piled her entire doughy bagel into my mouth, still on my hunkers, then heard footsteps stopping at the doorway.

— Evan?

From over there, no one could see my desperately grinding jaw, hidden as it was by the fridge door, but the woman's voice persisted.

— EVAN.

I tried pulverizing the bagel with my teeth but couldn't chew quickly enough, then put my hand up above the fridge and waved, desperately trying to buy some time. I counted to five and tried to swallow the huge mass of under-chewed dough but it wouldn't fit in my craw so I spat it into my hand and arranged it into one of the egg holes in the top compartment of the door, a ball of dough marbled with damp, chewed salmon.

— Evan?

The stolen Snickers and yoghurt were still hidden behind the fridge door in my left hand as I stood up and saw it was not Sandy, but Melissa Byrne, a girl I knew vaguely from college. She had long Titian hair and wore floral patterned dresses and sandals. Once, a few weeks before, I saw her on Haight and we waved at each other. This time, we sat down at the lunch desk and she made coffee. I sipped, my throat raw from the recent bagel drive.

— That's mad you're working here. In our storeroom!

She lived a few blocks from where I was currently outstaying my welcome. And though she was somewhat surprised to learn that I was so close by, her jaw only really hit the floor when she heard that Pauric and Rory didn't have a TV.

— Well, you have got to come over then. Have you seen *Party of Five*? It's A-mazing . . .

I was being asked on a date! Immediately I visualized Melissa with a mouthful of champagne or more likely Cava, and felt faint. Was this it? After she rinsed her cup and went back to work, I devastated Sandy's potato chips and grapes, but left the Brie and crackers – I don't like Brie.

When Laura, Melissa's oldest friend in the world ever, opened the door that night and ushered me in, my optimism about sex and dating was quickly dispelled. The spring evening air outside was fresh and mild, but in here the heating was jacked up, towels had been rolled and placed at doors to exclude any vaguely cooling breeze, and heaters were being rubbed constantly with woollen socked toes. A tub of ice-cold Cherry Garcia was being passed and eaten with individual spoons. All four girls were in flannel pyjamas. One of the three-letter networks had decided to brand Monday night 'Must See TV', and this apartment had taken the commanding tone to heart. Here they sat in their pyjamas, me sweating in just a T-shirt as the credits for *Friends* rolled. This episode was 'the one where the monkey gets away'.

— Doesn't anyone want to go out?

— No. It's starting!

— . . . get a drink? Meet people?

— It's, like, a Monday!

The show was about friends looking for love in the big city. I thought of my parents watching shows like this at home. Did they think this was my life? On screen there were no girls in pyjamas obsessing over lip balm, and no foostering virgins among them. The living room smelled of Sudocrem, condensation dribbled down the inside of window panes and Camel Lights were smoked. *Friends* were aggressive daters, but never once in my life had I been on a date, nor had most of the people watching. If we had anything like as much desire for love or sex it was well hidden and found its only release through drunken collisions.

This show was about surrogacy in a big city, about how friendship could supplant traditional relationships and even the family unit, providing people got on well enough. It seemed to say it was okay not to have a nuclear family provided you had friends. For a guy whose longest relationship to date had lasted six torrid weeks and who was quite unable to fall asleep in the same bed as a girl, and who, when sleeping in a room on his own, regularly woke up convinced that someone else was in the room, or in the bed, and classed such a prospect as a nightmare, that was interesting.

— This show is actually kind of subversive, in a way.

— Jesus Christ, shut up, Evan. What did Rachel say?

— Couldn't hear it. Damn.

I rubbed a fist at the window and through the moisture could see a plane blinking in the night and beneath it the lonely lights on Sutro Tower blinking back, understanding.

These girls didn't like to sully their hands with dealers so next week I sat in a friend of Dead Dave's apartment while he weighed a bag of KGB. He was twitchy, in his late forties with electrocuted hair, and the walls of his apartment had been covered in toilet paper finger-pressed in amphetamine fury into turrets, ravines and forts over the months and years.

— So Dave tells me you're looking for a new place. I need a room-mate. Think about it.

The inspiration for his sculpture was thrust into my hands, a painting of a boat containing a dead body and moving towards a dark, forbidding island of cypress trees.

— It's by Böcklin. One of Hitler's personal favourites. So you want Al Green or Barry White?

The pot wasn't for me, but to assure him you weren't a cop, etiquette required that you speak about drugs in code, and get high with him. After he weighed and measured and we smoked one of his joints I had to turn away from that wall altogether, for fear of losing my sanity in the topography. But I couldn't move to leave, and by staying beyond that moment, the idea of ever leaving began to carry with it a kind of dramatic force that I didn't have the courage to execute, and then the awkwardness of that moment was replaced by a tugging sense of having over-stayed. Only after finally getting out of there, when I had a chance to check my watch, did I realize I had been with the dealer-sculptor for just under ten minutes.

After the credits rolled the following Monday, Karen turned the volume down.

— You got the doobage?

How I hated that word. I threw her the bag and she gave me three twenties.

— Karen, is there any chance I could stay here for a few nights, until I get somewhere of my own?

The girls glanced at each other and non-verbally trans-mitted the information that this would not be possible.

— Nahh. Don't worry about it! Honestly guys. I'll get somewhere. Just, I wanted to ask. You know that kind of way?

Holding it by the end, Karen shook the joint. She had only been in the city two weeks but had landed lucrative temp work, answering phones on the forty-seventh floor of 555 California, for a management consultancy. She threw a scrap of paper with about fifty characters on it over to Melissa and winked, lighting up.

— My email address. When you get yours we can email each other at work and it'll look like we're typing. And they just installed video conferencing machines in my office too. Pretty mad.

She laughed as she sealed the joint.

— The world is changing, ladies. So tell me about Milo again. He's become a wood-turner?

Room-mate Referral was a bright one-room office off Haight with a huge front window. Thick ring binders weighing down the shelves all around were arranged according to neighbourhood. Bernal Heights, Potrero, Duboce Triangle – the names were spellbinding. You paid a thirty-dollar fee per month to sit here browsing and if you liked a listing in any of them, you went to see the tenants. But competition was brutal, and the crop of room-mates a crap shoot. As I flicked through the hand-scrawled sheets, many hundreds of terrifying futures began to materialize. 'Must like ferrets, ink and 3 Mile Pilot. Deal breaker!!!!'. The pot dealer had an ad in one of these folders, and though I was up for new experiences I was pretty sure I wouldn't want to live with anyone who was willing to live with me. Of all of them, just one listing seemed reasonable, so I slid it from the transparent plastic sheath, folded it in two and stuck it in my back pocket, then, sighing theatrically at the fruitlessness of it all, I stood up and left. You weren't meant to take listings with you, but I didn't fancy my chances in a fair fight.

One short block up the hill on the other side of Haight, Waller Street bore its nature far more proudly, and well as it looked, it smelled better up here: of jasmine, not waffle cones and wee. This block between Clayton and Belvedere was sun-dappled, cool from the clouds brushing at overhanging trees. There was no foot traffic and precious few cars and it was settled in a way that called to mind a road from an American sitcom. I produced the listing from my pocket, found the right door and rang the bell. A car bumper sticker showed a dancing stick figure like The Saint beside one word, 'fukengrüven'. The door swung open.

— 'Sup. You here about the room?

The guy holding the door stuck his right hand up at shoulder height, palm out towards me, the way an Indian chief might say 'How'. He was short and stocky with black hair in corkscrew curls and he wore a Tribe Called Quest T-shirt, surf shorts and enormous Garfield slippers. Finally and with a sigh, he let the arm drop to his side. What I learned, and later forgot had ever been odd to behold in the first place, was that these guys high-fived each other at all times.

— So yo, it's Casey, man.

He might have been Puerto Rican, or Hispanic, but his manner was pure Bay Area.

— I'm Evan.

— Shoes off, and enter.

In socks, I padded down the hall behind him. The spare bedroom was first on the left, small and dark, looking out into a garbage chute, but clean, and with hardwood floors. There was no living room, just bed-rooms on the left of the long corridor and a tiny futon tucked in a recess on the right. And along the floor were hundreds of boxes of CDs and records. At the end of the hall I turned left into a bright kitchen and Casey sat at the table and gave me a glass of water.

— ASHER!

From the next room came the insistent thump of house music and on the wall, a huge poster bore the word 'Spundae'.

— So, rent is 350 a month. You need to get your own phone line installed, and we don't like smokers. Are you a smoker? YO ASHER!!!!!!

— I can smoke outside.

Casey stood up and took a tray of roasted red peppers from the oven. He set them on the counter. He worked in a record store, and the man making the noise in the other room was a DJ who ran something called the Sunset Boat Party. Each was born and bred in Marin County, just on the other side of the Golden Gate Bridge.

— ASHER!!!! So we run parties and we're super mellow. If you like house music then this place will work for you. Pepper?

— 'Sup.

The man who must have been Asher was smiling as he scratched his rumpled hair, leaning against the door jamb, wearing a towel around his shoulders. He looked like Neil Young.

— Check it out yo. Derrick just cut my hair. I guess he just texturalized it some . . .

— Whatever about your hair, Asher. This is Evan. Our new room-mate.

— 'Sup, Evan.

Once again, Casey offered me a roasted pepper with something called hummus which was the colour of butter. This time I took one and dipped it in the strange liquidy spread, and God, it was so much sweeter than I had expected.

I don't know whether you could have called it long awaited, but Wendy's were pioneering the square hamburger and I held one in an open-air mall in Fisherman's Wharf. Since paying rent and a deposit at Waller and buying a box spring and mattress, I was now the kind of broke that could make you laugh and cry at the same time, yet though it was cheaper to do so, something prevented me from making my own breakfast. Fruit revolted me and though the square cheeseburger was no oil painting, and so much limper than the picture promised, and highly inappropriate for breakfast, it was deliciously cheap. The Otremba money had come through, thirty-nine dollars after tax, and using it, I was sliding down the greased ladder of fast food breakfasts, landing first at the Arbecue, a one-dollar, five-patty heart attack, then plummeting past ranch bean burgers at Jack in the Box, nuclear egg burgers, malignant grey sausage circles and a cornucopia of potato triangles drowning in vegetable oil.

Within moments my folder had thumb prints on it and I watched three young girls in shorts and matching pink T-shirts skip by in a state of mutual enthusiasm, climb onto a stage with a public address system, and begin miming to a song by Debbie Gibson. Behind them, a billboard for something called America Online. Tourists gathered in misshapen clumps outside shops. What was I doing here? Every chowder vendor and crab joint was staffed by career waiters that pulled in three hundred dollars a shift in tips during the summer nights. My CV with the offer of conversational French, 5 Cs in the Leaving Cert and a love of keep fit and crime novels was an insult to their profession. With it, I was trying to suggest that a fool could do their job.

I succumbed to a Basic Light, igniting the second-to-last one from the soft pack in my pocket. Myth had it that 'Basics' were compiled from discarded fag ends, harvested from the streets of this town by the homeless. That the thought didn't bother me in the slightest should have been my greatest cause for worry. On the dais, the girls bounced and marched and sang with blank white smiles, dead eyed with stagejoy, and when they finished their number the tallest among them noticed me smoking and curled her nose imperceptibly as she bowed to the smattering of tourist applause. I crept behind a bush, and when I pocketed the lighter I caught my nail on the corner of a card of some kind, and pulled it out absently. I had forgotten all about Sam Couples, Evangelist. Those languid eyes. I had been praying for a job, but why not believe in technology? Sam's office was located about ten blocks inland from the very spot upon which I now stood, and the case for the future could only improve. It was at least as promising as slinging chowder or gutting one of those lobsters floating in the grimy tanks, their claws bound tightly in elastic.

I followed the shoreline south a few blocks towards Embarcadero until the buildings on my right shrank to single- and two-storey warehouses that revealed the sheer rock walls of Telegraph Hill, dotted with scree and huge rusty bolts that must have held the entire elevated neighbourhood above it together. Then I found Chestnut, a cluster of buildings ending at the foot of the hill, some glinting as they caught the sun. The location was implausibly photogenic, an establishing shot from a sitcom, framed beneath the phallic sentry of Coit Tower. At the front entrance to 150 Chestnut an Art Deco train carriage had been converted for the purposes of a meeting room and the warped, thick glass windows caught the rays. The vermilion brick building behind it enveloped the train car. Feeling greasy and reckless and having exactly nothing to lose, I climbed the wrought iron front steps and pushed in the doors.

Inside, lithe Aniston-ian women swished past cradling folders. At reception, one of them took the Evangelist's business card, glanced at the name, then paged Tammy Hong over the PA system. Behind her lay an open plan office floor in a converted warehouse. Red-painted I-beams flanked a poured concrete floor above which a cast-iron-and-neon replica of the ForwardSlash logo hung above the studio like a bright new sun, a bold diagonal slash emblazoned across it in white neon. Office doors were painted bright green and a first floor balcony ringed the perimeter with a second layer of green doors. Suspended above the milling workers inside that room, the sign looked religious. I didn't know what this place was but I desperately wanted to be a part of it.

— You know Sam?

A squat Korean worked a hand cruncher in her left hand. From lounging around gyms in school during lunch break, I knew that I couldn't close one of them properly with both of my hands. Tammy Hong wore skin-tight denims and high-tops, cracking repeated bubbles with her gum.

— I don't know about 'know', I mean I met him once and . . .

— Good enough for Sam, good enough for me. Scoot through here and I'll give you the tour.

My heart sank. More tours. More in the way of charity. Tammy pushed in the glass door and I followed her, noting her shoulder blades rising and falling as we walked and talked.

— Thanks for seeing . . .

— Hey, we're taping the show. You gotta to be quiet.

The show? A show? The evangelist only mentioned that his company built websites for the Internet, but passing the circular wooden staircase at the back of the room we paused to watch as a statuesque black woman in a trouser suit prepared to read something from what was undoubtedly an autocue. There were two television cameras on tripods, a small but industrious crew milling around, and

beyond the dark glass on the far side I could discern a
bank of monitors with men in baseball caps before them.
A voice counted down from five to three, then mimed
'two' and 'one' and pointed at the presenter who switched
on the full beams.

— It's rush hour on the information superhighway and
the worldwide web is turning into the 'worldwide wait'.
We'll show you why! And if life in the digital slow lane is
getting you down, we've got solutions to get you up to
speed.

In the centre of the studio floor, a television camera on
a huge arm rose and tilted away from four guys playing
foosball, to frame the wrought iron company sign. This
was an office *and* a TV set, in which some kind of zeit-
geist was being choreographed, bottled and sold – a
television show about 'the Net'.

Tammy brought me past two smart-casual workers
playing an arcade game called 'Tekken' in the corner. That
must have been a part of their job. Behind another door,
a technician in flip-flops was testing a pair of night vision
goggles, motion sensors attached to his hands. Tinny
music emanated from each room we passed, Pavement,
then Captain Beefheart, then Orbital, the treble from
each set of computer speakers blending with that of the
next. We jogged upstairs to the balcony level and Tammy
strode around the perimeter. Each door bore different sten-
cilled descriptions – /reviews, /labs, /hardware, /gaming,
behind which young men in flannel shirts were typing.
But in this American sitcom about a young, thrusting

business, the walls didn't shake when a door was slammed – they were made of bricks and mortar.

I was ushered into a room, Tammy sat and cracked her knuckles and gum and studied my CV without laughing. Behind her, monitors and a keyboard. This was an edit suite.

— We're about convergence here. Creating a new cross-platform world of entertainment. TV plus Web equals us. Or so we hope. So tell me. Who is this 'Evan' guy?

She dabbed at the corner of my CV with a pinkie. For a moment I thought I don't know, then she sat on her hands, leaning forward to indicate that she meant me. Beneath her jeans her thighs bulged impressively. I stacked Milo's bold moves against my last few weeks cut adrift, traipsing around on the Wharf.

— Apart from what's on my CV? Let me see. I love people, honestly, and I learn quickly, you know, and I work hard; I love working, seriously.

— Can you drive?

— Umm, no.

She wrote 'no car' on my CV.

— Do you know Chyron 5?

Tiny, tiny details. How would she get ahead if she couldn't see the big picture?

— And you can't drive?

— Is that bad?

— Well, it's not good.

From a place unknown, a swell of fierce emotion

crashed over me, scaring me with its force. It was time to push my dwindling stack of chips into the middle and turn over my hand.

— Tammy, all I can offer is hard work. I learn really fast, and I love television. I'll learn how to drive. I'll do anything. I'm good at . . . just . . . working. The thing about me is that . . .

— Stop, stop, stop.

She was smiling in a kind way, as if my prostration at her New Balance running shoes was cute and all, but that really, I didn't have to do it any more. I was offered temporary work on a week-by-week basis for three days a week, moving furniture, building shelves and running errands, for six dollars an hour, and I was saying yes before I had calculated that with this commitment to ForwardSlash I wouldn't be able to take another full-time job, even if I found time to score one. I didn't know what a forward slash was, but I knew with absolute certainty that this was it.

— Yo, people! Employee number 21!

She shouted it down to the studio floor.

The hours immediately after were lost in a state of ecstatic mooning; wandering among seagulls quarrelling over stale tacos in corporate parks, reading menus at restaurants to which I would doubtless be squired for business lunches. I had found a job. On Market the traffic was stopped and a procession of red-and-gold open top buses crawled past. A walrusy man with a moustache waved a flabby paw at them.

— Excuse me. What is this all about?

— The Niners.

— 'Niners'?

— Yeah guy, the Niners. They just happen to be Super Bowl champions?

We watched fifty identically hewn footballers waving, having overcome a team of similar lunkheads from a city nearby, their victory valueless beyond the purely symbolic. The gold rush team could have been kids in basements rolling eight-sided dice and role playing, and as the procession rumbled past, the faces of the workers in the crowd were set to polite tolerance of the interruption. Football was all well and good, but down here, the rest were fighting a real war, for an invisible territory that until that day I hadn't known even existed.

— Go Niners!!!!

I walked so far up Market that it became pointless to do anything other than continue the rest of the way home. When I was young I had been playing barefoot on the rocks above the beach in Galway when my eye caught a greenish glint in the sand. Thinking it something of value, I jumped down to inspect it and landed on the broken neck of a Seven Up bottle hidden in the sand. What I had seen was the rest of the bottle, and when I limped back to where our families' towels were arranged and held my leg up for my mother under the crook of my knee, the blood drained from her face. I was big for six, and leaving baby Danny with my sister, Mum carried me all the way up the forty-three steps to the lane which led to the

houses without stopping once. On the way, she told me
not to look over my shoulder, but I did once in the early
stages of our trek, and I saw the thick towel swaddling
my foot, drenched in warm scarlet and dripping copious
globs onto the sand. That evening in Dublin, it took a
series of intricate stitches around my big toe to prevent
me from losing my foot, and climbing the hill towards
Haight-Ashbury, the space between big toe and next
biggest throbbed, and I felt something that might well
have been homesickness. When you're panning for gold,
the glint in the silt that catches your eye could always be
a shard of glass, buried there, waiting.

Day one of the job and walking up Battery, part of me
very badly wanted to run the other way. The mind plays
three-card Monte with our motivations. This was a definite end to something, an end I had wanted, but now I
couldn't remember why I had wanted so badly to give
away what I had before. Why hadn't I gone up to the
forest and carved wood with Milo? Once more the city
was fogbound and beyond the incline of Battery a wall of
grey cloud hugged the cliffs of Telegraph Hill. Somewhere
beyond lay the future me, my own shape and size but
spectral, and always on the move, out of reach, his face
averted, dipping around a corner just when I seemed to
have caught up with him, my outstretched hand reaching
for his shoulder. I had so many questions for him.

After the left turn onto that dead-end block of Chestnut, a guy in jeans and trainers began to materialize,

leaning against the bonnet of a rusty blue Chevy Malibu, and in a town of coffee shops serving espresso drinks for a couple of dollars, he was drinking something home-made, something poured from a tartan-patterned flask of the kind I hadn't seen in years. He had greying hair in a cow's lick, wore a baseball shirt, and when he saw me approaching, pushed himself off the bonnet and loped on over with a smile, pointing to the flask on the roof of the car.

— Greetings, sir. You want a cup of joe?

I shook Fred's hand and from the car radio, I could hear 'What a Fool Believes'. He poured me a hazelnut-smelling coffee, and we listened to Michael McDonald.

— Man, how does he get all the way up there?

I lit a smoke and Fred cocked an eye at me.

— You like the Doobies?

— I love the Doobies!

— You got another of those?

I handed him a cigarette and lit him up, and he drew on it then looked at it ruefully.

— Every night I quit and every next morning, I get the jones at just this time. Oh well.

— You like 'Livin' on the Fault Line'?

— Yeah, man. As long as it doesn't crack . . .

Just as I began to contemplate a quake right there and then and how Coit Tower would come slamming through the canopy of fog, Tammy came out and leaned over the railings, gazing past us at the misty morning. All facing out and arranged on Fred's car, it felt like we were posing for an album cover.

— Sumbitchin' weather, huh?

Fred flung the silt of his joe into the ditch at the foot of Telegraph Hill.

— I don't know about that, Miss Tammy. It's good for lifting.

— True . . .

Tammy dangled two black Velcro back supports off the railings.

— You guys met each other already?

We each took the bait, Fred strapping himself in, grunting.

— Yes, ma'am. Me and the young squire here share a weakness for AM radio.

— A dying breed.

Tammy smiled. It was clear she regarded Fred fondly, as you might an eccentric living in your apartment building. I spied a large flatbed truck reversing onto Chestnut with a puny warning beep. Then, remembering this was work and clearing her throat in a series of hoarse barks, she began to break it down for us.

ForwardSlash had just acquired the adjacent health club, a series of huge, interconnected buildings, and over the coming weeks, our job was to furnish it for an influx of workers who had all this stuff to do on the Net, but nowhere to sit and do it. And after we facilitated the upsurge in numbers, we would then be responsible for replacing every old computer in the building with new ones, and the old computers would be given away to charity. Fred was charged with finding the charity, and in a town of perfectly good TV sets and three-seater leather sofas abandoned at nearly every intersection, it didn't surprise me that once the equipment was replaced, the company was supremely uninterested in its final resting place.

The beeping stopped, the driver jumped down from the cab of the truck and once Tammy signed his forms, we threw open the back and 150 thick slabs of pale, smoothed but untreated wood lay there, almost breathing. A more distant beeping sound began and another truck was now backing up, this one apparently loaded with steel table frames to support the slabs. Fred traced a finger over the stacked, grainy ends.

— How will history judge all of this, Evan? A waste of wood?

— I take it you do not at this point in time have an email address.

Fred leapt into the truck bed and bent over.

— That is correct. Now. Let us lift and build things. Count of three? One, two . . .

It was hard to gauge it just by looking at them, but those tables were heavy – solid blocks of pine, slightly smoother on one side. It took two people to lift one and the best part of the morning to get the first delivery off the truck and stacked upright against the building walls.

As we laboured, sometimes talking, sometimes not, my nostrils filled with the raw, sappy smell and I had to wonder whether these materials had been chosen on purpose. In this state the desks were made less of wood and more of freshly dead tree. The real source of things, the point of origin – wasn't this what Sam the Evangelist and all the rest of them wanted us to disregard? To buy into his vision of the future, didn't we need to forget about the value of holding things? Wouldn't we have to be happy with 'stuff' bought without prior touching, worn without measuring, eaten without tasting? Would the buyer live a million miles from the moment of creation? And if so, why the raw wooden desks? Maybe it was their idea of a joke, planted to offer people pause, when the moment came. Maybe late one night one of the coders punching ones and zeros into a machine set atop one of these beautiful altars would stop, run their fingers over the wood of their desks and consider what, in exchange for all that was being lost, would be gained by this charge into the future. Maybe then they would put their cheek to the tree and weep, because there were rings to be counted on each slab, the history of life before the axe fell. Didn't carnivores cry in abattoirs?

At noon, I sat on the front porch smoking, my back screaming, hands raw and splintered. A burly Indian in a billowing denim shirt stepped out, cadged a light and settled his frame on the concrete steps beside me. He crossed his legs on the step beneath him, an enormous coffee-skinned Buddha smoking silently, his eyes sullen and dark. After a few minutes of silence, he glanced at my Velcro back brace.

— The man bra.

— An insurance thing, apparently. I'm not used to all this lifting.

— Irish. What do you do normally?

He had the formal English accent of Indians, with a hint of California.

— I want to work in TV.

— Why aren't you in LA?

I told him about Ireland, then about Milo, and how working for Tammy was my assured entrée to this world. In response to all this convoluted logic, Raj snorted with derision.

— Brother, I'm gonna give you some advice. You can forget about TV. In a decade, given a choice between the TV set and the computer, people will be ditching the television set.

— What about 'convergence'?

— So you read the brochure. That's a company line, a 1993 idea to help stupid people imagine how it's going to go down. But they will not converge. One will replace the other.

— What about the TV show here though?

— Advertorial.

I attempted a sage nod but Raj knew I knew nothing.

— The show is advertising for the website. Think about it. Providing thirty minutes of branded content a week is cheaper than buying a thirty-second spot to advertise a website in prime time on the network. But that's exactly what it's doing.

— Doing what, though? Where's the money?

We watched a fresh-faced boy in a suit climb past us.

— Driving traffic to the site. Listen, you don't have to understand the mechanics to get in on this. Half these guys can't boil an egg and they're making twenty times what you are. They are the Boomtown Rats . . .

He winked, then stood, flicking his cigarette away.

— Listen, if you're in any way smart, it would take you maybe two weeks to learn HTML and you could start making bank. You don't look like a lifter. Ditch the man bra, come by the labs and I'll lend you a book.

Right then Fred's Chevy Malibu pulled up in front of me, 'Abandoned Luncheonette' by Hall and Oates playing on the tape deck. I thanked him and left. Raj shouted after me, waving at Fred.

— Back the right horse, man!

It took a couple of days for me to pass some kind of test and be introduced by Fred to what he called the Royal Scam. At around noon we were returning from the local post office where we had delivered two loads of parcels, and were pushing the empty hand carts through the national headquarters of Levi-Strauss – that pillar of American manifest destiny. This complex lay around the corner from ForwardSlash, an ochre cluster of brick buildings that reminded me of their pre-distressed jeans. In front was a tinkling water feature, some aggressively kempt lawn, a raised patio, and gazebos built to accommodate the chinoed herds, and on the fringes of all this artful urban planning lay the Levi's staff canteen.

Given that he had two daughters and an ex-wife to support and was working on the same paltry wages as me, Fred was an unbeatable guide to the best places for cheap lunch. We hid our mail trucks behind a topiaried bush and pushed through the revolving door.

— I don't have any money.

Fred let me catch up with him, then whispered in my ear.

— And you don't need money if you work for Levi's. Just say 'corduroy'.

The Chinese deli with the two-dollar bacon muffins, the three-dollar burrito from the taqueria on Bay behind the projects, the burgers from the U.S. Café in North Beach, these were all contenders, but nothing is cheaper than free. We took a pair of trays laminated in plastic faux denim lino and began pushing them past an array of deliriously good food options. Fred began to load up and everything he took, I took too. Baked potato. Pizza slice. Five types of salad. That way, when we were busted, we would do the same time.

— Corduroy.

I had my code word ready, but the lady at the checkout didn't even look up.

At the table by the window, I tried not to keep looking around and waiting for the tap on the shoulder but Fred was utterly unconcerned. I had put him at thirty-five but it turned out I was at least ten years under. To escape the murderous white winters of North Dakota in the 1970s he joined the army, and after honourable discharge, he and his young family (he got married at seventeen, had his first daughter at eighteen and his second at twenty-five) settled in West Portal. When the marriage ended, Fred moved into an apartment in the Richmond district and now spent his weekends playing softball in a league that included the inmate team of Vacaville prison, and chasing Asian girls. He used to drive a cab for the Veterans cab company, but stopped the night he picked up a fare from Candlestick Park, where the 49ers played. His fare was a cameraman, who told him that his job was to rake the crowd and find the pretty girls and frame them nicely for the director. Fred speared a fry and smiled.

— Pardon my language but when I heard that, I damn near shit little green apples.

He had wild tales about taking acid and going to see the Who live in Omaha, and liked to say 'shoot' and 'darn', and things that were good were 'terrific' and never 'awesome', and no one was ever 'dude'. They were 'sir' or 'my friend' or 'good buddy', and though he never blanched at my effs and blinds, apart from those little green apples, never again did I hear him swear. Not until the very end.

Back at the office, the IT department blazed a trail for us, running wires through every inch of the building. Over the following weeks we ferried slabs to the end of these green, blue and yellow tendrils and mounted computers on them. The new building was still an old gym, parquet floor, hoops, even a faint smell of sweat clinging to damp cold walls. Our trainers squeaked like those of athletes as we built desks in the bleachers, on the corridors and beyond the three-point zone. Every desk we built was occupied by a dewy-eyed graduate, and every time we built a fresh row they were annexed – the company couldn't hire people quick enough to write all the code that was required to colonize some invisible mountain range at the end of all the coloured wires, and plant the ForwardSlash flag atop it. Fred mopped his brow.

— You know, I've just figured out what this scene reminds me of. A natural disaster.

— I thought you were going to say the Gold Rush.

— That too. Did you know this: when residents of this town learned about the gold upriver, at first San Francisco became a ghost town. Yeah. Everybody deserted their hotels, shops, businesses to head for the hills and look for gold. It was only when the gold-diggers from the rest of the country came to town that the city itself boomed again.

— So by not learning about computers, we're some-how ahead of the game?

— Very possibly.

— I love your optimism, Fred.

He hefted another slab to standing.

— Not nearly as much as I do.

Into the fourth then fifth basketball court we dragged the slabs and when they were full we populated the old reception, its turnstile entrance retained as an original fea-

ture from all the way back in 1985. We didn't put desks
in the shower cubicles, but only because Tammy informed
us with a frown that it contravened 'some dumb health
and safety by-law'.

As with all real work, the end of days was the best, sitting on the railings at the bus stop island, in the middle
of Market in the magic hour, hands splintered, the ocean
wind on my face. I'd hardly built a chapel out on the
prairie, but certainly, along my ancestral line somewhere,
was buried a trace of Presbyterian work ethic. I felt whole-
some.

A few stops along from where I had boarded it, the 6
Parnassus came to an abrupt halt at the Civic Center, the
bars which divined electricity from the city grid unmoored
and clattering impotently against each other. It sometimes
happened under the stress of a sudden turn or an arc too
wide. Normally, the driver stepped down and reattached
them manually, impervious to the murderous hatred
steaming from behind windscreens of honking cars on all
sides. This time, though, he wandered off in a loping
stride, resplendent in black leather fingerless gloves and
standard issue brown suit. A woman shouted out the
window.

— Uh uh. No you didn't, driver! No you didn't just
walk away!

But he had. The bus was full, and after a few moments,
people started to talk. Natives here had no problem hearing their own voices in public – their unabashedness just
another gorgeous cultural anomaly. The skinny camp man

with the Macy's employment tag caught the eye of the girl with the skate T-shirt and the sweat bands.

— This is hella funny.

— . . . Nuh uh, dude. I'm super late right now.

Behind her, a couple of blonde women were engrossed in their own conversation, unaware that we had even stopped, or that anyone was listening, or that it mattered a damn what they heard, or thought about them.

— I know a lot of chill-ass guys, like these two gay guys I met, and I scored them pills for like five bucks from Sierra.

— Hey, you talk to Stacey yet?

— Yeah, I talked to her. And I'm all, 'It's my vagina, you bitch!'

And behind them, a young black man sang along to the CD in his Discman.

— 'I'm stalkin', walking in my big black boots' . . .

Then he saw a guy he recognized on the street, whipped off his headphones and leaned out the window.

— Yo, you gonna sell me another bag of just shake or is there buds in there?!

The dissonant chat seemed to send a message – we complain, but really, we are happy. Everybody loved their President, their beautiful streets, their work and money, their gods and their futures. People marched for the 'Mission Yuppie Eradication Project', which encouraged members to vandalize SUVs parked in the traditionally Mexican neighbourhood (MYEP motto – 'you've had your burrito, now fuck off home'), but here everything worked.

There wasn't really anywhere to go and get properly angry in this town. I never wore a Walkman any more. Some passengers began to moan loudly, but I could have stayed among them for ever, listening.

Our driver finally reappeared, clutching a packed McDonald's bag in one hand and a 'Big Gulp' in the other. Behind the bus, he briefly set his dinner on the ground, connected the wires, then bounded back on, impervious to the bickering. Other buses swung out on the widest possible arc to get by ours, their passengers smirking or waving.

— It's all right for all of y'all. Y'all are going home for your dinner. I gotta work.

A Chinese woman boarded with a live chicken under her arm. The driver stuck out an arm.

— No livestock on the bus, lady. Step down.

She looked at him quizzically and he pointed at the beady-eyed chicken, then shook his head.

— No livestock.

— Is food. Dinner.

He laughed and held up his McDonald's bag.

— Nah, lady, this is dinner. That's an animal. Not on my bus. Step down.

It dawned on her what he was saying and she set her bag down, wrapped both her hands around the chicken's neck and wrung it. After holding it tight for a few seconds, staring at the driver, she let the chicken's neck drop like a length of garden hose, its eyes these cruel shiny buttons gazing down the bus at us. As she fed a dollar bill into the machine the driver shrugged, hit the button to close the door and she walked on down the aisle, past shocked commuters, at that point reconfiguring their dinner options. Finally we moved up the hill quietly, so far from home, grateful to be connected once more to the pulsing grid of a blue electric city.

— Those are potatoes?! Oh, my God, that's so sweet. You're such a bachelor!

Asher's girlfriend Nikki padded into the kitchen and I put a tea towel over the pot and stood in front of it. I was wearing my most amazing suede Adidas trainers and an X-Large T-shirt, but standing next to her still felt like a lumbering farmer. Could you be a bachelor at twenty-one? Nikki was a masseuse, had long black hair and gothic make-up. She opened the fridge and leaned in, her boyfriend's old Sonic Youth T-shirt riding up to reveal a tiny black silk thong. She smiled over her shoulder, post-coitally, and took out a chilled bottle of cranberry juice. She kicked the door closed and leaned against it, holding the glass bottle between her legs and screwing the cap open, then lifting the bottle to her mouth. A drop of cranberry splashed onto the T-shirt — of course it did — and when she lifted it and licked the stain I glimpsed her bare belly, the front of her thong, and she saw me looking.

My poor spuds, cowering there behind me, under the damp tea towel. People here saw them not as a staple but an elective, a quaint and unsophisticated variant ranking beneath squash, roasted peppers and eggplant in the desirability stakes. I was a lumpen spud and Nikki was arugula, whatever that was – lithe, sexual arugula. She couldn't have been less than twenty, but around her, I felt like a weird, clammy-palmed uncle. It was difficult not to resent that.

— Are you coming to Stompy?

I knew this was a nightclub that Asher sometimes played at. But I wasn't much of a one for clubs. Milo called them fascist aerobic workouts and everything to do with dance music in Dublin had been dirty, Sides on Dame Lane a grubby dungeon full of scrawny ravers, the music dark and hard. The graffiti outside the Dolphin's Barn flats back home summed it all up – 'rave to the grave'. I grew up with guitars in the living room and people drinking whiskey out of mugs, and it helped for me to identify as a drinker, because you could do that to the exclusion of things that I didn't want to do without people knowing you didn't want to do them. Besides, it was 6 p.m. on a Thursday and I had to move desks in the morning.

— This is tonight?

— Sure is. You gonna drink a little juice here before-hand?

She wasn't holding any juice out towards me so I hadn't a clue what she meant, but I decided to play it real cool. I forked a spud and inspected it.

— You know, I might just do that.

— You're always in your room eating your dinner. We never get to see you. You should stick around. It'll be fun.

She padded out in the direction of the kick drum.

I lifted the damp, loamy tea towel, smelled the pot, then wiped my condensated cheeks. Until now, my roommates' presence in the apartment had been represented only by the rattling of plates and cups on the kitchen shelves, or a bleary morning encounter en route to the bathroom along the corridor. They did most of their living in their rooms, where each had Technics 1200s, stacks of records and twin bay windows that looked out onto a wildly overgrown communal garden tended by the upstairs neighbour, that everyone referred to as The Jungle. Their rooms looked out into The Jungle but mine was at the front, a box room peering out into the trash chute and a stairwell between us and our neighbours. Already, at night, I had been woken by bags of trash clattering into the huge wheelie bins outside my window, from the apartment above. But man, I loved it here. I had a shelf in the fridge, another in the cupboard, and I had a job.

— 'Sup, dude? Smells hella funky in here.

A burly white guy with dreadlocks held together with a wristband had materialized and was offering me a high five. I took him down awkwardly, our fingers slapping weakly. He swung a plastic bag off his back, and as I began spooning out my potatoes onto a dinner plate beside my one desultory chop, he began pouring a carton of juice into a Pyrex jug, then from his backpack adding a Ziploc bag of white powder. In his hair was a huge, bright green bud of grass. Throughout the ceremony, each of us concentrated entirely on the other's creation.

— You're the new room-mate, right? The Irish guy?

— Certainly am. Is that the juice?

— Sure is. You down?

I nodded and we stared into it. Tiny chalky islands of white powder floated on top.

— I should add apple, huh?

He went to the fridge and I gazed into the cloudy mix. Asher padded into the room and saw me and the mix.

— Holy shit, yo Casey, the juice is here!

The juice was fruit juice mixed with MDMA, and all of the apartment had been waiting for this. Now Nikki and Casey came in, and others began to issue from the walls. A slender black guy with the most open face drifted in wearing a sarong. Then Casey's sister came in with an Indian guy, and we all looked at the juice, then a guy in an XLR8R T-shirt arrived with a friend called Pepe and another fellow whose name I didn't catch. I found myself quite unable to eat. We stared at the Pyrex jug, moon-struck, as the man with the bud behind his ear lifted it up and grinned.

— You like cocktails, Nikki.

— You bring the cock, I got the tail.

She took the jug and drank some, set it down and padded out, and after a beat, everybody whooped. Casey stirred the mix with a spoon, then produced two empty Arrowhead water bottles and very carefully siphoned the bright juice into them. He closed the lids and shook them like maracas, dancing around the room.

— All set.

One by one, the people involved took small gulps from the bottles and passed them round. Pepe was last before me, and slid it over towards my plate of potatoes. I took it, drank a mouthful, and everyone whooped again.

— . . . Western and Eastern religions, different schools of thought, healing modalities . . . spiritual self-improvement services once only available to those living in the jungle . . .

Twenty minutes later, as the guy in the sarong slowly explained to me in words that sounded rote what it was that he did for a living, I became high.

— . . . my clients are European royalty and celebrities, and impoverished inner-city children.

What? By now the spuds were in the bin and the decks in Asher's room were playing, this music making sense for the first time. Someone handed me water, and I was so relieved that he had stopped talking. Then the dread-locked guy came out of the toilet waving a stick of Nag Champa in front of him and holding his nose.

— Every damn time I roll on X! You might want to give that an hour.

— Way to bust my groove, man.

The man in the sarong curled his nose and I noticed that his skin was unbelievably, almost weirdly smooth.

Nikki wandered in and I must have looked distressed. She saw me holding the bottle of juice and came over, beginning to rub my back. Her hand was supercharged with electricity and I shivered and shut my eyes. When the skin of her fingers brushed against the skin of my neck, my entire body quivered.

— You're feeling good, right?

— Unbelievably so. It's like . . . I can't . . . It's not just . . . it's something else.

— Just let it happen.

— But it's so . . .

— Relax.

— It means something, something else. It has meaning. In my life.

She took the juice and looked at me kindly.

— You never realized you were in so much pain. Right?

With my eyes I asked her how she could have known that, but she just did.

— It's okay, sweetie. You're with us now.

Three a.m. and orange streetlights in the South of Market District lent warmth to the pallid faces. I lit a cigarette from the one prior, drank more water and chewed my gum. Leaning against the wall the thud of deep house music worked its way across my shoulder blades, the confluence of bass and 808 pouring down my spine in waves. If I concentrated on that vibration, my eyes would close again and my mind would begin to float away, so I stood away from the wall. We had hand stamps to get back in, but the door staff were watching out for drinkers now; my old team. They were the ones starting fights and spilling Jaeger on the pretty girls inside, frustrated by the asexual dancing and the lack of action, unlike the pale skinny boys clutching water bottles and leaning against the wall beside me, those of us drawn to this scene from UC Davis and Chico State, and from Dublin. Inside Stompy, time had folded into itself under a wave of progressive, hypnotic house music. I must have been dancing in there because now I was drenched in sweat. Beside me was Nikki's friend Anna, tiny and Asian, and whose strawberry lip gloss had left a sticky print on my cheek. Now Casey and the guy in the sarong bounded out excitedly.

— Let's get our swim on!

A small wall-mounted television set playing an infomercial for the Ab Blaster. A fan plugged into the far wall, in front of which the Sikh proprietor was slumped, in short-sleeved shirt and wife-beater. Behind him, a beaded curtain covering the doorway to the family bedroom. I could make out two small children asleep on a mattress within. This was The Pacific Motel on Lombard, the main artery connecting the city to the Golden Gate Bridge. Everything about this was funny as, together, we crept past the window on our hunkers, giggling. We rounded a corner to the water's edge. The pool was kidney-shaped and lit from beneath, teal water covered with a film of sleeping insects. Surrounding it was the two-storey motel building and a walkway around the top floor. Casey wasn't swimming but Nikki and Anna stripped before any of us had our shoes off, diving into the pool as one and surfacing at the far end, Sapphic and sleek.

— Come on, you guys! It's awesome in here.

Wrestling with his leather sandals, the guy in the sarong fell over with a thud, to peals of laughter shushed away just as quickly. I stripped down to my underwear, catching a glimpse of Anna, who waved. I dived in and everything stopped as I gasped at the cool, beautiful depths. My boxer shorts slipped past my ankles, floating towards the deep end behind me. This happened at a school swimming gala once, years before, and I could remember the shame then as I surfaced to jeers from the gallery. Back then I had abandoned the race without a second's thought, plunging back down away from the race to retrieve my togs and even managing to dress myself in the chlorinated depths. Now it didn't matter so much. I was in California. Sails clacked on moored yachts in the distance. Rain, fog and shimmering puddles. Whether it rose up or fell down, the whole city always yielded to the molecular caress of water.

I breached the surface and there were Nikki and Anna, smiling. After a moment of paddling beside each other, I noticed the ring had slipped from my shrunken finger, but before I could begin to scan the bottom of the pool, Casey shouted at us from the first floor balcony, buck naked. His preferred mode of entry was the bomb dive and he landed with an explosive splash and shriek, displacing waves of water and causing lights in the bedrooms around the balcony to switch on. The ring was given to me by my parents the year after Danny died. It had been my grandfather's, his name was Daniel too, and Dad had given it to me to remind me of Danny for ever. When the water settled I looked down to see whether it would glint from the bottom, but I couldn't see it and couldn't be sure I even had it on me after the club. Anna then noticed that I had lost something and joined me, and together we began to scan the tiled floor, walking towards the deep end in baby steps, all eyes looking down. Then I saw that it wasn't just my finger that had shrunk. Holy fucking shit. My penis hadn't looked like that since I was nine.

— Forget it! I'll get another one!

I splashed at the water violently with both hands, laughing falsely, and then I swam to the far end, dived under, retrieved my boxer shorts and put them on while treading water. I reached the edge and crawled out of the pool, suddenly sober. I could continue swimming, but what was going to happen afterwards? And if I screwed it up and they learned that I was, at twenty-one, still a virgin, wouldn't I then lose them as friends?

The day before, I had set up the desk of a beautiful girl in work called Maggie. She was twenty-three and friendly, and I knew she was single because she had told me at some point during the installation, but even as I dragged her 486 Hewlett Packard out of its Styrofoam casing and plugged it in, something in the way she moved so fluently around the desk, the way she bent to answer the phone, the way she requested frozen yoghurt from another girl who was going to grab something at the shop, it was all too assured. These women were liberated, modern and super-confident, had moved beyond the awkward years of fumbling ineptitude and premature conclusion. Maggie and I sat in Harrington's after work smiling, wedged between a group of her girlfriends, and a man came by selling roses, but she needed a rose as much as she needed a wilting rube on top of her.

— No thank you. Roses are lame.

— . . . violence is blue.

— I'm sorry?

— Emm, nothing, just, words . . .

Maggie was entitled to her orgasm, she knew what to do to get it, and she didn't have any more time to waste. Even if she couldn't tell it from my veneer, it would take one night with me for her to find out that I wasn't the answer, rather a weird and somewhat upsetting question mark. And then all of work would know too. As I saw it, the bind was simple. I was now far too old to lose my virginity at any point in the future.

It didn't strike me as odd that I hadn't slept the previous night, until I got off the bus to work, and a black Land Rover with tinted windows pulled alongside. I kept walking, my hangover arrived and the SUV was keeping up, so I started to walk faster. Then the window buzzed down and a man was inside wearing shades, glancing over, then slowing down even more, so that he was now right alongside. It was Sam, smiling, fresh and pressed, his sports coat hanging in the back seat area behind him. My heart was thudding.

— Where are you headed?

— Into work, actually. Thanks to you! I've been wanting to thank you for that in person.

— Hop in. Unless you're not allowed to ride with strangers.

— Aren't you going to offer me sweets first?

He moved something off the passenger seat and spoke sternly.

— You're in America now, Evan. Perverts here offer 'candy'.

— Sweets, candy. Are all US perverts this pedantic?

— I speak only for this pervert.

After the door shut I did my best not to thank him once more for the job. That kind of obsequiousness gets old. But what else to say? For quite a while, we just drove. I wished the radio was on, then wondered if it could be turned on. It was stiflingly hot in here too. Could I lower the window? I began to concentrate on just sitting there, as hard as I could.

— Hey, thanks again for the job.

— You're welcome. You working hard?

— Like a dog. And you?

— I always work hard. Not that you can tell. This is my third start-up. They're always the same, like a competition. Who can stay latest at night, 'lunch is for pussies', yadda yadda.

— It is great to be working, Sam. I really owe you.

— I'll be sure and call that in.

He smiled.

— Thanks again.

He laughed before answering, his inflection inferring but leaving unspoken the 'as I said'.

— You're welcome, Evan.

I wiped my palms on my trousers. We drove in silence and as we pulled onto Chestnut, he slowed down to let the receptionist cross the road. She beamed. Sam whispered.

— God, you must love it here. Young, good-looking, all these babes, and with your accent. I can only imagine.

— Ah, well now . . .

It was so hot in this car.

— You're blushing, young man. Are you breaking hearts?

My mouth was parched.

— God. I don't know about . . .

— The Irish accent is so musical, it's hard to believe you'd ever do anything grown-up and really bad. You know what I mean?

My scalp began to itch and a bead of sweat rolled down my back.

— Well . . .

— The way you talk. It's wonderful, so innocent.

— I don't know . . .

— I'm not being patronizing, at least not deliberately.

I know you're an adult. But you could just read the phone book to an American woman and she'd jump your bones there and then.

— I'm not sure . . .

Now sweat rolled down my nose. He opened the doors with the clicker and finally we plunged down into the cool relief of darkness, cruising between pillars, looking for a spot.

— What age are you, Evan?

— Twenty-one.

— I am *more* than double your age. Where did it go? Let me give you a piece of advice. Get married late. Stay in the game for a long, long time and wait until you're good and ready.

— Okay.

— Get some experience under your belt. So to speak. Where were all the parking spots?

— Okay . . . .

— You're probably already cutting an erotic swathe through this town . . . am I right?

I felt like I was being held underwater, this panic clearly a chemical residue from the night before. And for the first time in my memory, the car park was full. What could I say?

— I dunno . . . hey, thanks for the lift, Sam.

— No problem.

I smoothed my trouser legs and tried very hard to breathe.

— Seriously though, thanks. Thanks a million.

APRIL 1995

Mickey took a turtleshell comb from his back pocket and spat on it, then restored his comb-over. Standing on the roof of ForwardSlash, Fred and I awaited the prognosis.

— The problem is the roof is sagging, is what that is.

Apparently Fred's friend knew all about repairing roof leaks and that's why he was up here with us, but it felt to me like charity. Mickey must have been fifty-five, his potbelly tight as a drum, and he elected to belt his faded Levi's below the waist. He spent all his days out at the racetrack in Oakland and sometimes if there was a three-man job to be done, Fred would call him up and get him over to lend us a hand. When Fred called, Mickey always answered.

A huge puddle had gathered on the roof and we began to sweep it towards the drains with coarse yard brushes. But the rain storms had been fierce, drains were blocked with leaves and twigs and had to be cleared by hand; Fred's and mine. Mickey poked at his drain doubtfully with a broom handle. Fred was on his hands and knees, digging and chatting enthusiastically.

——You see, he's called the Unabomber because he's supposed to target universities and airlines, but today, the letter said that he has no beef with them and he's sorry about the losing-the-limbs snafu.

Only that morning, the *New York Times* had published the 'Unabomber' manifesto, and Fred had devoured it with ghoulish fascination, not entirely in disagreement about his principles, if not the execution.

— He's really mad at technology companies. I told Devon in the mail room about it and when I left, he was actually sniffing packages. You reckon anthrax smells?

— I reckon if you can smell it, you're already in a spot of bother.

Fred held up a fistful of rotting leaves and I presented the bin bag.

— Think about it, Evan. You deliver mail.

Down the weeks and with endless patience, Fred had taught me the difference between Phillips-head and regular screwdrivers, how to lift heavy objects and where the FedEx office was. Mickey kept asking Fred whether he could get him in to work at ForwardSlash full time, as a handyman. Fred said he'd try but that they already had two, and when he gestured to me to make that point, Mickey let me know with a glance that he didn't think much of my credentials. Fred and Mickey were simpatico, drank together at the local bar, The Lodge, around the corner. And there, no doubt, an odd story about my lack of nous had crept out.

The place smelled earthy and fresh, and after a long

morning the drains were cleared and most of the water displaced to the street below. Up here, we couldn't be seen from the street, only by those on top of Telegraph Hill. The sun had dried out the roof, and we began to pour hot tar from buckets onto it and sweep it flat with old brush heads. I looked over at Mickey, sunning himself on the far side of the roof, brush head idle beside him. He had cast himself as our foreman on account of knowing about tar and rain, and was thereby entitled to do nothing. And if he was sleeping, I wanted to wake him up.

— Hey, Mickey, next time it rains, won't this just happen again?

He didn't open his eyes.

— I sure as hell hope so, kid.

The next time I met him, Sam saw me before I saw him. I was walking across Levi's plaza alone, pushing my empty mail truck back to the office. And unlike the others all around who hurried about in twos and threes, laughing at an office joke but laughing distractedly, he was leaning back on his elbows, eating an ice cream, holding but not using the handkerchief in his spare hand. For everyone else, lunch was borrowed time; borrowed and repayable that very afternoon, but there Sam almost-lay, faintly amused by something that no one else knew.

— Top of the morning.

— There he is. Hiya, Sam. Having your ice cream . . .

— Sure. Who doesn't love ice cream?

I kicked the mail truck to standing. I wanted to compliment him on the way he looked, but I couldn't, because it wasn't about the way he looked but the way he *was*, and as such could never be properly conveyed. It was how he ate ice cream on his own because he wanted ice cream. It was experience, breeding, power, or the confluence of all three. It was casual, ineffable and utterly hypnotic.

— I might have to get one of them.

— Go do that. I got Tonto right here.

I had meant much later, when my work was done, but he had already draped a protective heel on the tyre of the mail truck, the store was directly behind him, and for some reason, free will elsewhere entirely.

Back on the roof, after a concentrated thirty-second spell of work, Mickey leaned on his brush, squinting into the sun and breathing heavily. When Fred and I had tarred our areas we began to encroach on his, now literally doing his work for him. When I came closer Mickey stopped me, his hand on my arm.

— Stretch it out, man. We're on the roof. We're getting paid by the hour.

I went back to tarring and he went back to sunning himself, now using my new bag as a pillow. The Forward-Slash bags had arrived that morning, black record bags with everyone's email address stitched on the flap. evanb@forwardslash.com – my bag was free advertising for the company, but momentous nonetheless, and after Karen's, the first email address of anyone I knew. When I mentioned this in a letter to my mum, she wrote back to say that she thought the local library in Dublin had a computer with email on it. We were going to try and send each other a message that weekend. Now Mickey rearranged my bag as a kind of pillow and noticed the email address but said nothing, and appeared to be sleeping until a few minutes later when he craned his neck up to see us.

— Man, you're going too fast. Stretch it out, man. Tell him, Fred. Tell him to stretch it out.

Fred kept working but didn't answer, and this caused Mickey to sit up, confused.

— Yo, Fred. Tell him. You're in charge. Tell him, man.

Mickey waited for a response from Fred and Fred made him wait, then turned to me.

— Mickey likes the roof, Evan. You oughta know that.

He laughed, and continued working. Mickey looked at Fred accusingly.

— What? You don't like the roof? I'm the dumb one now? For not wanting to break my back up here, on a part-time gig?

Fred never stopped working the tar.

— That's all right, friend, but I'm a little different.

— How so? You better than me?

— I never said that.

— So what then? You don't like the roof?

— My baby girl doesn't like me on the roof. That's what.

Fred had already told me about his youngest daughter and how she wanted him to get a proper job like her friends' daddies. Mickey went to rearrange his pillow again.

— 'Evanb . . . something . . . forwardslash dot com'. The hell is that?

I stopped sweeping and looked over. Up here was a literal place, and tarring the roof with Mickey was tarring the roof with Mickey. All that existed was that which could be touched. I looked down at the pale band of skin where Danny's ring used to be.

— It's a bag.

— I know it's a bag, slick. What's this is what I'm asking?

— That's my email address.

Mickey laughed.

— What, in case some nerd on Muni wants to date ya? Some guy?!

I went over and took his pillow from him and threw it away to the side of the roof, making sure that this time the email address side landed face down.

— Aww, I'm sorry, Evan. Did I hurt your feelings?

Fred kept sweeping.

I met Sam again in the plaza but this time I was sitting down to smoke and he walking by. He sat down without speaking, his eyes trailing the parade of feminine calves sashaying past, and I began to notice them through him. Looking at two girls, each throwing long gamine legs ahead, their hips swivelling on a tight central axis beneath a wrapped miniskirt, both of them glanced at us and away, then again at Sam, then smiling at each other, walking on by.

— You got a girlfriend, Evan?

— Umm, no.

He had smiled directly at the women, unabashed, knocking them out with it.

— You're single?

— Yeah.

Staring at the ground, the same prickle of awkwardness began to dance down my spine. What, I wondered, was the alternative to those two? In the semi-conscious life of manual labour, noticing him around the office, I'd found myself examining his smooth hands, once or twice lingering in parts of the building where he might be. And he seemed to find me around the place too, and always chose to stop and sit down beside me.

— You get to my age, and increasingly you realize that what you are attracted to, more than any particular type, is youth.

— I . . .

— Yeah. Blooming youth in all its forms.

Any response bubbling up within me was allowed to float away, unuttered. I wanted to disagree, but couldn't.

— It's wild, that power. And they won't even know they have it until it's gone.

On Friday in The Lodge, Mickey, Fred and I watched OJ sitting in the dock, hollow-eyed and mournful, being bickered over by lawyers and judges, an errant pet. The trial had briefly edged out the never-ending baseball game on the main TV set. I wanted a pint but Mickey instructed us to drink the specials, those well drinks like Jack & ginger and 7 & 7.

— That's the move, kid. Cheap as hell. Don't buy brands. Never buy brands.

I obeyed him, because down here was Mickey and Fred's domain, and down here they spoke in a more lugubrious tone, to a sympathetic cast of regulars who were over forty and ruddy faced, slumped non-athletically at the bar, watching infinite baseball games through drooping lids. Down here I was a 'tourist', by which Mickey meant not those in degrading plastic ponchos huddled around damp maps on Pier 39, but the bright young things of ForwardSlash.

This was a local bar. Here, no one gave a shit about pagers and if pressed, all swore by the 'art form' of writing letters. Here you could learn about buybacks, drink free shots, and hear stories from the school of K-Mart realism – tales from the racetrack, the dockyard and well remembered weekends in Baja. Patrons were disdainful of the future, their cynicism curated by a fleshy bartender in his forties with an ever present Oakland A's cap. At the end of these sessions, Lodge regulars oozed from their stools, past electronic darts machines, spicy wings, plastic gingham covers and ash trays overflowing with stubbed Parliament Lights. They melted into the night, home presumably, to dusty kitchens, mouldy sheets and stacks of yellow newspapers, the provenance of longer, more melancholy stories to come. I hid my computer bag under my stool and prayed that Mickey wouldn't bring it up.

When Raj joined us at the bar, I saw Mickey shoot Fred a what-the-hell look, but Fred ignored him and Raj never noticed, and F. Lee Bailey spoke, Mailer-ish, tough – by now I knew every lawyer's name. Over the course of the televised trial, judge and legal teams were slowly ascending to the thinner air, their own features adorning *Vanity Fair* and *National Enquirer* alongside those of their clients. The nature of celebrity was changing and I wanted to say something to Raj about the persuasive power of television, but it would have been petty to mention our first conversation, so I kept schtum. Until recently, Bailey and Johnny Cochrane had been neck-and-neck in terms of profile, but now Cochrane had raced ahead by holding up the alleged attacker's glove and imploring 'if it does not fit, you must acquit'. When she heard a replay of that moment before the break, a deflated woman with a slash of scarlet across thin mottled lips tapped the counter for a refill and snorted in derision.

— That's fucken' hip hop.

Everyone knew that OJ was guilty as sin, that the black community was looking for an injustice equal to that of Rodney King a few years before, a second wrong to make it all right. But in The Lodge, it wasn't about race. The Juice was a son of the city, and though no regular could bring himself to suggest that he was anything other than guilty, their fascination with his fatal flaws endured because of who he was and what they had watched him do from these very bar stools, two full decades before. For them, time itself should have been in the dock.

After the baseball went back on, two senior TV producers called Stacey and Kenny arrived along with Maggie, whose desk I had built a few weeks before. They ordered their drinks beside us at the counter, and they ordered for the imperious Diandra Hooper, presenter of the TV show, queen bee for the horny drones who spent their days and night punching code. In person, she was Nubian to the core, Pam Grier, but Diandra's on-screen persona was ushered weekly towards a caramel skin tone suggestive of tanned white person at least as much as whited-up black woman. Raj joined them at a table at the back, then beckoned us over for a drink. Mickey sized up the offer with a gimlet eye.

— They the big swingers?

— Pretty much. Come on. Let's go over and say hi.

When Fred stood up I did too. No way was I staying with Mickey, who swivelled back to the TV set.

— Clever boy. Don't forget your little bag.

At the table, Diandra was comparing OJ's glove to Desdemona's strawberry handkerchief. I had heard all about her from a TV editor whose name I never caught, a guy who, when he encountered me smoking outside the building with Fred or Raj, would insist on talking to me about 'colleens' in a disgracefully bad Irish accent. And when he did so, he would mostly talk about Diandra, and what a great piece of ass she was and whether I was going to 'hit' that. Another guy joined the table, a big man called Charlie wearing a tight black Aertex revealing thick muscular arms, with (in what I considered an ironic counterpoint to his appearance) a high, sibilant and soft voice. His brown hair had subtle blond highlights and was gelled back stylishly from a widow's peak. I had never hung around the senior producer caste before so I stayed quiet, drinking and listening, until someone asked me if I wanted another drink.

— I'll have a wee one.

Stacey pounced.

— Did you say 'wee'?!

— He did. 'Wee'! I'm sorry, but that is adorable.

The table exchanged a look. Charlie leaned forward.

— Hey. Can you do me a favour and count from twenty-nine up?

Diandra was smirking and I didn't understand why, but I was willing to do pretty much anything for a seat at this table.

— Emm, twenty-nine, thirty, thirty-one, thirty-two . . .

They were laughing, Charlie uncontrollably, Stacey with her hand in front of her mouth.

— . . . thirty-three . . .

— Turty-tree!!!!

Diandra could contain herself no longer.

— Stop, seriously, oh God . . .

Thankfully, someone changed the subject and ample, denim Kenny told a story about interviewing a former mayor of the city called Harvey Milk for the local news, right before he was assassinated. Kenny played the part of Godfather of Bay Area Television right down to his cowboy boots. Though he ran the TV show at work, he harboured a dose of scepticism about the Net, even though it was clearly going to be his meal ticket from now on. Charlie seemed to have known Harvey Milk too.

— At least now you have your 'Self Pursuit' question.

— What's 'Self Pursuit'?

— It's 'Trivial Pursuit' but with yourself as the specialist subject. So Kenny's question is: 'Which murdered politician did Kenny interview just before his death?'

A round of Self Pursuit began and it transpired that Raj had played table tennis with the singer from Devo. When Charlie's turn came he read from an imaginary card.

— How many of the Village People did Charlie Helm sleep with?

The answer was four – Charlie never scored with the Indian or the construction worker.

Sitting among hip, wry TV producers, Fred might have noticed a few rueful glances from the bar, or else he was just a good guy with loyalties to observe, and drinking buddies that were needed on the weekends. After a while, he excused himself in his usual courtly fashion and rejoined Mickey at the bar. As he left, Raj glanced beyond him.

— Ho. Check it out.

Standing at the far end of the bar with a tight smile was none other than Hardy Townsend, the CEO of the company, right where Fred had just rejoined Mickey, and beside him Sam. Though those sitting were a decade older than him, with Hardy's arrival, a minute but undoubted shift in behaviour rippled around the table, a stiffening of postures, more concentrated stirring of drinks with straws. Hardy was a prototype, combining the patter and aggression of a salesman and the technological brain of a coder. In appearance, he managed to be gym-fit and nebbish, and though I had never spoken to him, from watching his dealings with others, he could be smooth and gawky, an occasional dinner companion of Al Gore who was also capable of outbursts of childish pique.

The discussion moved on to what might become obsolete within our lifetime but the rest of the table kept glancing over at Hardy, and me over at Sam, who waved. I waved back. Stacey thought eating meat would become obsolete – she was vegetarian. Then we were talking about weight and Kenny was telling us about a morbidly obese friend of his who wrote for *Seinfeld* and believed the quality of his writing to be index-linked to his weight.

— It's tragic, actually. He knows it's killing him, but he can't do anything about it.

Stacey drained her drink.

— Why doesn't he just go on a diet and write for *Mad About You*?

— Okay. What's everyone drinking?

Now Sam and Hardy were standing in front of us and the CEO himself was holding a notepad and pen. After we ordered, he brought everyone back their drinks and Sam carried over a tray of Jägermeister behind him. Raj sniffed his dubiously.

— What's the big occasion?

Hardy smoothed his tie and produced a flier, clearly delighted that someone had bitten.

— Two reasons. Firstly . . . the new Oscars!!

He slid it across the table and Kenny read it aloud, proclaiming it grandly.

— 'The First Annual ForwardSlash Internet Awards'. Really?

— Yeah, really. And the second, bigger reason is this. Top secret information, but we're all friends here. So let's just say it seems that the possibility of an IPO by Q4 '95 is now more of a . . . probability!

Everybody clinked, shot and grimaced. Soon after, Hardy went to the bar for another round and Kenny picked up the flier and smirked.

— 'The new Oscars'. I wonder, in ten years will we be asking each other who won 'best Java applet' in 1995?

After we began to talk about technology, things got a little hazy. Everyone wanted to strike a chord with Hardy, the wolf lounging among us in sheep's clothing.

— The cinema. A disc the size of a CD will hold a full movie.

— The communality of cinema cannot be replicated.

— When you say 'communality' all I hear is people eating popcorn in my ear.

— The art work has to be small scale now . . . before, it had intrinsic value. I can remember buying albums and studying the gatefold for weeks, *deciphering* shit, on my bedroom floor.

— The problem with CDs is they're not even an improvement on cassettes.

— The future of music is about it no longer being a physical object, just a digital file.

I snuck a glance at Sam, we clinked glasses, and then I knew I was drunk because it didn't seem to surprise me that from all the way over on the other side of the planet, Róisín walked into the bar, clocked me with a wan smile and glided over.

— Fancy meeting you here!

— Hiya chicken . . .

The way she had arrived, the way we hugged, and from the manner in which I introduced her to Sam, it appeared as though she was my girlfriend, and this assumption was fine by me.

Róisín got my address from the Morelands because Tom and Sheila had been given it by Milo, as his own. When I told her about him and Dave and the bus in Mendocino, she didn't bolt immediately to the Greyhound Terminus, just smiled in that knowing way, and searched my face as she liked to do. Earlier, Róisín had met Casey at my place, who told her about ForwardSlash, and down at the office they had told her about here, and now . . . she twirled the sticky-looking cherry round in her drink and popped it in her mouth, owning the joke of it as sexy. Sam laughed indulgently and something contracted in my rib cage. Because it had taken me a while to find it, I didn't particularly want to share this scene, this evening, with her. Róisín rubbed my arm fondly.

— I am sorry for landing in your lap like this. Is it okay?

— Are you kidding? It's great to see you.

— I called you a few times but it just rang out. And the voicemail had a stranger's voice.

— Asher. I share a line with him. I need to change that message.

— You don't mind if I crash? My bags are already there . . .

— . . . Course!

Róisín and Sam got to talking. This was making me woozy, not to mention the continuing reappearance of Jaegermeister. I excused myself and tried to play darts with Diandra and I could tell I was drunk because sometimes my dart wasn't even making it to the wall where the board was mounted, diving limply onto the floorboards with a dull thunk and shudder that seemed crudely metaphorical. I was trying to find a level of sobriety that would allow me to rejoin the table, but the plummeting darts and continuous shots confirmed that I couldn't, and then it was too late because Sam had left.

After the bar closed we said goodbye and Róisín, Kenny and I stumbled back to ForwardSlash. We groped our way down the stairs to the dark underground car park, but before going down I glanced back over my shoulder and saw that the light in Sam's office was still on. We threw on the basement light and bleary heads popped up in the back windows of cars.

— What's that all about?

Kenny waved his key around then pointed it at us, swaying.

— Product launch. There's no point in going home if you're coming back in a few hours. But we . . . we are not working tomorrow and I . . . I am giving you guys a ride home. Ergo, get in.

— I think you're a little too drunk to drive, Kenny.

Typical fucking Róisín. She had just met him. She didn't have the right to say that. He was much older, and these were my friends. And everyone in this town drove drunk. Róisín was walking back to the steps. Kenny jabbed at the car door with his key, then shouted.

— Ro-sheen. I command you. Look at this machine.

He hugged his car, head leaning on the roof, smiling dumbly.

— My sweet baby.

A bleary coder looked up from the back seat of a Honda Prelude a few bays over. Róisín climbed out of view.

Even though I couldn't have done it, driving in this town looked easy. Left, right, stop, pause – no winding lanes, no weird blind turns or intersections with large gnarled trees in the centre. No farm animals crossing and no boy racers – a mathematical grid. Still, not for a moment did I acknowledge that there was an angel on my shoulder, although by the end Kenny was driving with his hand covering one eye, 'to cut down on some of the traffic'.

When I turned the key in the door, I got a shock.

Róisín wasn't there. I shouldn't have left her to get a taxi alone on her first night in town. If she had called one, why wasn't she home now? I decided to stay up for her but ended up falling asleep on the futon, which was technically going to be her bed. Then it was six in the morning and I had slept in my Pumas, and my feet were swollen, hot and tingling. A wave of relief washed over me when I peeped into my room and saw Róisín asleep under my covers. I took fresh clothes out to the hall, showered, dressed and ate, overcome with a flood of curiosity. How did she get back? Where had she been?

— Wee turty-tree!

Charlie beckoned me in without looking up, watching TV, long slender legs thrown up on the desk in his new office and a laptop open beside him. His finger absently brushed the click wheel from time to time, keeping whatever was on the screen alive. He had been up here to consult on our TV show before, but I couldn't really say I knew him apart from being aware that he had slept with two-thirds of the Village People. Behind him, a framed *X Files* poster hung on the exposed brick wall, a remnant of a predecessor who had been too technology-oriented to deliver eyeballs. ForwardSlashTV was haemorrhaging viewers and with his stuffed Rolodex, Charlie's mandate was to use the stars to bring 'em back.

In the far corner a TV showed the action from Crufts Dog Show and as with every office in the building, it was impossible to tell if the occupant was remotely busy. I bet that was never a problem in years gone by when, regardless of your position, if you had a TV set on in your office and were watching a dog show you were almost certainly skiving off. Before, if you were bored in work and you wanted to kill time, you had to read whatever came to hand – instruction manuals, the phone book, the brochure for the coffee machine. Now all leisure was research or looked very much like it, and new media work was supposed to be pleasurable, particularly in a company as youthful as this one. The man glancing up was either researching a forthcoming interview with the webmaster of crufts.com, or was bored, or really liked dogs. If it happened to be all three at the same time, Charlie had scored himself the perfect job.

I coughed.

— Yes. I have a new computer for you, and some shelves to assemble.

— Say, what do you guys do with the old computers?

— We take them away and wipe them, then give them to a charity.

He turned back to the television and only then did I notice the black Labrador snoozing beneath the desk. Charlie gazed dreamily at the TV set, then cooed.

— Oh, Evan! Would you look at that adorable Afghan?

I watched a lank creature with leg fur resembling designer slacks trot up the green baize carpet and turn on his paws smoothly, mane flowing like Christy Turlington's hair. The dog looked like a snob, somehow.

— His coat is so sleek!

— My, yes. It absolutely is.

The judge began to inspect the mouths of competing hounds, leaving Charlie to turn to me and watch for a moment as I tore at the cardboard of the flat-pack shelves.

— So you build stuff that actually matters.

— That depends on how important these shelves are, Charlie.

— Very important. Vital things will go on them.

— Well, how shall I put this . . . I'm keen to get into making things that don't matter . . .

— Be aware, Evan. The shelving unit will last longer than this technology television moment.

— Don't say that out loud around here. You'll be sectioned. Or put in jail.

— I'm already nuts. I'm from LA.

— Ahh. I should probably go down there to get into television, right?

I hefted the CPU and monitor onto his desktop and he slid his still-folded legs to one side to accommodate them, considering whether to say something. I laid the shelving flat on the ground, knelt down and began an inventory of bolts, the snoozing Lab beside me.

— Have you met my boyfriend?

I looked up. Charlie was studying his laptop screen intently.

— No. Have I?

— Carlo. He's starting work here tomorrow as a runner.

— No, I haven't met him yet. I'll certainly keep an eye out for him, though.

— Here's a picture online so you'll know what he looks like.

Charlie nodded at the screen, inviting me over. I put the screws on the ground and went around to his side of the table. This Carlo had his picture up on the company intranet already? Mine wasn't up there yet, and I had been here so much longer!

I was expecting a young, pretty guy, just out of college, but on screen was an ursine Hispanic man in his thirties with a fat handlebar moustache, and it took the briefest of glances to confirm that this picture had not been posted on the ForwardSlash intranet. Carlo was posing in front of a hot-pink background, topless save for an ornate embroidered black waistcoat. Above his head, in a slashing font, 'Carlo Grant stars in 69 Meat Street. Woof!!!!'

— Okay, great! Now that I know what he looks like, I'll keep an eye out.

I moved back to the far side of the desk.

— But look at the beading on that waistcoat. Isn't it divine?

Charlie was whispering and peering at the picture in a manner that demanded I come back and inspect it. I did, very badly wanting a job on his show, and once I was able to affirm that yes, the beading on the waistcoat must have taken a great deal of time to hand-stitch, he coyly scrolled down, revealing his boyfriend's naked lower half and his enormity. A noise not unlike a gasp escaped me, and Charlie smiled at my uncontrolled, pure confusion – if confusion can ever be said to be pure.

I began to reassemble, moving planks of wood noisily, hearing the continuing commentary from the dog show while the silent presence of Charlie grew ever louder. Never before had I seen the erect penis of another man, let alone one the size of an emu's neck. And I remembered a story Stacey told me about Maggie, the young, pert Jewish New Yorker with stunning breasts whose desk I had built, and who was drinking with us and Kenny in The Lodge the night before. There were five producers on the TV show, four of whom had worked in the industry for a decade and were in their mid-thirties. Inexplicably, the very young, just-out-of-college Maggie had been hired as the fifth, after managing to convince Kenny to help her produce her idea for a story. As pitches go it was hardly game-changing stuff. A man on a motorbike with two computers strapped to the panniers and a web camera mounted on his helmet was crossing America and recording his adventures in a series of flickering, low resolution images and a diary on the Internet.

Kenny couldn't do anything about content but as an ex-editor and cameraman he was a master of form, who could make the ugly nuts and bolts of a story like this one shine by virtue of the way they finally looked. Stacey told me how he stuffed that piece with picture-in-picture, wipes and transitions, sharp music cues and hyperactive camera work and afterwards, rumours abounded that in exchange for his wizardry at the keyboard, he had been afforded the opportunity to handle Maggie's warm globes. Even to an envious young man like me these whispers sounded like sour, sexist nonsense. However, on the morning after Maggie's trial edit Stacey told me how she jogged from her apartment into work, and happened to be coming out of the shower when she met Maggie, wearing nothing but a towel and a curdling, mortified grimace. Stacey held the shower door open, thinking it odd that someone as confident as Maggie could seem that prudish about nudity – until she got back to her desk on the studio floor and learned that it wasn't about that at all.

As she was firing up her computer, Stacey glanced at the edit suites on the balcony floor above, and right at that moment, perhaps prompted by the trilling start-up sound of her Macintosh (which Fred swore was the stolen opening chord to 'Squeezebox' by the Who), Kenny stepped out yawning, barefoot, hair tousled, zipping up his pants. By the time he saw her and beat a retreat back into the Avid where the makeshift bed had been arranged, Stacey was already furiously typing 'ohmygod ohmygod ohmygod ohmygod' onto the keys of a still-booting computer. Until Stacey told me about Maggie's rapid ascent to the higher rungs of ForwardSlash, I had never been aware that people in the real world slept their way to the top. To me it was the stuff of daytime television, where American lovers had evil twins and entire seasons were shown to be dreams after all. But now I lived in California, had

I disappeared into the magic land of TV? Was I now obligated to live like a character from *Knots Landing*? Was I able?

I stood Charlie's shelves up and leaned them against the brick wall, then wiped my hands and tried to think. At that exact moment, Sam Couples happened to be passing by, and waved in. I waved back as Charlie glanced up, and craned his neck to follow.

— Just who is that furry little Dreamjew?

I began loading the old computer and cables onto my mail cart, desperate to leave.

— I dunno. Some guy.

— Say, Evan. Do you think I could hold onto that? It would help if I could work at home.

— We're supposed to give the old equipment to charity.

— Maybe I could make a donation to the charity and take this one home? You know, I'm looking for an assistant. We're onlining the first show of the new season and we could try you out there, swapping tapes, and see how we go.

— Really?

— Sure. But you might need to talk to Tammy. I'm scared of her.

I couldn't tell whether Charlie ever intended to make a donation, and because I didn't know what else to do, I took the old computer off the mail truck and set it back against the wall.

— I'll talk to her, and you can have that, but don't tell a sinner.

He smiled and turned back to the TV.

— Thanks for the pretty shelves, 'turty-tree'. I love a guy who's good with his hands.

The man crawling on all fours along Folsom in the dog collar might have been pushing sixty, but the companion tugging hard at the attached chain was younger, his bare torso stuffed into a black studded waistcoat. His jeans had been fundamentally altered so that bare ass was exposed, and this master-and-pet scene was being played out indifferently, as if they really were dog and owner on a constitutional stroll. When I was a baby my sister would pretend I was her pet and walk me around the house, and with his combed-over hair and hanging gut, the man on his knees reminded me of my school Economics teacher, but in no other way was the scene at the corner of Folsom and 10th relatable.

I turned to say something to Róisín, but she pretended (I know for a fact she was pretending) that she wasn't surprised, and that nothing about the scene was remarkable. I was beginning to understand the knowing smiles that played across the face of Charlie and Alonso who also worked at ForwardSlash, when I told them my plans for the weekend.

— You're doing what?

— The Folsom Street Fair. A bunch of us are going. It's like a big party. Sunday. Bands.

— I know what it is, honey. I don't wear a suit and tie every day.

— Well, nor do I. I've already been to Gay Pride, you know.

Alonso was short and tubby with a trim moustache, and when he grabbed the back of the seat at his freshly assembled desk and rolled it over, commanding me to sit down, I thought he was going to give out to me. I sat down, and leaning over me, his hands on his knees, he examined my features with a dramatic, concerned frown.

— Sweetie, you can forget about Gay Pride. Folsom Street Fair makes Halloween in the Castro seem like Disney on Ice. And Halloween in the Castro makes Gay Pride . . .

— . . . I've been down the Castro too.

— Well everything's dandy and you've seen it all, so.

He stood up and raised his eyes to heaven, then stalked past Charlie.

— You talk to him.

Why was everyone able to assume that I was this sexless leprechaun? Couldn't I have been a poly-amorous Celtic stud (even if I wasn't?). I wanted to stove Alonso's face in and Charlie could tell.

— Don't mind him. It gets a little wild is all.

It was ten deep at the bar on Folsom and Dore, a hot room of menacing signifiers: beards, tattoos and shaven heads. Here, though, any threat was undercut by smiles and winks. Queuing for a drink I saw a man on his knees in front of two others in the backyard. The standing men's trousers were around their ankles but they were chatting as if they were getting pedicures instead of head. I was sweating by the time I made it back outside and when I found Róisín, she was sitting on the kerb watching the street life. Holding our plastic cups of beer, I stood away from her for a moment and watched her, arranged small and neat on the sidewalk.

Róisín was beautiful and she seemed to like me enough to stay around for a while, and her liking me was a big part of us getting along so well together, if not everything. She had been on the futon in the hallway for weeks now. Casey and Asher didn't seem to mind – it was me who felt in some way detained by her presence. It wasn't that she was begging to hang out with me, certainly not. Róisín had plenty of friends in this town, many more than I did, in fact. Days would go by without me seeing her and I began to think she thought she was doing me a favour by hanging around. We would meet up after I finished work in the evening and eat some food, maybe have a drink, and everything would go really well. Then at the end of the night, I'd say goodbye and go next door to my room and wonder whether by leaving her to sleep on the futon in the hall I was doing the right thing, and if not, how exactly she wanted me to play it.

It wasn't as if she wanted to sleep with me or anything like that – events back in Dublin had formed part of a revenge subplot and nothing more. I knew that men operated at many levels of subtlety beneath those of women, and in the field of non-verbal communication, Róisín had few equals. She knew that my dumb loyalty to her boyfriend would force me to admit to Milo what had happened, and in this way she would be able to communicate to him that she was totally over him, without ever having to say a word. Of course she had asked me to promise that I would never breathe a word about this to another living soul, and even though it was clear to me that she desperately wanted me to tell Milo, I knew that she needed to ask this favour of me just as badly, to add the gloss coat – her as an honest, mortified young woman who had been temporarily overwhelmed by passion. And when I did confess my sins to him, drunk in Murio's Trophy Room, he snorted with laughter and lit a cigarette, thinking of something and turning back to me.

— You're grand, Evan. Don't sweat it. I'm just glad it was you and not someone . . . more . . .

— Someone more what?

— Nothing, man.

— Come on, man. More what?

— Just . . . someone else.

Now, sitting alone amid the chaos of Folsom, her boyfriend up and gone, her friend-by-default me, she looked vulnerable and I ached for her. When you aren't near somebody, you could love them so much more – I hated myself for that, but it was undeniable. I went over and gave her the beer. She was holding something tiny and precious between her thumb and forefinger and when I sat down beside her she made to put it in my mouth.

— Here.

Rather than accept whatever it was as she was suggesting, I put the beers down, sat beside her and took it gingerly, examining it in my palm. A square of paper with a tiny cartoon strawberry. Róisín sighed.

— It's acid.

— Oh, shit. Have you taken some?

Róisín opened her mouth and slowly stuck her tongue out, revealing one of her own. I examined the tiny square of paper. She didn't like it, the way I cared what other people were doing. I couldn't even smoke pot but I hated being disapproved of by her. An elderly man with a resemblance to Terry Wogan passed by, naked. The fifteen steel rings encircling his scrotal sac elongated it to about one foot, his nuts straining against the very limits of human flesh. I handed back the acid.

— I can't. I'm sorry.

She took her half out of her mouth, took my square back from my damp palm and wrapped them both in a cigarette paper.

— You can always take yours without me.

— I can't, actually.

She put them in a tiny handbag and narkily snapped it shut.

— Why not?

— It's no fun tripping on your own.

We sat in silence on the kerb, me the hopeless square responsible for ruining her day. The silence between us became unbridgeable, and I was so glad when a punk band called Pansy Division invaded the space and drowned it out.

Róisín was worried about Milo. That morning there had been a shouty phone call, but typically, she had refused to tell me what it was about, saying only that she didn't want me to worry, and also, that it was up to Milo to tell me himself about the problem. He hadn't told me and she couldn't do that for him. It would be a betrayal of trust. Well, that was that, then. I had spoken with Milo on the phone a couple of times but we kept it short. He had blindsided me, left me bereft, and though the rational side of my brain knew I had no claim over him, another part of me felt the loss more keenly for that very reason.

Had it been a month before, when she had arrived, I probably would have encouraged her to go upstate and find him, and you know, talk some sense into him, get him back down here to the city to validate the decisions that the rest of us were making to stay on the straight and narrow. But now I had a job and an apartment and all these people around me, and some sort of direction in which to head, and it was good to know that whatever he was shouting about on the phone, Milo clearly hadn't found the answer, and that by arriving on my doorstep and not his as expected, Róisín hadn't found an answer either. Misery loves company. Everything we knew about each other we knew from osmosis, not from telling or ever asking, and now that we were locked in some kind of competition to be happy, he would never tell me his problems and I would never tell her mine.

A tap on the shoulder and I turned around, and it was true – Alonso from work didn't always wear a suit and tie. Today it was a steel mesh jockstrap, and he had an arm around a petite Filipino boy. Both were smiling that same knowing, maddening smile.

— Raul, this is Evan – he works in my office, and he's Irish.

Raul whispered something to Alonso and Alonso nodded. There was simply no way I was betraying shock or discomfort. Because sitting down there on the kerb it was right at my eyeline, I decided to jump right on in with I-Spy.

— I love, love, love your jockstrap!

— It's surprisingly comfortable.

— I didn't expect to see you here, Alonso.

— I never said I *wasn't* coming.

— Róisín, this is Alonso who I work with and Raul.

— Aren't you a doll. Are you guys . . .

— She's my girlfriend, yeah.

— Really. Well hello, miss!

A flicker of confusion crossed Róisín's features as she shielded the sun from her eyes. They waved goodbye and made their way through the crowd towards the bar, Raul turning around and blowing a kiss. Róisín blew one back, smiling.

— Why did you introduce me as your girlfriend back there?

— You know the way, with the whole thing. It's easier.

A fat man in a black leather cape came over, devil

horns glued onto his bald pate. For our delectation he presented a tattoo encircling his bicep in red ink, in German. In a camp Gestapo bellow, he translated: 'he who fights with monsters should look to it that he himself does not become a monster. And when you gaze long into an abyss, the abyss gazes also into you.' With this, the caped crusader bent over, whispering in a cutesy voice,

— That's Nietzsche, kids.

He overbalanced, sending our drinks flying.

The clock radio said 4 a.m. and I was peeling off a sock when a knock sounded and Róisín entered unsteadily, smiling. Even drunk, she managed to be willowy.

— The futon is just so bumpy.

Before I could answer she shut the door behind her. I tried to shrug like it didn't matter to me but it was more like a spasm. I looked around and didn't realize until I saw it through somebody else's eyes that the room was something of an embarrassment. A cactus in the corner that definitely needed dusting. Clothes slumped from where they had hit the backboard of the far wall. A box of cassettes, grubby trainers in a lonely row. I hadn't even unpacked – I had no furniture into which I could pack whatever it was that my bag still contained.

Even though it was just a box spring on the ground with a sleeping bag on top, a saleswoman at Nordstrom had bullied me into buying a valance for my bed. Now I noticed how it made the bed look like a giant limpet stuck to the floor, splayed fabric gathering whorls of hair and dust. I dived under the sleeping bag, then worried about what that said or didn't say, and whether I did or didn't want to say it. Perhaps because she was drunk, Róisín took her clothes off slowly and deliberately and when she turned to the bed, I slid over to the far wall, off the only pillow. She climbed underneath and we lay there in silence.

— Can I smoke?

Apart from wearing shoes, this was the issue about which Casey and Asher were the most militant. There was to be no smoking allowed in the apartment. Nada. No. Absolutely not.

— Sure.

We lit up and I pictured us in a film, thinking how from above, this pre-coital terror could be mistaken for post-coital bliss. Was it really about the couch next door being lumpy? When we put out our cigarettes I yawned, feeling small and brittle, a little cold and entirely awake. Was this a moment to seize? It didn't feel like it, or how I imagined it would feel when the moment came. Róisín rolled over and reached down the front of my boxer shorts and I rolled over towards her and we kissed, my head leaning against my left arm. Because my eyes were open, beyond her head I could see my own left hand sticking up in salute. I closed my eyes and focused on my right hand which had begun fiddling with her bra strap, attempting to invade a cup, then straining against the limits with a finger or two, then finally stumbling around the back, a drinker locked out of his house, checking the windows and doors.

Then my hand began venturing south. My fingers were inside her knickers now, canvassing opinions from the electoral body and moving or staying put according to the exit polls. As my hand continued working, feeling her thatch on my wrist, our kissing became a little less clinical and a little more ardent. The mechanics were working, maybe. I kept on the move, but gentle, playing around in a way that I desperately hoped was pleasurable. In reciprocation, Róisín's hand found me hard and began to play with me, my testicles, and then with my perineum. She moved to allow herself in there more fully and then she plunged her index finger inside my ass. I actually yelped with surprise, then pulled her hand away, trying and failing to laugh it off. She rolled over onto her back and we lay there in silence for a good few minutes.

— I don't get you guys.

— What do you mean?

— You always like to put your fingers inside girls, but when a girl tries to do it with you, you become all weird.

And I thought I would be thankful when she broke the silence.

— Well, it is a different matter, isn't it? I'm the man.

— What?!

— It's . . . an ass. You know?

— What difference does that make?

I hadn't a clue what to say, so I began to kiss her again and moved on top of her. She spread her legs to accommodate my torso and we continued kissing, but I was leaning above her and it felt as natural as dangling from a cliff. My instinct wasn't offering clues, and when I rolled onto my side to take off my boxers, I instantly lost my impulse. My head was thudding, and I very badly wanted to be alone now, in another room, in another house, or maybe in a bar. Róisín ran her hand through my hair, smiling sadly.

— Hey. Penetration isn't everything.

But for a petrifying virgin, what else was there? She laughed and reached for her cigarettes, lighting one for me and passing it across to where I lay, backed into the wall. Only then, now that I had no prospect of doing it for real, could I begin to fake a good night's sleep. There were so many possibilities that could account for the accumulation of disappointing nights like these. I am drunk, I am high, I am sick and frigid, I am insane . . .

The clock read 6.20 a.m., a grey, cold dawn streaking through the blinds. Soft rain dusting the foggy window, Róisín sound asleep, the room smelling of smoke. Sometime in the night she must have put her T-shirt back on, removed her make-up and climbed back under the sleeping bag, so I had slept a little after all. I crawled over her, taking care not to wake her up. This was a fraught moment. Many of the best excuses that could reasonably have held the night before I could no longer hope to use in the cold light of morning. If I was sick before, was I not now better? If drunk, was I not now sober – if a little hung over? If I had been tired, had I not slept well? From upstairs, a sack plunged down the chute into the steel wheelie bin beneath my window. I froze, glass smashed in the yard and a bird flew off, but beneath me, Róisín didn't stir. I got out of bed and carried the clothes I needed for the day into the bathroom, and inside I dropped the pile on the floor and vomited against the bowl, shivering, my stomach heaving tensely, hands on wet tiles. The shower hid the sound of further retching and I began to warm up under the jets, smelling my room-mates' shampoo and stale smoke particles as they ran from my hair, the grit and dirt of me disappearing through the plug hole, for now anyway.

Fred and I chugged up Market in a rental truck, heading towards the residence of an ice sculptor on South Van Ness. Since accepting Charlie's offer, I spent half my time working as a runner for the TV show and the other half with Fred. These days Mickey was getting more work with Fred, I was working more than ever for the TV show and everyone was happy. But today Mickey was sick, it was the day of the First Annual ForwardSlash Internet Awards, an ice sculptor had been commissioned to create some-thing to sit on top of the cold buffet table in the venue, and Fred and I were tasked with ferrying it down there and setting it up.

Queues of people were forming outside stores on Market, wearing rain macs and holding Tupperware. On the same day as the first Annual ForwardSlash Internet

Awards some big band clearly had the temerity to announce a tour or release a new album. It made our company's grand gesture seem small and I was sorry for Hardy and us as a company. Judging by the crowds queuing and the apathy with which our award ceremony had been greeted around town, it felt like evidence that we had misjudged the extent to which people wanted to fall in love with computing after all.

For much of the day I kept hearing that Rolling Stones song 'Start Me Up': on people's computers, in the shop at lunch while I was standing in line for my burrito, even in Kenny's Porsche as he rumbled by us in the morning with a loud beep. People liked the old stuff. Having spent Easter at Fred's apartment I could attest to his taste for the past. In his neat, small one-bedroom in Outer Richmond, the cassette tape ruled, and no microwave was used in the preparation of turkey and trimmings. The moment of purest modernity came when his ex-wife sprayed UHT cream on his youngest daughter's apple pie for dessert.

— Viva Las Vegas!

Fred's wonder and surprise at this new thing was not for the sake of his youngest daughter. So what would happen, I wondered, as his ex-wife smiled somewhat sadly at him and he poked at the pile of sugary cream, beaming, what would happen when he finally admitted the 1980s into his life?

On the drive we listened to *Zuma* and, rounding a corner, could see the sculptor standing on the street as promised, wearing protective gloves and waving us into the parking spot, using the chisel in his right hand. The sculptor was tall and hairy and smelled of sweat. His beard was bound tightly at the chin and punctuated thereafter by elastic bands at intervals, so it resembled a chain of sausages. Fred and I were to transport the fruits of his labour directly down to the Pier. It was a good four hours before the awards were due to begin and despite the rain showers, the day – and the van – was stiflingly warm.

— Gentlemen! Follow me.

His wife was Japanese and bowed deeply as we passed her. We were led down a flight of stairs past blowtorches and an Oriental broadsword of some description and into the garage area, where a huge form stood on a plinth, swaddled in thick silver foil. It was perhaps twenty feet by five, and all around it the floor was slick with ice and sloping gently towards a central drain. I could see my breath. Fred scratched his head.

— That as heavy as it looks?

— Almost exactly.

I couldn't wait to see what the sculpture was – an ice computer? An enormous ampersand? The sculptor chuckled because getting it down to the venue in one piece was not his job. He slapped the foil.

— So that cover creates a dead air space. It will buy you an hour or so for transport time and for set-up. Once that foil comes off, the detail should be preserved for a four-hour event. It doesn't start to look like mush until long after that. Your award show is at eight, right? And it's four now? So you get down there and get set up for six then whip that off, you should be cool.

He opened the garage door and gently, with minute, coaxing shoves we hauled the block out to where the van was. Once we opened the back, it took all three of us beneath it to load it on, then strap it down.

— You guys might wanna get another body down there to help you unload. I'd go with you, but I got a last-minute order for a Windows 95 launch party. Busiest time of the year.

— Oh, yeah? When is the Windows 95 launch?

— Are you kidding me?

— No.

— You haven't seen the crowds?

— I mean, yeah, we've seen crowds, but that's for the software?

Fred took off his baseball cap, scratched his head. We may as well have been chewing straw. The sculptor clapped his hands over his mouth, then shouted upstairs.

— Michiko! C'mere. You say I live in a vacuum!

We drove much slower going back, to preserve our cargo but also so Fred could gawk at the people, as if we were on safari and they another species.

— Look, Evan. Fans of software. Standing in line.

TV crews on Market were vox-popping people who had stood all day to get their hands on this . . . thing, which as far as I could tell, would allow them to perform the same jobs in a slightly different manner. For a technology TV show this was the equivalent of an election, but even the major news outlets were there. Queues were snaking around entire city blocks. The software even had a song, that horribly turgid pastiche of their own work by the Stones which had been chosen, no doubt, to target the boomers outside. The atmosphere was feverish. Skies had darkened throughout the day and as we pulled up to the warehouse, thunder cracked and a series of rain storms began. Now those who weren't filming the midnight launch of Windows 95 were being filmed in the rain, waiting for the product.

The ForwardSlash Internet Awards were being held in a warehouse right on the water, a black tie affair to be compered by Diandra Hooper. Presumably in the absence of genuine broadcaster interest, our own cameras were filming the event, and the ice sculpture was to form the centrepiece at the buffet area outside the hall, for before and after the presentation. Fred and I enlisted the help of two IT guys that had been setting up projectors and we four lugged it into position, mounting it on the drip tray, around which a buffet table was arranged. The room was long and narrow and closed off to the outside with a large black scrim, and after the caterers arranged the food around the table and left, only Fred and I remained.

— Should we take the cover off?

— We should probably wait until the last minute.

Fred wiped his hands on his shirt.

— Well, I guess the beauty of ice sculptures is there's nothing to bring back. If you don't mind hanging out to take off the cover, I might return the van. That okay, young Evan?

After Fred drove off, I left the smaller, newer reception area and parted the black scrim that had been hung to prevent us from getting a peek and wandered into the main room. It reminded me of an abandoned roller disco and smelled faintly of fish gut. But carpets had been nailed to the floor and pigeons ushered out, and though basic, the long room with the vaulted ceiling had a dramatic impact. I tested the echo. It was huge and creepy, and up there under the eaves, something flew off. A glitter ball dispersed silver shards and huge circular tables were set throughout the perimeter, and on the far side of the empty floor stood a stage and a huge screen. I sat at a few tables, deliberately desynchronized some place settings, then went back to the reception room. I went outside to smoke, came back in and wandered some more, then when the alarm on my watch went off, I began to remove the foil slowly, circling the huge buffet table like it was a maypole, gathering foil in balls and setting them behind me on the ground, taking great care not to knock anything over.

The sculpture was beginning to catch the rays from an artfully placed dado light on the rafters above, and as the wrapping revealed the bottom then the middle, a representation of a person or people began to emerge. I unwrapped the last of the foil, stood back and drank it all in. Rising from a spume of icy waves was the wily, smirking face of Hardy Townsend. The ice sculptor had captured perfectly his bullet-proof confidence, the small-eyed glint and the immense cranium. But walking around the back of it, there was a second figure on the far side, inlaid, and drawing closer I saw that it was Sam, an incredibly lifelike Sam, facing the wall.

I pushed aside a tray of Ahi Tuna and tested the buffet table for weight. It suggested that it could take me so, stepping up onto it and holding the sculpture by the base, I pulled myself up level with this man. From beneath, the perspective of Michelangelo's *David* is perfect, because his head is slightly bigger than the rest of his body, to account for foreshortening in the eye of a person walking around the base. But from up here, the proportions of Sam were eerily accurate, a recreation of lips and jaw and Adam's apple. There was that luxurious hair, a little long all over, and the smile which was ever so slightly come-hither without smugness or conceit. But I had drunk in these features in person before and he was an overweight, older married man. I had been down on Folsom and seen what was on offer, and there, among the super-effeminate boys in the T-shirts and the burly musclemen, there were neither Sams nor men who liked men like Sam.

Which left me here, staring at a pair of majestic, frozen eyes, willing me to draw my face closer. I moved in and kissed him with my eyes closed and was overcome by how cold his lips were and how unlike a real kiss this was. Then I remembered it was a sculpture, and realized with panic that I was stuck to him and quite immovable. I tried to work myself free by pushing my tongue between the ice and my own lips, but then my tongue got caught, and as the frozen lips recognized their trapped prey and tightened their grip like a once-kicked limpet, to pull away from the sculpture quickly became an impossibility. Standing up here, my feet between ceviche and swordfish, my mouth already numb, I was properly stuck, and any time I tried to move, I could feel the fabric table cloth beneath me shifting slippily, and when I tried to move with a little too much vigour the glasses began a tiny ominous rattle of their own and I had to stop altogether. And it was impossible to escape that reflection, offered back by a glassy simulacrum of pupil, like I had been checking my teeth for spinach on the back of a restaurant spoon.

My tongue was burning and the only relief was in pressing it further onto the ice, which stuck it there even more. Now the tip of my nose was stuck too and I recalled one mountaineer in a book that had lost his nose to frostbite. For a few minutes I stood still in a rising panic trying to breathe warmth onto my captor, trying to get Sam's mouth to melt sufficiently to set me free, but he had trapped me good and proper. The lips I had so desired before were now pillowy manacles, the glassy stare a grim affirmation of my darkest ever thought, still unutterable, though there was no denying I was where I was because I was who I was. I tried to cast a glance down at my feet and see if there was anything on the buffet table that could be heated and lifted by foot, something I could manoeuvre up here to help me wrench free, but it was impossible to see down there. All I could find was Sam's unblinking gaze and me frozen within it. I had to escape.

I wrapped my arms around the sculpture and tried to decapitate Sam from it at least, but ice is ice; brittle, sure, but tough enough and freezing against the bare skin of my forearms, which I had to make sure not to get stuck to it. The sculptor had said it would take four hours for the smallest details to begin to melt. I howled in a way that scared me. I continued breathing on his mouth and tried to think. Assuming I had the strength to do so, if I pulled the entire thing off the table and onto me, there was no guarantee that the part connected to my face would disengage, or that I wouldn't be mashed beneath it, into a horrendous, fleshy Slush Puppy. I tried to take comfort in the fact that I still hadn't destroyed the food, but if I didn't alert someone and get them to help me, I could still be here when the scrim on the door was removed and the entire company – plus wives, life partners and spouses, and Sam (SAM!) – moved into this room. I had to shout for help. If someone came in I could tell them I had done it as a bet. I could always say Fred was here, and he made me do it, and then he had . . . run away? No. But the alternative was much worse.

— I come back later?

Jesus. A voice had sounded behind me and I turned around to the right, and instantly howled at the ripping sound emanating from my lips.

— No, no, don't move. I help you.

The figure hove into the corner of my eyeline and I could make out a Guatemalan woman in her early forties leaning against the table, wearing the light blue smock of the cleaning company, a half-full black refuse sack by her side. I recognized her as the regular night shift cleaner from ForwardSlash. Clearly she had been dispatched down to the Pier to give this place a hoover and a dust before tonight began. She was tattooed, her brow with two large gothic dollar bill signs in greenish-black ink, her right forearm with an intricate portrait of Tupac Shakur, his Crip bandana in a bow about his head. She had a gold tooth and was holding an empty office bin. Judging from her slackening jaw she was trying and failing to come to terms with what she was seeing. Was there any remote chance that this type of behaviour was customary in Guatemala, like a Cinco de Mayo thing? She disappeared.

— Nghhh!!!

She reappeared.

— No. Wait! I get hot water.

I found the idea of being told to wait ridiculous. She gathered the sack around her back and moved away again.

Was it now over? No. I had been caught. She would set me free, but after, she would talk to someone, and what would she say to them? Who would she talk to? Had she met Sam? Oh, God. Almost definitely. Would she connect this to him? Probably. The sculpture was that good. Once I had been steamed off it, she would be able to recognize his face and maybe she already knew him. Sam worked late sometimes and was exactly the kind of hail-fellow-well-met charmer that would natter with the cleaner as she vacuumed and dusted around him. Would she tell Sam about this, and if so, how exactly would she phrase it? Did she speak enough English to convey the situation, or did he understand enough Spanish for her to really go for it?

When she came back the cleaner was carrying a basin of hot soapy water, and a mug emblazoned with the words 'PointCast'. She set the basin down on the edge of the table, took the cup in her hand and filled it, then gently stood up on the table, between the lobster tails and the Mary Rose sauce. She moved close to my face. She lifted the cup above my forehead and gently, like at a christening, she poured the hot water down my face, and as it sluiced down around the contours, I could feel it blend with the melting ice of the sculpture. There were tiny cracking sounds and I could feel my nose coming free. I licked at the warm water with the edge of my freed tongue, then ran it over my lips, which came free also, and for the briefest moment before they lost their contours Sam's lips felt warm too and I swallowed some water. She stood down and moved the basin away, then gave me an arm and helped me down. I stood back from the table, wiping my hands on my shirt front.

— Thank you. Needless to say, that was a bet. Where's Fred? I'll kill him.

I wiped my mouth with my hand and it came away bloody.

— That was a bet. You understand?

She shook her head, smiling. She went to take the bowl away but I gestured that I wanted to keep it to wipe my face. When she went to leave I stopped her.

— Umm, I don't know what you saw exactly, but whatever it was that you think you saw, do you think you can be quiet about it? I mean, can this whole . . . thing possibly be just between you and me?

Her blank face.

— The two of us? Here's the deal. I'm sure you like your job, and I certainly like mine. You like your job? Te gusto . . . trabajo? Yes? Great! So do I! I love it, I absolutely love it. I mean, I don't understand half of what goes on in work. I guess the buzzword is convergence. You know, television plus internet equals FORWARDSLASH!

— I don't know.

This was hopeless.

— So, our secret, yeah? God, I wish I knew the Spanish for secret . . . What happened in there. Can that secret be between you and me? Something we have? Secreto?

— A secret.

— Yes. A secret.

I repeated the word 'secret' and this time held a finger to my lips. She shrugged and left, and using a napkin from the buffet table and the bowl of hot water I cleaned away the blood. Sam's mouth had melted away, and the bottom of his nose, but his eyes were still clear, witnessing, unblinking. I climbed the table once more and using the 'PointCast' cup, poured the water over them, watching bloody tears sluice down his cheeks, melting him away into blankness. Then I got back down, straightened the buffet table and left.

I spent hours that night sitting by the cliff at the top of Telegraph Hill, thinking about what I could do to fix it, but I couldn't think of anything. Those glass eyes had seen me, and I had seen myself in them. It was four miles to my apartment in the Haight, and by the time I pushed off for home, it was getting on for eleven. The streets were quiet and slicked with fresh rain and I cut through North Beach behind Columbus Avenue, passing the many adult movie theatres. Without realizing before that I would, I went into one and parted a curtain, behind which sat booths like those that used to deliver passport photos, but with doors. I shut the door behind me. I had never been in a place like this before. On the wall in front there was a screen, and to one side of it, a roll of greasy two-ply toilet paper. On the screen, a menu of pornography and a coin slot. I fed a few dollars worth into the slot, and from the menu chose a video in which a group of hirsute Turkish men of all ages stood masturbating in a circle while in the centre, an older man and a young woman had vigorous, passionless sex on what looked like a yoga mat. Another first.

Outside, a queue was snaking down Columbus towards CompuLand, and then the bells of St Catherine's struck, off in the distance. A voice on a loudhailer asked everyone to stand back, and for a moment, nothing at all happened. Then, a clap of thunder, and the doors of the consumer electronics stores, the book stores and the record stores around all of the city yielded on their hinges to the slavering hordes rushing in and grabbing at sky blue boxes. Striking bells announced the dawn of the age of enlightenment. It was now. The rain was confetti. Windows were flung open and love declared loudly to the stars.

Even though the Tonga Room at the Fairmont Hotel was indoors, Milo was waving from beneath a bamboo gazebo, gulping something out of a coconut shell. He was stringier than before, no longer burly, cheek bones protruding. But although the coral necklace hung a little looser around his neck, as did that profusion of wristbands and the rings on his thumbs, he was still Milo, and when he stood up, I laughed at the familiarity of it all. I saluted him formally and he bounded over to meet me. It had been months since I'd clapped eyes on him and when we hugged a tear escaped, spilled as much for my own loneliness in the intervening period as the missing of him. This ambush of me by my own emotions was mortifying and behind his back I made sure to wipe away the evidence with my sleeve.

— The fuck happened to your lips?

— Bloody cold sores.

I laughed and then he pointed at my blue Ben Davis

pants cinched with a shoe lace, the tie stolen from Casey's room, the heavy wool jacket of the sort favoured by Civics teachers.

— Ready for your day in court?

I thought we'd have to dress up on account of this being the most expensive hotel in the city, but Milo didn't even have a jacket over his *Houses of the Holy* T-shirt and he smelled faintly of patchouli oil. Still, something about the way he carried himself precluded any problems with dress code. He owned the place. The mistake had been everyone else's.

Without knowing what was in it, I ordered one of his drinks, which was a zombie, and after the hollow clink of our coconuts, we drank and kind of smiled at each other. The Morelands were here on holiday, and Milo, Róisín and I had been summoned to The Fairmont, where they were billeted for the duration of their stay. Milo and I had this tradition of drinks before drinks which had endured down the years. Even if other people suggested drinks prior to a party, we'd meet for drinks before those drinks, a pre-gaming ritual that always kept us one step ahead of the posse, or behind. Róisín was coming in an hour, parents an hour after that. Milo twisted a napkin.

— So yeah. Tom and Sheila are splitting.

— Jesus. Are you okay?

— They haven't met other people, and they're still going to be friends, but that's why they came over. Of course, that's not what they said. Tom gave me the whole

'I've always wanted to see San Fran, and do the thirty-one-mile drive round Monterey', or whatever-the-fuck. Apparently he even brought his golf clubs . . .

— So they're on holiday together? That's nice.

— I doubt it. I wouldn't say Sheila's going to caddy for Tom. Nah. I'm not seeing that.

— God, I'm shocked.

— It happens, Evan. They're adults.

I knew it happened. I knew they were adults. I was just looking for something to say.

— I suppose they stayed together for me. When I left, that was it. Only child, you know?

Not long after Danny died the Morelands asked my parents if I would like to go on a holiday with Milo and his family and I replied that I wouldn't enjoy that at all. There was nothing to think about, because when I was thirteen, I didn't know him. There had been that incident with Fr. Browne and the catapult, but soon after he had moved on to secondary school and that was that. His parents knew my parents and I knew who he was but we weren't friends and anyway, he hadn't asked me himself – his folks had, and that wasn't likely to endear me to him. At first, the children of parents who are friends have a difficult time of it, eyeing each other up warily from opposite couches, squirming in their good clothes. My parents were surprised that I was willing to turn down the opportunity of an all-expenses-paid week in Greece during a wet and dismal Dublin winter, and they relayed my lack of interest to Milo's parents, and I expected that to be that. But that wasn't that at all. The following week, Mum returned with a counter-offer: she would buy me a guitar if I went. I had thought it was charity on the Morelands' part – to get me away from home, give my folks a break and give me something to distract me from Danny, but now that guitars were being offered my going revealed itself as an act of charity, from us to the Morelands.

Everything in the little resort was white, pavements bleached entirely from sunshine and the restaurants with white-washed walls. After we arrived, Milo and I were sent out onto the beach, from where we could see the apartment curtains drawn in the middle of the day, and not opened until a matter of minutes before we were due back. On the beach that first day, Milo solemnly informed me this trip was 'make or break' for his parents. That first night I can recall Tom and Sheila both being in great form, laughing and drinking and cracking jokes with us. When the men with guitars came by our table, instead of enduring them with shy grins like our family would have done, Sheila stood up and sang along to one of their songs, something about owning a donkey.

But something changed between them after that first night, something that Milo could sense, and dinner thereafter was a little more tense, and he always wanted for us to be excused. During the daytime Sheila Moreland liked to sunbathe and was reading a book called *Riders*, which bore a picture of a female butt covered with the stretchy white fabric of jodhpurs. More often than not it was an olive-skinned guy called Toni who served us, spelt just that way, who used to hang around at Sheila's lounger after serving and chat with her and us, if we were there. He was around to serve us dinner too, and used to make Sheila laugh a lot. Tom didn't seem to mind, but Milo took an active dislike to Toni and one night lying in adjacent hotel beds, the fan whirring and the night too sultry for either of us to get to sleep, I asked him about it.

— I just don't like him. That's all. I think he's a bum-boy actually.

— Do you?

— Yeah.

— Still, he gives you free ice cream.

— Doesn't mean he's not a total benny.

The way he turned to the wall and pulled the covers around his shoulders, it was clear that this particular subject was closed, now and for ever.

For the rest of the week everyone seemed to spend more time apart than together. Tom was more into the town than the beach and would be gone nearly all day. Sheila lay on the beach basting herself and drinking Diet Cokes, and we had the run of the place, pretty much. I was there to occupy Milo and give them space. He had other friends that I knew from the year ahead of me in school, but they were cut from a different cloth to me. During that week I chalked off a number of firsts. First drink, my first attempt at waterskiing, and on the second-last night, Milo and my emboldened self snuck out of the apartment, went to a disco and met two English girls of our age who wore brightly coloured string bracelets on their wrists and became our girlfriends (my first proper girlfriend).

On the last day, we were playing table tennis for a neat pile of drachmas on the side of the table – the remainder of our spending money. The game was marshalled by the girls, and deadlocked at 19–all. The ball bounced high and inviting on my side and I prepared a vicious swipe and smashed it past Milo, past the table and through a gap in the top of the wall of the shower room behind.

— 20–19!!!

I ran inside to get the ball, splashing through the disinfectant puddle at the doorway, cold water seeping into my foamy flip-flop soles. Inside, one cubicle was locked and the ball might have dropped in there – it wasn't in or beneath the rows of sinks, in the bin for hand towels, or in any of the drains or nooks where muscular Greek spiders congregated to build their homes. The falling water behind the door sounded hollow, as though the cubicle was empty, but when I leaned down I saw one – and then a second – pair of feet in the stall, each facing the other. Though the sound of cascading water was loud I could now hear gentle moaning, and then I saw swimming togs in a ball lying on the shower cubicle floor. I stayed crouching, looking at the four ankles, my knees wet, shower water raining down, listening to the sound as it gurgled into the drain. What was going on?

I felt a gentle tug on the back of my T-shirt and noticed Milo was standing beside me. When you are bad, you learn things you wouldn't otherwise come to know about, and that kind of knowledge can carry the heaviest weight of all. He winked at me and crept into the adjoining shower stall and I followed. In our stall was a small wooden bench for resting clothes and towels and from the stall next door, the sound of cascading water was louder, as was the breathing of whoever was within. We were smiling at each other as we prepared to peek over the top. Milo and I each stood on the end of the bench, counted to three using fingers, then slowly raised our heads to the top of the brick wall separating us from next door, then lifted our heads over and looked down.

Thank God Toni's eyes were closed, because his head was tilted up towards us. His togs were hung on the hook at the door and he was standing under the shower, with his right arm behind his head and his left holding the head of a figure beneath him. Rising and dipping under the cascading water was the unmistakable form of Tom Moreland, naked. Toni's muscular, tanned stomach moved up and down as he worked his groin in and out of Milo's father's face. We stood there for a minute, listening to the shower water raining down, and then I felt a gentle tug on my arm and noticed Milo was already standing down off the bench and motioning for me to do the same, his cheeks drained of tone. Like any young boy I would have given literally anything – the money resting on the table outside, the guitar I had been promised for going on this holiday in the first place, my own life – to be allowed to continue to watch. For horny voyeuristic boys of all ages, such a sight was the Holy Grail. But this was Milo's dad.

Dutifully I stood down and as quietly as we could we crept out, our feet squelching on damp, bleached water.

Outside, I swept the coins off the table and gave them to Milo. He pocketed them wordlessly then walked past the girls and off towards the hotel.

— What's going on? We're going swimming, remember?

— He's feeling sick. I better go. See you later?

I ran after Milo but he had already disappeared, so I slowed my pace down to a walk. My head was buzzing from all the information, and I kept walking, trying to process what I'd just seen. I wandered down the length of the hotel apartment block, and a lizard slunk out from under a bush and ran across my path. My head was down and scanning for more when someone jumped out from behind another privet hedge and pinned me violently against a wall, their hand a vice around my neck.

— If you breathe a word about that to anyone I'll cut your fucking throat in two. And you know I fucking will.

For a moment I thought it might have been Tom Moreland himself.

— I'll fucking kill you and bury your body in a field.

Was it Toni the waiter?

— I'm not letting you go until you promise. Fucking promise, Evan. I swear to God.

I couldn't speak, and instead hissed the words he had wanted to hear in a low voice that was almost science-fictional.

— Oww. Jesus, Milo, that really hurts. I can barely breathe.

When he saw the fear in my eyes, Milo finally let me free and I dropped to my knees, weak and winded. And once more, he was gone.

That night at dinner, Toni was back, flitting around the table and sweeping crumbs away with what looked like a hair comb, dextrously lighting candles and slinging cocktails. Milo had excused himself and it was just me, Sheila and Tom and I was still carrying around the image of two naked men from earlier, because there was nowhere I could put it. I barely knew where to look, for fear someone might guess that I knew what had happened. I was terrified. But Tom appeared oblivious and so too was Toni.

— Where is the other handsome boy?

— Milo is sick – or possibly sulking because it's our last night and he doesn't want to go home. Isn't that right, Evan?

Sheila was drunk, gesturing sloppily with the glass in her hand, spilling ash on the table cloth.

— That's not right, Mrs Moreland. He really is sick. He got sick earlier.

I never contradicted her and she could tell that something had shifted. She looked at me as if she had never seen me before in her life.

— I beg your pardon. Are you okay?

— Fine thanks. This chicken is brilliant.

Milo had to know where my loyalty lay. And as Toni

swept off, I watched Tom watch him go. How had I not noticed this before?

Later that night I lay in bed endlessly replaying the vision of Milo's dad naked, the wet shower water pelting his shoulders and his own hard member peeking up beyond his belly. We had lain there in silence for hours and I knew from the way he was breathing that he was awake.

— Milo?

He didn't speak or roll over, and in truth that made it much easier for me to go on.

— I just want to say that I'll never tell anyone about today, and I don't mind that you grabbed me around the neck, even though you made me sound like E.T. I'll never let another soul know about what we saw. You can count on me.

He turned around and I was shocked to see that he had been crying.

— Promise?

I did promise. I did.

The next time I met Milo and Tom it was summer and they were on an adjoining fairway to that of my dad and me, on the day of a father-and-son competition at the golf club.

— Give me patience.

Tom Moreland hid his face with his hand as Milo swiped ferociously at his ball, lying obstinately buried in the heavy rough, impervious to all the exertion going on above it. A little knowledge is a dangerous thing, and what Milo knew and could not mention was to affect him profoundly from that day on. It was neck-and-neck as to who was enjoying it the least. I hated the buttoned-down conventions and codes in a place like this, but my dislike paled in comparison to the extent of his. Again he swiped, then again and again until he was slashing wildly at the grass with no hope of ever connecting. I was hardly better but I had poked my ball up our fairway in a series of grubby little strokes until finally it bounced onto the green.

My dad smiled and went over to Milo. He put a hand on his shoulder then bent down, picked up the ball and dropped it out onto the short mown grass of the fairway with a smile.

— It's no fun at all in there. Give yourself half a chance.

— Kevin, that's breaking the rules.

I couldn't believe Tom Moreland was giving out to my dad for giving Milo a drop. Having smiled a 'thank you' at my dad, Milo had already walked over and begun to address the newly liberated ball on the edge of the fairway. When he heard his dad disputing it, Milo didn't look back, just bent over, picked up the ball, walked over to the rough and placed it in exactly the same little nest of tough, weedy grass, and addressed it again, in its old resting place. He drew back his club as if to behead someone, and drove it into the ground. Through force alone, the ball squirted out onto the fairway and rolled down towards the river on the left-hand side. Milo shoved his club into his bag.

— Happy?

Tom Moreland smiled at my dad, as if to say 'kids!'. Then the two dads marched on down the fairway ahead of their sons, happy that they knew so much more than we did, and the two sons followed on, wishing to God we knew a little less.

By the time the Morelands arrived in the Tonga Room, a half-dozen coconut shells were gathered on our table and Róisín was with us. It was the first time I had seen her in a few weeks too. Shortly after the Folsom Street Fair, she declared that it was time to stop sponging off Casey and Asher (and me, I had to extrapolate) and find a place of her own. Sheila Moreland waved a jewelled hand and as they walked over, Róisín grabbed my arm.

— Your lips look sore. Do you need some lip balm?

— I'm good.

— C'mere. Don't leave me alone with them, will ya?

After shaking Milo's hand, Tom stood back from him and looked genuinely shocked.

— Jesus Christ, son, where's the rest of you?

Once Sheila had managed to stop hugging and stroking him, she stood back and clapped a hand over her mouth too.

— You're half nothing.

Tom pumped my hand and gave me a friendly punch on the shoulder.

— Evan. Great to see you. And Róisín. How are you, my dear?

They kissed on both cheeks, Sheila offered Róisín a limp hand, and then there was some being looked at and lots of feeling itchy, then a round of please sit down, then cocktail menus were passed, then the waitress arrived and we did the ordering and the rating of each other's orders and then there was the long wait for the drinks, punctuated with sighs, lots of sighs, and when the sighs ran out, one or two 'so!'s. At last the drinks came and we clinked.

— So. You two are sharing a place?

Sheila must have known that now he was back, Milo would be staying at Róisín's. Who at this table didn't? Clearly Milo decided somebody didn't and that it was an illusion worth preserving. He linked my hand with his and patted our hands in a parody of a couple.

— We certainly are. We're very happy. Aren't we, dear?

I took my hand away. Given what we knew, that was a little pointed, a little cruel.

— So if those two are living together, where are you staying, Róisín?

— I'm in a little place of my own, Sheila, about five blocks away from 'the boys'.

— Aren't you very independent?

— We're all adults now.

She glanced at Milo, then we set down the cocktails and said 'so' and fell silent. There was a rolling clap of thunder and rain fell into an artificial river in the middle of the room. For far too long we laughed at it, the most grateful recipients of this ersatz wonder.

After grilled Anderson Ranch lamb cutlets and a round of forty-dollar scotches, we were back in the Tonga Room, and as was the way with evenings with the Morelands, everyone was drunk, and Sheila dragged me onto the dance floor in front of a savagely bored steel drum band. Over dinner they had asked me about my job and I explained the Net to them, reluctantly, since right across from me Milo was twisting his napkin, aware that as his parents listened, they were wishing that he had contented himself with a job like mine. Sheila was, at least.

— You're a dear friend to Milo, Evan. Thank you for that.

— He's a good friend to me.

— I'm sure he has his moments.

— He told me about you and Tom. I'm really sorry.

— I don't think it comes as any surprise. We've been separated for longer than he knows. I know he's not living with you, Evan. I think Milo thinks we're religious but we only went to Mass for his sake, which is another joke. Gawd. The games we play.

Over her shoulder, I saw Tom chatting to a waiter. Sitting there without the apparatus of business or golf or wife or sporting event, one hand tanned and the other pale from the golf glove, he was lost, doomed in future to walk behind a caddy-piloted buggy in Pebble Beach, looking for a ball that no one would watch him hit, writing a scorecard that no one would ever read, failing once more to defeat himself.

— You don't need to worry about Milo. He knows who he is.

Sheila's face was about six inches from mine.

— That's quite profound. Hey, are your lips sore? They look sore.

The music stopped, the waterfall began and I went back to the table. Milo swapped Róisín for Sheila and Róisín beckoned Tom over to her. I ordered a zombie and watched them, and though they danced apart from each other, Tom and Sheila could still have been a pair. Sheila allowed herself to be spun by her son in uncertain, anti-clockwise circles, eyes closed as she leaned back, while a few feet away Tom spun Róisín, and his eyes were closed too. If only they knew that each was thinking the same thing as the other – please, please take me away. Let me rewind and do it over. Wouldn't that have brought them closer?

Weeks before, I shunted Róisín's bags into a fairly unpromising shell on Masonic at Haight and since then she had stayed beneath the radar, but having said our goodbyes to Tom and Sheila, we made for her place, and the results of her nesting were clear. The living room was small but bright and the kitchen stocked with food and functioning appliances. Besides the odd concession to student life – tie-dye sheet tacked over the window, well-thumbed copy of *A Prayer for Owen Meany* on top of the toilet, a wind-up set of chattering teeth – Róisín's place had a discernible aesthetic, governed by more than whether a sofa on the street had not been yet been pissed upon by a dog. Pieces of furniture matched other pieces, throws complemented artwork and rugs brought rooms together.

We had been in the kitchen drinking Vendange from cups, but during one of his patented dreamy upward gazes Milo noticed what looked like an attic door, directly above the fridge. Róisín had no idea where it led, but now he was back in town and Tom and Sheila out of the picture she was restored to her insouciant self, and when we asked if we could check it out, she just shrugged. With him on my shoulders I walked Milo over towards the door. With the heel of his hand he pushed a few times until the paint seal broke, then the flap was gone, hands grabbed him from above and he was floating high into a blue rectangle of hanging stars.

— Holy shit! Hello everybody. Mind if we join you?

— Come on up, dude!

Not only was it roof access, but access to a party that the neighbours were having, high above Masonic. I helped Róisín up, then scrambled out myself. There was about twenty of them, mostly tattooed, in their twenties, in Vans, flannel shirts and Ben Davis work wear. Laid out on the crunchy tar lino were a record player, deckchairs, a large umbrella and a keg of beer. As girls in floral dresses and Converse floated up out of the hatch in ones and twos, Jeff Buckley was singing, 'Lover, you should have come over'. Fairy lights were strung from TV aerials and behind the clouds hung a vestigial reminder of the moon.

One guy in heavy-rimmed spectacles wrote your name on a blue plastic cup and that was your cup for the night. Anyone without a named cup was a crasher and couldn't drink. We queued for the keg, and according to his cup, Seth stood in front of us. He was stern and unibrowed and insisted it wasn't a party, but a wake. The revellers were mourning the end of the 'zine to which they had all contributed for twenty-six editions, one called *East Bay Hey!* This guide to the Oakland punk universe was being discontinued in print form and made into a website. Seth handed me a copy of the last edition, a loosely bound bundle of photocopied pages with hand-drawn comics and reviews hammered out on a typewriter.

— It's becoming a whole 'nother thing now and a lot of us are pretty bummed about that.

Milo peered over my shoulder as I flicked through the pages and for the duration of my sconce Seth stood beside it, his open hand hovering above protectively, ready to snatch it back. Milo nodded gravely.

— Hmm, yeah . . . the unique hand-craftedness. It's really sad. I'm Milo. I'm a wood-turner.

Seth looked at me to see if he was joking. I shrugged. I mean, it was true on some level.

— You know, it dudn't mean half as much when it's pixels. But hey! No one can stop the onward march of 'cyberspace'.

Milo and Seth shook hands and he grabbed back the 'zine.

— Ink is dying, people.

Milo turned to me and grimaced, as if he had some tough news to impart.

— Yeah, the Internet is bullshit. Sorry Ev, but it just is. This town is being brainwashed.

Seth eyed me warily.

— Why is he saying sorry to you?

— Oh, I work for ForwardSlash. But all I do is build desks. Out of wood, so . . . there's that.

— 'ForwardSlash'. We've got one of yours here. Tali.

Seth handed me the nozzle and gestured over his shoulder.

— She's responsible for the online deal-io. Swing by when you're loaded up.

When we wandered over to Seth he introduced us to a girl in her mid-twenties, small and brown-skinned with mod haircut of wispy bangs and tiny, green-framed glasses. She exuded fierce intelligence without the defensiveness of the under-sized, and she didn't stand up.

— Hey, Evan. You work at ForwardSlash?

— For my sins. I've seen you around the building.

— You'll protect me when all these Unabombers get wasted and try to hurl me off the roof.

Mark's Keyboard Repair was playing now and with the sound pulsing like a lava lamp and this view of the park, it was all kind of devastating. We sat at the very furthest edge of the ledge, legs dangling over the abyss. Milo rolled a joint.

— So Tali, tell me this. Why kill the natural, organic 'zine? Just for kicks?

Milo had asked the question, but Tali smiled at Seth.

— We're not killing it. It's not *murder*, Seth. What's the best analogy?

— An iron lung?

Tali laughed.

— It's migrating. That's all. It will live, but somewhere else. It's a decision voted on by all of us, and it's simple really. You can have greater reach online with a fraction of the cost. And no trees die, so that's good, right?

Here, she winked at me, and Milo saw.

— Yeah, but you need a computer to read it. So only nerds can read it. Rich nerds.

I winced at the pejorative use of the 'n' word. Clearly, in the intervening months Milo and I had been standing on different tectonic plates, and without realizing it before, had been moving apart. There were no nerds any more, only people who got it and people who didn't.

— The web is only as strong as the people that use it, and computers are expensive, and right now, people are using technology mainly to talk about technology. But as it evolves it will get stronger, and will facilitate all kinds of discussions way beyond that. And it is going to grow. It's going to explode, Milo. You'll be online in a few years, believe me.

She shouldn't have said that. Milo hated anyone thinking they had something on him.

— Yeah, well I like to see people when I'm talking to
them? Thanks all the same.

— You don't like phones?

— You know what I mean. Seriously. Fuck's sake.

Tali looked at me then at Róisín, with her eyes wide.
She hadn't encountered this degree of childish hostility
before, and I was surprised too. Seth stared at his 'Seth'
cup, and I at 'Evan'. A bus rattled past below me. Róisín
leaned over to Tali, a little drunk, her arm draped protectively around Milo's shoulder.

— Tell me this then. Sister to sister . . . computers are
all well and good, but will the Net ever do something for
us, in here? Where it actually matters?

Róisín put a hand on Milo's heart. Tali took a deep
breath.

— 'Sister to sister', I think it will.

— How?

— Well, what's the thing that you cherish most in the
world?

Róisín looked at Milo, but he was staring down at his
dangling feet, still angry. You could tell that Róisín
thought she had the answer.

— I cherish love. Nothing is better – more important –
than love. And technology can't improve that. I mean,
I saw a comedian on TV the other night talking about
how, in the future, there'll be a thing you plug into your
keyboard that you can stick your wang into and have

sex with a virtual person? I'm sorry, but that's not love to me.

Milo laughed and Róisín looked at him, delighted. God, I hated them for their certainty. Tali put down her cup.

— What if you loved something that nobody else loved? What if you were so lonely, so shy, so repressed that the only way to relate to someone was online? What if you made a connection that way? Would that connection necessarily be bad?

Milo looked up and snorted.

— It would be bad, yeah, that you were such a fucken' loser that you couldn't find a single person in the real world . . . it would be sad.

— What if you were just shy, Milo? Or gay like me, from a country like mine – like Iran – where my sexual preference is punishable by death, or stoning?

In the war of the chilled liberals, that just about did it.

Across the road, a male figure moved through a living room, holding a bulbous wine glass, then sinking into a sofa beside a woman and running his hand through her hair. I love looking into windows. When I was young I used to cycle around my neighbourhood at night every Christmas, looking at the decorated trees in each living room. They look so much better from the outside, framed by a window. Everything does.

— What if you couldn't find 'the one' in a bar or a club or in your home town?

Milo put an arm around me, leering at Tali.

— Like old Evan here . . .

— Seriously. What if you had never found anyone like you, never knew another 'you' existed?

I could feel Tali looking at me, wanting me to wade in on her side, and she was right. Imagine lifting off this surface and flying right across these streets, brushing past windows illuminated warmly from within, where curtains billowed in the night. Imagine finding the right window and zooming in. And what if you could get inside, but preserve the feeling that the outside view had given you, the virgin view, unspoiled by the grubby patina of real life?

— All I'm saying, Ro-sheen, is it's not about relationships. Not yet. But as more and more people log on, the chances of you finding someone to talk to, even about the very specific things that only you love, can only improve. Even if it's just music, or tech, or politics, or travel. That's all I'm saying. And in enough years . . .

— What?

— It will deal with love between humans. Eventually, it could alter the human condition.

I shivered. It was getting cold up here. Tali wrapped her scarf around tiny shoulders and smiled.

— It could change the architecture of the heart.

Then she stood, put a hand on my shoulder to steady herself, then patted me and walked back towards the keg. She called out behind her,

— I'm talking about the end of human loneliness. But I'm drunk, so don't listen to me.

AUGUST 1995

Now that I worked for Charlie in the TV world we didn't do it often, but on the rare occasions that Fred and I still operated as a duo, we knew how to work those mail trucks. Rolling down Sansome, we could have been competing in the rhythm gymnastics section of the blue collar Olympics, sending them waltzing left or right with a desultory glance of the hand, caressing them into elevators and down ramps with a brush of arm or hip, without the appearance of any effort. A young woman and an older man were walking towards us, and as we drew closer, I saw it was Róisín, and beside her Sam, and they were talking and laughing, together somehow, luxuriating in each other's company, and the sight caused me to stop abruptly. Fred ran his truck into my heel, breaking our spell.

— Hey, is that your lady friend?

I bent over and rubbed my ankle. Sam was eating a miniature tub of Ben & Jerry's with a luminous plastic spoonlet, tie draped over his shoulder. For some reason he reminded me of a schoolboy, and there was something else about them that looked off, and it took me a while, squinting in the sun, partly obscured by a large brown UPS van, before I finally got it. It was the body language. As they loped along he said something, she laughed, then he sort of leaned over and bumped his shoulder off hers, unbalancing her in a funny way – as if they knew each other well, instead of hardly at all.

Fred continued trundling his hand cart towards them, unaware that this meeting was in any way incongruous. I stayed put as he passed, watching them say hi to him and walk towards me. Since the incident with the ice sculpture I had vowed to stay away from Sam, forcing me to break attention towards his habits, but it wasn't easy. I couldn't handle the sick feeling in the pit of my stomach whenever I was around him, and even when I was chatting with the mail room guy and Sam walked by with a sheaf of papers and patted me on the head with them, I just smiled and went back to my business, heart twisting. All I wanted to do was spend time with him – doing what, I didn't know exactly. By now our father–son, mentor–pupil dynamic was carved in stone. Sam would never be able to continue a friendship with me if he knew how I liked him. He would run a mile. When he materialized beside me in The Lodge, at the mail room, on the street, being so close to what I wanted and being allowed to remain there only if I never once reached out and touched it, was driving me mad. And now that I could no longer bear it, it seemed he was always around. In fact, if it was remotely possible that Sam was as odd as me, then I'd have said he was following me, but no one was as odd as me. That I did know.

The day after the incident with the ice sculpture, in the foreign language section of 'A clean, well-lighted place for books' I cobbled together a sentence and transcribed it onto the back of an *SF Weekly*: '*Cuando usted me vio con mi cara pegada al hielo, era una broma. Gané mucho dinero para hacer eso. Pero gracias*' it read, and though I had already forgotten what it meant, the first time I saw the cleaner again, from my jacket pocket I took the scrap of paper, fixed a smile and made to walk towards her and recite it. But the strangest thing happened on my way over. She looked up at me, and her lack of recognition was so natural that I found myself walking by and fetching an entirely unwanted glass of water in the kitchen. She had even moved a vacuum cleaner aside to let me by, and standing by the sink in the kitchen, I was baffled.

Was it possible that she didn't recognize me? Perhaps she encountered such a panoply of depraved activity on her nightly beat in the offices of this city that my sad, arctic clinch had barely registered on the scale. Since that night, I had been haunted by vivid dreams in which I had killed her then somehow disposed of her body, and each night the manner in which I did so was different. One night I'd sling the corpse into the cliff walls of Telegraph Hill like it was a shot put, and it would dangle out from behind some scree; I'd have to climb the sheer face to rescue it, and I'd wake up scrabbling at my bedroom wall. Other times I'd steal a ForwardSlash helicopter and drop it out at sea, and once, I cut the corpse up and served it to the employees of Levi-Strauss with roasted red peppers that Casey had insisted upon adding. After that I looked up the number of a therapist in the Haight-Ashbury area but never booked a visit, and when the cleaner blanked me, I had to ask myself whether it had been a dream. Maybe they were cold sores after all.

Róisín saw me crouching behind the UPS truck and waved, then Sam saw her waving and waved too. I had applied all the rigour I could muster to staying away from this troubling vision and yet there he was, right back in the thick of my world, calm as you like. Clearly the man had no feelings.

— Drop something, Ev?

— My pen. How ya doing, guys?

— Everything's grand and brilliant, as you'd say.

Róisín laughed at Sam's Irish accent and I lit a cigarette, aiming for nonchalance. When Róisín lit one she really nailed it, exhaling to the sky, restoring a lock of hair behind her ear.

— I was just telling Sam here that I've never been in California during the fall . . .

It's so fucking easy for you. The pair of you.

— . . . I'm really looking forward to it. You've never been here for the fall either. Have you?

— That's right, Róisín, I moved over here in January, as you might remember. So yes, I have yet to experience *autumn*. But I'm looking forward to it.

Sam smiled.

— Have you guys been out there on the water yet? In the bay?

— We took the ferry to Alcatraz once. Me and Róisín and *Róisín's boyfriend* Milo.

— I'm sailing on the bay this weekend . . .

Nobody had missed a beat. I was impressed.

— . . . it's a lot of fun. You should come out.

— We'd love to.

Róisín was answering for us both, but she wasn't wrong, or not fully wrong.

— What are you guys doing this weekend?

— I don't think I'm doing anything. Are you doing anything, Evan?

— I'm going on Sam's boat in the bay. Don't you have plans with your boyfriend?

— I'm not entirely sure that I do. Do you?

Róisín narrowed her eyes. Sam flapped his tie back down his shirt front.

— Great! Maybe see you both on Saturday!

He walked off and she looked after him with a smile, then at me.

— He's nice.

— He's married is what he is.

I wheeled my truck past, leaving her to chew on that.

It was only a Thursday but that night the Haight 7 was much more packed than usual, crawling up the street at Buchanan, the last big climb before Lower Haight. Jerking forward, it always felt as if we mightn't make it up there, and when we finally reached Fillmore, loads of Deadheads boarded, stinking of weed. We struggled up the second slope before Upper Haight and by Masonic, the neighbourhood was thronged. Camera crews glided along the sidewalk, their swinging wide-angle lenses like the mouths of whales, swallowing algae.

By now the Deadheads were nothing more than an occasional curiosity for the local news, who might visit them once every year for vox-pops about the launch of a new ice cream flavour. I only understood that tonight might have more import when I saw a CNN cube around the foam microphone of one reporter, standing outside the Goodwill Store. CNN? National news? Could Windows 96 be out already? The reporter was jumping from foot to foot, preparing to interview a skinny guy with peroxide blond hair, designer eyewear and a Grand Royal T-shirt, who hadn't bothered to dismount from his Schwinn.

— Isn't this a terribly sad and tragic day for this neighbourhood?

The reporter thrust the foam mic head towards him and the guy laughed bitterly.

— Not if you have to live here it isn't.

— How do you mean?

— I didn't identify with his music. When anybody passes away it's sad . . . I guess, but the Dead is not a big deal to the residents. Although, it looks like there'll be a whole lot more panhandling and public urination around the Haight now. So that kinda blows.

A Deadhead who had been listening and was leaning

against the wall of 'The Pork Store' threw a hard bagel crust at the man's head. The camera panned to find the thrower.

— Hey, shut up, geek. That's disrespectful.

— To who, freeloader? The homeless? The *genuinely* homeless?

— Hey, you're a fucken' dick, man. I am genuinely homeless.

The camera swung back and forth, the homeless guy standing up to confront the man now cycling off. He spat in his wake, then screamed after him.

— You can eat my balls, shit bird!

The camera swung back to the reporter who aimed manfully for compassion.

— And there you have it. Late last night, in a treatment centre by the name of Serenity Knolls, a tribe lost its leader. At the age of fifty-three, Jerry Garcia passed away. And grief? Grief is unconfined. On Haight Street, among the Deadhead community, I'm Loren Spitzer. Stewart?

On the next block I saw Milo before he saw me, the darting eyes, the absence of shoes, and in that instant whatever bond we had finally vanished. I tried to recall him in Dublin and thought instead of Sebastian Dangerfield. Whenever anyone spoke about books, Milo's eyes clouded over and you could tell he wasn't listening any more, but waiting for his chance to wade in and talk about how he loved no book with the passion that he loved *The Ginger Man*. He had read it about twenty times, and not much besides – but made it seem like he had sailed on the seven seas of high literature to find that no other piece of writing had the beating of it. And in life he vouched for Dangerfield's boozy charms with equal fervour, climbing drainpipes that led to nurses' quarters, singing and brawling in early houses, hurling florid obscenities at the stars. But now in my mind, all those traits were given back to the rakish character of fiction and the skinny guy on Haight with the long thinning hair, the one accepting money from a stranger and scratching absently at his tummy; he was a penumbra. The old, *real* Milo was gone for ever and there was no promise left, apart from one that was already broken.

Within half an hour we were sitting in The Jungle, *Odelay* by Beck giving way to *In Sides* by Orbital. Milo ran his hand through his hair and made the sound of someone sucking something from his teeth. I knew there was nothing stuck there.

— I was cruising up and down the Haight for hours, trying to remember which block you lived on. I'm glad I ran into you!

— I bet you are.

It was only a Thursday, but as was the way with Casey and Asher, a swirl of names and faces abounded – a constantly morphing cast of DJs, masseurs and promoters, some of whom I had first befriended in my kitchen. I looked with pride at the number of people wandering in and out of The Jungle. Skinny club kids exchanged high fives with each other in the hallway, lounging around in their socks, fresh and placid. About ten of us were

arranged on cushions from the sofa, chasing the inexorable progress of the evening sun. Through bedroom
windows, Asher was passing out bottles of Tsingtao, and
Milo accepted another.

— Yeah, just my luck. I get back up to camp and pretty
much the moment I arrive, the shit hits the fan. It's the
blues, man.

By virtue of his long-standing tenancy, The Jungle was
the domain of our upstairs neighbour, an acid-fried Eng-
lishman with lank matted hair who paired hobnailed
boots with tracksuit bottoms, and reminded me of John
Martyn. As he repeatedly told me upon finding me smoking on the front stoop, he had lived in this building since
Janis Joplin had been a tenant. Since then he had planted
thousands of plants in The Jungle and dug a narrow,
undulating trail in and around them, a winding path that
sank to ten feet deep at some points, then rose to the top
of a tiny hillock of vegetation at the back, like the papier
mâché sculpture I remembered seeing on a drug dealer's
wall. Sheer cliffs, dark valleys. In this town, the architecture wrought upon the subconscious mind of all these
freaks – by all these different drugs – was exactly the
same.

— How's Dave?

— Long story, brudder. Basically, there's this guy on
the next hill over in Mendocino who has a serious weed
farm. And down the years he built this pyre out of stuff
he wasn't using. Like empty bales of fertilizer, pallets, all
that stuff. And the pyre was getting on for thirty feet high

in the air. When I first got up to the woods, Dave brought me around to him to introduce me, so they wouldn't be suspicious if they saw me swimming in the river or wandering around looking for manzanita wood. Anyway, this guy was a Deadhead too, and he said that the day Jerry died, he'd light the fire. Well, yesterday, Dave was carving out front and he got this strong smell of burning, then he noticed smoke rising in the air. Plumes, man. You don't need a TV to get the news . . .

Upstate they all knew Jerry was sick. Dave started his own bonfire, and in that ceremonial pursuit he was not alone. Apparently, during the previous months and years, in the wake of persistent rumours about their totemic hero's health, Deadheads discussed what they might do on this sad day. On Dave's first pyre, sticks, leaves, mud and newspaper were dragged together by him in a fevered scraping at the ground with feet, then bare hands pulling at scraggy tree roots, and as Dave watched those licking pagan flames, sweating and muddy and briefly sated, from under the cover of his sleeping bag Milo watched him watching it, feeling for the first time like a tourist. This was private grief.

Though not a drinker, Dave produced a bottle of scotch that he kept under the bonnet of the bus, and Milo joined him by the fire, putting an arm around his friend. Dave cried a little, and they poured some on the ground for Jerry, and by then, dirty mattresses and a cupboard had hit the fire, along with records by any band that weren't the Dead, then many by the Dead themselves.

Within a few hours, smoke from hills between Santa Rosa, Ukiah and Chico intertwined in the hazy blue skies above Northern California. More and more grey tendrils reached up from further north and south, a network, a cloud of carbonized songs and memories, stored up there for eternity.

At noon, Milo made his way down to the stream behind the bus. On the far side Kerry Phipps owned five caravans but only slept in one. The other four were permanently guarded by underfed German Shepherds that he could hear barking already. Before he reached the chicken wire perimeter, he prayed that they were on leashes, and before he even reached the encampment he met Kerry, pointing a rifle at his gut and chewing beef jerky. Kerry wore a pair of dungarees and a Phish T-shirt beneath a savagely long red-and-grey beard. He uncocked the gun when he recognized Milo and after a brief conversation took his money, and came back twenty minutes later with what he swore was coke but was undoubtedly two wraps of crystal meth. In The Jungle, back-lit by the plunging sun, Milo smiled.

— Dave's a bit of a tweaker after all.

They spent the day doing bumps of meth and drinking, heaving car tyres onto the fire, while a boom box sat on the dirt, a cassette of *Workingman's Dead* playing wonkily, mangling its tribute in the dark. After a while, Milo watched Dave try to rip makeshift wooden guttering off the side of his bus for the purposes of further burning and put a reassuring arm on his shoulder.

— If you keep burning, you won't have any stuff left.

Dave caught him with a sucker punch that sent him flying into the fire. Milo landed on hot burning rubber and barely managed to scramble away. Dave screamed at him,

— Get the fuck outta here!!!!

Milo went down to the river and washed and then, cooled off and sobered by the water, made his way back to the bus. His hand was slightly burned but it could have been much worse. Dave lay in the bare earth, eyes wide open, a rope of saliva falling towards then rising from the darkened arid soil beneath his mouth. Without realizing before that he would, Milo put on his bag, patted Dave on the shoulder and walked in the direction of the highway.

He didn't have to tell me how he knew it was over because when you know, you just know. Out in The Jungle the sun was now below the tree line, the city smelled of smoke, and that track by Josh Wink about a higher state of consciousness began to emanate from Asher's room. Milo smiled ruefully and lifted our last beer to his lips.

— Tell you, man, I'm cursed.

All of Haight-Ashbury was still in bed, coupled and entwined behind shuttered windows, further shaded from the sun by the boughs of sighing foliage. On the road, a squirrel nibbled at a discarded Babe Ruth beneath a car wheel. It was 8 a.m. on Saturday morning. I cradled a coffee in my hands. I had to wake up – Sam was picking me up any time now. My eyes were shut, neck caressed by a shaft of sunlight and I could feel my head dropping. I should have stopped by Róisín's and asked her along – after all, she had been invited too. But back in the city, seemingly for good, Milo had stayed with her the previous night, and with that, it would have been odd to swing by and disturb her with a reminder of that invitation. Besides, I was still smarting.

We had been meant to meet up the night before, and I waited for a good hour outside Specs in North Beach, trying to remember Róisín's phone number, then trying to find a payphone that worked, then calling and hearing it ring out, then going into the pub and drinking on my own until my doubts about whether it had been my fault or theirs gave way to the numbing fug of drunk-and-alone. When I got home I stole Casey's beer from the fridge and slipped out to the furthest corner of The Jungle, sitting on an abandoned deckchair, drinking and looking at the stars. Negotiating those holloways was hard by day but in the dark, tunnels of briar and overgrown cacti reached out to grab you, and out there it sometimes felt as though you could turn a corner and feel sentient branches closing behind you, wrapping their whispering boughs together and demanding that you press on and try to pierce the blackness.

The low hum of a catalytic converter, filtered strains of talk radio, a sharp beep. I thudded back to waking life. Between my feet, the huge to-go cup lay on its side, lid miraculously on, but shipping a puddle of brown liquid through the drinking hole. Sam's SUV had materialized and was neatly parked in front of my place. Hoping to convey childlike enthusiasm I jumped up but far too quickly, and blood broke the storm walls, pounding at my temples. The woman in the passenger seat looked angry, as if they had been fighting. But when I stood she noticed me and turned on the full beams, waving brightly. Lustrous auburn hair framed a neat face that bore traces of Mediterranean heritage. Somewhat predictably, Sam's wife was beautiful.

She wore something that smelled of vanilla and under her gaze, it took me five goes to shut the back door.

— I hope you brought your sea legs!

— Hiya, Mrs Couples.

— It's great to meet you! And call me Lida.

I will never be able to do that, I thought.

— Your girlfriend not coming?

— Emm, Róisín? She's probably still in bed.

— Probably?

— She's not really my girlfriend.

Lida looked at Sam, but he didn't look surprised.

— I hear she's very pretty.

— How are you this morning, Sam?

Sam glanced in the rear-view as Lida turned back.

— Looking forward to a day on the water.

This was the weekend, couples time. Lida must have resented my presence. If she never got to see her husband and didn't like sailing and had gone to all this trouble just to hang out with Sam, I really shouldn't have been there, and with her there and with my hangover I didn't particularly want to be there either. Maybe that's what they were arguing about before I climbed in the back seat, but with such chirpy American women it was impossible to tell.

— Listen, I just want to thank you for bringing me sailing today.

Lida put a hand on her husband's shoulder and gave the line to Sam as he drove.

— I'm not a water person, but I heard you guys were joining him and I thought, you know . . . eww! That's gross!

She was looking past his shoulder and Sam and I caught a glimpse of a homeless woman crouching between two parked cars at the corner of Page and Central, the fruit of her labours a honey-coloured liquid hurdle through which our fat wheels now splashed. A chopper buzzed past high in the sky, searching for me among the rooftops in raking lines. When you are catastrophically hungover, what coffee gives with one hand it most certainly takes with the other, and I was now awake but overcome with dread. I focused on the horizon, already seasick.

Despite his insistence that the correct term was docked, really, Sam's boat was parked, parallel parked in front of Safeway, in a long row flanked by identical boats, with hundreds of other identical boats stacked in identical rows beyond, the wood of walkways creaking in the water. I carried luggage onto the deck while Sam busied himself on board with knots and gasoline and Lida took a Dramamine, washing it down with some banana Odwalla.

— Ro-sheen. An unusual name.

— I think it means little rose.

— Little Rose. You hear that Samuel?

It began to dawn on me that this wasn't an idle day trip at all, and that somehow, I was collateral in an argument between husband and wife. My being here and Róisín's absence meant someone was gaining something and someone else losing.

The deck could seat four and had a 'nautical' theme: stained wood slats, blue and white cushions, sample knots in a mounted glass case bolted to the wood-panelled wall of the cabin below. Before we left the marina, Lida put on Sade. Once the relevant knots were tied and untied we put-putted slowly out of the dock in reverse, executed a three-point turn among the rows of boats and thereafter put-putted forward at 5 mph. Within minutes we cut the engine, Sam raised the sails and now we were borne along on a decent gust of wind, out towards the centre of the bay. The water undulated smooth and unserrated. Hundreds of other small vessels were dotted around in the near distance. We weren't moving particularly fast and it felt less like sailing than a mid-tempo amusement ride, bouncy and seemingly set around a secure central axis. Even as I wondered whether the Dramamine had been excessive, I heard Sam trying to persuade Lida to concentrate on the horizon, but she was looking green, and before we made the acreage of water between the bridge and Alcatraz, near the millionaire homesteads of Sausalito, she had made her excuses and ducked below.

— How you doing there?

Sam was steering and I turned my face, drinking in the bracing wind. We had been silent for a good five minutes.

— I'm gonna be honest with you. I'm a little hungover.

— Is the motion of the ocean upsetting you?

— The fresh air helps.

He sat down, with the tiller between his legs. He was wearing khaki cargo shorts, revealing brown hairy legs.

— You know what you need? A swim.

I checked to see if he was joking but he wasn't.

— A swim? Can you do that? Just jump overboard?

— I take a swim nearly every time, right about here. Go on!

The water churned black, green and white. He was right. I was completely methylated, and if not a literal punch in the face, I needed something just like it. I stood up unsteadily and made to go down to change, then remembered Lida was there. Sam noticed with a smile.

— I won't look.

I began to strip off unsteadily, stopping at my boxer shorts. My skin was goosebumped from the wind, which was whippy. It was colder now and already I was more sober than before, enough to regret the decision to swim. But Sam was smiling and seeming to dare me, my clothes were in a pile at my feet and deep water was one of the few things that didn't scare me, so I trod carefully towards the back of the boat, my toes occasionally clawing between thin wooden slats. At the stern, I put a hand on the sail and raised myself up to the platform beside which Sam was steering. I adjusted my waistband and caught my breath.

— Are you doing it?

— Just watch me do it.

— Okay, then. Three, two . . .

I jumped and hung there, and then plunged down and God it was cold; heartstoppingly cold, and so quiet beneath the breach. I kicked down, wanting to stay under for as long as I could manage. After five, six, seven strokes the water was pitch black and heavy, and I pulled through it, pushing myself down until my eardrums pressed back. Someone told me you couldn't swim from Alcatraz to the shore because of the cold, and down here I could well believe it. My lungs had emptied themselves with the shock of impact, and I was ready to breathe the air again. I righted myself and pushed up, breaking into the light with a gasp.

What a view. That golden bridge a mile away, the boat framed perfectly between its two vertical stanchions. Sam waved from the deck. To my right, Sausalito and Tiburon, then beyond that the Berkeley hills. I trod around to the right and saw Treasure Island and Yerba Buena. Beautiful. I spun back around and swam towards the boat. With ten fast shivering strokes I reached the back of it and grabbed a foothold on a tiny rope ladder with wooden steps. Sam reached down an arm, I gave him my hand and he yanked me up to the side. I threw a leg over and in standing onto the back seat, slipped on a foam cushion and overbalanced into him. He caught me and had a towel in his hands and wrapped me in it in one smooth movement, steadying me with hands that rubbed warmth into my arms and back.

— You looked good in the water there.

Then he let me go and I looked at him. He looked away and took the rudder again and I stood back, a towelling pupa, swaying a little. I climbed down back to my clothes pile.

— You enjoy that?

Over my shoulder I told him it was great, my head buzzing. I dried and dressed myself in silence, in the chaste, restrained manner of a young girl at the beach. That spongy detergent taste of towel. I laced up my trainers, draped the towel over the entrance to the hold to dry, and turned back towards Sam, who stood at the tiller completely naked.

— Take the wheel?

His chest was brown and hairy around the pectorals and his large, dark nipples. A thin line of downy hair ran over his stomach towards his midriff, and the skin around his paunch was tanned and taut with smooth rounded weight. Beneath his belly was thick and pendulous from the waves. His sick wife was in the hold, and all he was now doing was waiting for me to walk towards him and take the tiller. This man really knew how to play the odds. When I reached him I fixed my gaze on the handle and took a firm hold. My mouth was salt dry when he whispered from behind my back,

— Hold steady. You lurched it quite a bit there. Just hold the tiller straight and true. The wind is blowing from the far side, so if you keep a firm grip of it, it'll stay static. You don't want it to fill the sail. You got it? I mean, it couldn't be easier, right?

He was behind me, gripping the tiller with his hands, his arms over my arms, and could I feel something grazing against my lower back? I had to turn around but just as I did the pressure disappeared and two pale soles were enveloped by water.

Young men at home couldn't wait to act old, and old men never did anything spontaneous. Youthful behaviour in those who are older seemed American, and if it was possible to be deliberately spontaneous, that was Sam. Holding a tiller for the first time, watching him surface and wave, then swim vigorously back towards me from about fifty yards away, I felt more Irish than ever. In this country I fretted about things so much more than those around me who might have had real reasons to worry. Middle-aged businessmen snowboarding and smoking bong-loads of weed, Steven Spielberg wearing trainers. Was it in defiance of something they felt about the creeping advance of time or because they really were free? Nobody wanting to be old was one thing, but wasn't it a race you couldn't win? In that moment I resolved to do something deliberately youthful once he got back on board, and with this resolution came a welcome kind of light-headedness and a pounding of my heart. Enough speculation, enough of purgatory. I would have to help him out of the water and he would be naked, and when you touched a naked man, didn't that have to lead somewhere real? I felt giddy.

Out in the water Sam was really going for it now, but he wasn't making much progress. The tiller was perfectly straight and yet we were now about 100 yards from him. And then he stopped, cupped his hands to his mouth and shouted something, then began to swim again, front crawl now as opposed to the more decorous breaststroke of before. It's hard to tell whether a boat is actually moving out on the great expanse of sea without having something static to compare it to, such as the only person who knew anything about sailing floating, shouting and swiftly receding into the distance, about 150 yards away. Watching Sam's bobbing head on the horizon, it became clear that despite his instructions, or because of my inability, we were now moving at quite a clip, heading west towards the Golden Gate Bridge, after which the Pacific Ocean beckoned. And me in charge? God, no. Not me. I looked up and saw a full billowing sail.

Sam was smashing his arms through the water then stopping and shouting something at me, then swimming again in quickening, choppy strokes that looked very much to me like panic. Now he was a speck and I couldn't hear what he was shouting because Sade was crooning closer to my ears, those smooth laconic vocals sounding a horribly ironic counterpoint to the operator on deck. A rolling blanket of cloud grazed the top of the bridge and out of nowhere the sky darkened. I looked at the tiller and it was exactly where he had instructed me to hold it, but he was now a good 300 yards back, floating on an infinite billow of water, and I laughed when it finally dawned on me why I was still a virgin.

When I was young, it seemed to me that as long as my darkest impulses lay unacted upon, then I would be safe, protected and uncondemned. I was raised a Catholic, and would pray nightly for my family's health, in exchange for my own good behaviour. But I had faltered, and now, at the exact moment I had decided to yield to subconscious desire, the moment in which Sam hit the water, the elements had conspired to send me scudding away from him, the sail above now billowing vigorously in a way I hadn't noticed before. The boat would rise and he would be within my range of vision, then we'd plunge down the far side of a swell and he'd disappear. I craned to catch a glimpse of him. He was 300 yards away and we were now under the bridge. Something was being communicated to me by the skies themselves. Did I understand what was involved with giving in, exactly? Did I get it? Did I?

— FUCK! Okay, I won't!!!!

— You okay, Evan?

A voice issued from below. During the entire interlude I had forgotten all about Sam's wife. Even if Sam made it back to the boat, the possibility of a moment between us was now gone, and in response my tone was irritated.

— I'm fine. Stay where you are.

— It's really rocky now. What's going on?

Her pale head peeped out, followed swiftly by the rest of her. The bridge blocked the sunlight from the deck and above us road traffic howled and clattered past. Now we were flanked by immense golden stanchions, and it was Stygian, wet and dark. The huge, cruel blocks of concrete were more than twice the height of the boat, and we were carving through fog between them, away from a sterile aquatic playground in which people wakeboarded and had fun, and into the other side and the cruel immensity of the Pacific Ocean, where people died.

— Jesus. Where's Sam?

— He jumped out. For a swim. I did it first, then he did. He says he does it all the time. We're meant just to be floating, but we're going miles away from him now and I don't know what to do. I've never sailed a boat before. Have you?

— We need to turn it around somehow.

Lida was shouting over the wind and on her face I saw for the first time what it was like to love someone more than yourself. Sam was hers, and out of sight, alone and in the water. I might well be going to hell, transported across the sea like Böcklin's shrouded figure, but to her, his was the greater peril.

— Really? Are you sure?

— We can't just sail to Hawaii!

On the face of it, turning around was the move. But we were past the bridge now and out in the ocean proper. And if we continued into the wide grey expanse, the chances of us not sinking actually increased, in a way. The

boat was important to our safety and I just didn't want to
smash it off anything – rocks, or another boat, and the
idea of trying to pilot it back to San Francisco through
the notoriously choppy waters under the bridge and
avoiding yachts, pleasure cruisers, passenger ferries – not
to mention the bobbing cranium of Sam himself – was
fraught with danger. Even if we got back to him, how
would we stop so he could climb back in? How did that
happen normally?

And still, the music; the oozing fretless bass and sleazy
late-night sax arching an eyebrow at our life-and-death
confrontation on the deck.

— Fucking Sade. Can we turn that off?

— Pull the tiller. Pull the tiller the other way to the way
it is now.

— But it's right in the middle.

— Well, pull it one definite way then.

A flash of anger and panic. Holding the tiller steady
between my knees, or as steady as I could, I took off my
life jacket and tossed it to Lida. She put it on and zipped
it up. A freighter sat out in the ocean and I was shocked
by how much bigger it was than a few minutes previous.
I began to shout over the gathering wind, mostly to keep
myself thinking about something.

— Do you know anything about sails? It seems like if
I loosen the rope at the back of this one and pull the tiller
towards me, the sail will swing around and we'll catch
the wind from the other side. Wouldn't that send us back
towards the shore?

Lida took the tiller. At the back of the boat, the sail was secured to a silver post by a complex knot. My hands were cold and it was wet and it took me a few minutes to loosen then free it entirely, and when I did it swung violently to the far side, catching a strong breeze and narrowly avoiding Lida's head. I took the tiller back from her. Behind us, that was Baker beach. We were way out.

— If you sit down a little lower, I'll pull this all the way towards me and see if it turns us back. Lida, we're going to be fine. Don't worry.

She sat down, I pulled the tiller and nothing happened. It moved back to where it was, so I pulled it again with maximum force and the boat lurched violently to one side, the sail whipping around the other way, narrowly avoiding her crouching form. The boat banked sharply to the left and a huge wave crashed over the side, drenching us as we leaned close to the water. She was violently sick on the floor and over the side.

We were tilting hard now, almost parallel to the receding shoreline, which continued to reveal more of itself at an alarming rate. The waves broke across us.

— I think I should try and get it back the way it was.

Her silence gave assent and I pulled the tiller to the other side. The sail whipped past me and the boat righted itself a little. Now we were heading to the wide expanse of ocean but it was somewhat calmer.

— Is there a radio below deck?

Lida hugged herself and nodded yes. I signalled for her to navigate and made my way below.

213

It looked like a police radio, though I couldn't recall how I knew what they looked like. I unhooked the handset and pressed the button on the side.

— Mayday.

For some reason, that word embarrassed me and made me wonder whether it was an exaggeration. Could we not do something elementary that would return us to the car park by the supermarket where all the boats were parked?

— Emm, hello? Can anyone hear us? We're on a boat heading out into the ocean, and neither of us knows how to sail. It's a long story . . . Can anyone hear me? Over?

I waited, but there was no sound. Cupping the handset in my hand, I sat down and tried to think. I pressed the button again.

— Hi. Umm, mayday, mayday. We're in a boat with a white and blue sail just maybe a mile beyond the Golden Gate Bridge. Or a kilometre. I don't know what that is in knots or furlongs, or whatever . . .

The boat keeled heavily to one side and I was thrown across the cabin, hitting my head on a shelving unit. I dropped the radio and a bottle of Famous Grouse flew out of a cupboard and smashed to smithereens at my feet. Paper plates Frisbee'd across the room, as if issued from a tiny clay pigeon machine.

— Ffffp, ffffp ffffp.

— EVAN!!!!

That was Lida screaming. Something was happening up top. I gripped the sofa and rails and pushed myself up to standing, then struggled onto deck. To my horror I saw that Lida had abandoned the tiller entirely and was now waving frantically at something with both arms, jumping up and down like a queasy cheerleader. Once I cleared the cabin I turned around and saw a larger boat scudding across the water towards us.

— My God, Evan. Your head.

I put my hand to my forehead and it came away claret. There was blood on the deck but help was at hand. As the boat drew alongside, we saw Sam, wrapped in towels and wearing a rain mac. Clearly, he had hailed another boat to pluck him from the surf and follow us out into the wide ocean. I was pleased to see that he looked stricken with guilt and worry, and not enraged at my own incompetence. As the boats drew closer he smiled a little guiltily.

We tied our boat to theirs, then they boarded ours. Lida slapped him on the face and then they hugged, him wrapping his towels around her as he had with me before. It was over. One of the guys from the other boat took ours back to the shore. As we cruised back towards the supermarket someone dressed my forehead with butterfly bandages, and someone else served Lida, Sam and me a kind of broth from a sachet. Lida and Sam kind of had their quiet time together and I sat a little further away, trying to read the bilious wake and knowing the feeling in my stomach for what it was: pure jealousy.

Dreams are malignant, tumorous, fatal. That night as I slept we were back on the deck, and Sam was gripping a sail near the stern, his face upturned, drinking in the sun,

deliberately bringing us away, because he really wanted
to. Lida was far away, just . . . gone somewhere else
entirely. And I was in the hold and trying to climb on
deck so that I could be near him, but every time I thought
I was there, in the confounding manner of all dreams I
wasn't reaching that final step up into the brightness at all
but was below the water, down in the murk of the sea.

I love the agility of the subconscious, how it is nimble,
dancing about, resetting obstacles, constantly moving the
furniture around. I am below the water and can see the
outstretched hand grasping down through the gloom,
trying its utmost to save me, and then there is light and
something does grab me, and I wake up screaming, back
on the front stoop of the house on Waller, still waiting for
a day on the sea. My claws are bound in blue elastic
bands. Eventually he'll come and jerk me from scalding
water, break my shell and casually scoop out my insides.

I stationed myself at the machine room door. Thursday
night. I wasn't sure whether it was allowable for a bottom
rung tape operator to sit down in the TV control room
during the moments when he wasn't working. By now
Mickey had been covering for me so often that Tammy
had hired him full time for the maintenance department,
and after weeks of photocopying scripts, walking his
black Labrador and collecting his dry cleaning – and even
though he wasn't here tonight – Charlie had made good
on his promise to get me into this hallowed space.

I leaned on the door frame then rejected the impression that conveyed and stood straight, then removed my hands from my pockets then fretted about where to put them. Hands looked so odd just hanging there by one's sides. Briefly I folded them, but that seemed sullen so I crossed them behind my back. Now it was weirdly military but at least it was dark in here. Beyond the door lay a humming electronic hinterland of tape decks, open mouthed and hungry for information. Kenny sat on a dais, feet up, fiddling with his pager. I had already put the wrong tapes into the wrong decks on a couple of occasions and the editor had been snippy enough about it. I still didn't know his name, but he was in his fifties, had sandy long blond hair and thin arms and wore denim shorts, flip-flops and Oakley shades suckered to an elastic band around his chicken neck. Sometimes the most obvious signifiers of relaxation are offered by the most uptight souls. I was loosely dressed and tightly wound, moving behind this artfully created cloak of concealment, and you can't kid a kidder.

On the monitors, a legion of Diandra Hoopers blinked out, some versions of the presenter in colour with time code, and others small and black and white. With its blend of science fiction nerdiness and celebrity tattle, the perfect story on ForwardSlash.tv would have been an interview with Tom Cruise in which he launched a website to reveal to the world that he had been probed by an alien. But despite the proliferation of advertising for Netscape and Lycos on Muni, the Net was still only on the radar of early adopters – those whose interests in computing far out-weighed their star wattage – those with something to gain by appearing on the show, and less for the show to gain by having them. And by now, most of them had already appeared – Thomas Dolby, one of the actors from *The Brothers McMullen*, the guy who played Luke Skywalker in *Star Wars*.

Charlie's arrival was supposed to bridge the empty years until the world migrated online. But the show was struggling, none of these men cared much for technology, and all would have preferred to work on network news. Writing the links for Diandra was Kenny's gig and now he hunched over a Compaq 486 in the corner. The images spooled backwards, her fluoridic smile reversing into exactly nothing under the hollow roll of the editor's track ball. The editor paused here then swivelled, a cruel smile curling the corners of his mouth.

— You would, though. Wouldn't ya, Irish guy? You sure-as-hell would. Get me Digi sub clone in deck 2, graphics master deck 1, sizzle in 3.

I pushed through the door into the nerve centre and swapped out the relevant tapes. From behind, the voice barked again.

— Then submaster deck 2, SP clone deck 4.

Every time I stepped into the control room I fretted over the destructive potential of 'erase'. Back in the suite, Kenny was reading something to the room.

— How's this? 'Everybody's talking about it. The Internet, the World Wide Web. Get online or fall behind.

Feeling a little lost? Fear no more. We'll show you how to get connected.'

The editor applauded sarcastically and Kenny ejected the floppy disk. The editor mashed some more buttons and cursed. He pinched the bridge of his nose.

— The fuck. That is *not* a submaster in deck 2. Are you drunk, m'lad?

Had I erased something? That was mistake number three of the night. My skin itching, I replaced the tape and came back in. Kenny came back with a sheaf of scripts, he and the editor laughing at a joke that had been cracked in my absence.

— I'm really sorry about that. Is everything okay?

— Sure, 'tis grand.

Kenny handed the scripts to me. I saw an address scrawled on top.

— Spin these over to Diandra, man. I'll do tape op.

— Sorry, Kenny. I don't have a car.

He produced a set of keys and smiled.

— Mine is the Porsche downstairs.

— Yeah, but umm . . .

— It is your job.

— I know that. But . . . can't we email it to her?

Kenny barked a laugh.

— Spoken like a true evangelist. Diandra's just a . . . figurehead. Maybe in like a decade.

Right then, the editor paused on another frame wherein Diandra's mouth made an O-shape.

— What does that remind you of, Irish guy?

He looked at Kenny for approval, but Kenny was frowning, waiting for me. And I was the runner.

The car park was dark and empty save for two cars: the editor's muscle car and Kenny's Porsche. I had driven a dodgem car in Funderland about ten years before, under the supervision of sullen Dutch boys who with their shorn-headed stewardship took all the fun out of fun fair ('Stop preshing the accelerator. Now presh it hard! Jesus Chrisht! Drive, mon!'). But a car with petrol in it? I negotiated the ignition, then the gear and the handbrake, and pressed on the gas, backing it out. Thinking carefully through the constituent parts of the driving experience I manoeuvred towards the exit, found the clicker for the gate and pressed it. Tentatively giving her gas, I lurched up the ramp, broke through the subterranean gloom and onto the street, and then I was driving alone in the San Francisco night, rolling to an intersection and scanning the streets for cop cars, my heart in my mouth as I spun onto Bay. After I passed through the Van Ness intersection the streets began to flatten out and slope gently downwards towards the Marina. I turned right at Fort Mason.

When the lights went red at the next intersection, I stopped and waited for an old man in a sky blue fisherman's cap to cross. The man waved and inched his way out into the road. Out here in the hanging fog, I began to relax a little, and then began to fucking love it, me working for a TV show and driving a Porsche round the streets of San Francisco in the middle of the night. The derring do!! What would Milo think?! He had found a job moving furniture for a company called 'Starving Students', and split his time between the futon in my apartment, Róisín's place, the bedrooms of a Puerto Rican dog-walker, those of a cellist who worked at Café Abir on McAllister, and a fourth who worked at a gallery on Minna. Caitlin the air hostess had also reappeared on the scene. So yeah, five girls on the go. But no car and no career.

The scar tissue on my foot began to throb, from where my foot had been cut all those years before – I had been feathering the brake with that part of my foot, so I released it. Marina Boulevard was flanked on one side by yachts and the water of the bay, and by wood-frame houses of the reclaimed ocean on the other. I could hear sails clacking. There was the jetty where Sam's boat was being repaired. That chapter had been forcibly shut by me now. I hadn't seen him since that day and on balance his absence from my life made things much easier. Could I begin to convince myself that I didn't ever want to see him again? Only if I never did see him.

I felt a bump in the car and my first thought was that I had been hit from behind, but then I looked out and saw that we had moved forward and the old man was now leaning across the bumper with his palms on the windscreen and staring at me with a wide angry face. What was he doing up there? I jammed on the brake and he slid down to a standing position, then bent over and examined his legs. Jesus. This was not a crash. I could not have a crash in this car, with no licence or insurance. This was a . . . thing, a thing that had happened at about five miles an hour. And what the hell was he doing? He'd dent the bonnet if he wasn't careful. He had dropped his Safeway shopping bag and his walking stick, and now he leaned over to pick both of them up. I threw my hands up at him. I was pretty angry but I managed to keep a lid on it because he was old.

The man walked around towards my window and beckoned for me to roll it down. My light was green. Maybe he wanted to apologize for still being on the road?

— What the hell are you doing?

I laughed. That wasn't an apology.

— What are *you* doing? I waited ages for you to cross. The lights have gone green.

— That does not entitle you to run me over, young man.

— Hang on. Let's not exaggerate. I lightly brushed you.

— I'm hurt!

— You know, I can't do this now. You are grand, basically. And I have to go.

— You can not just go. There has been an auto accident.

— No, there hasn't, don't say that. Just . . . don't be ridiculous!

It couldn't possibly be serious. I couldn't have cops here, without a driver's licence. And I couldn't tell Kenny about this, about my not being able to drive in the first place.

— Can you let go of the window? I have to be somewhere. Thanks.

I drove off, leaving him waving his stick in the rear-view.

Outside Diandra's I rolled to a stop and inspected the Porsche. It seemed fine. I rang the bell of an unremarkable pastel cube on a quiet street of pastel cubes, counselling myself as I waited. Crashes were swift, 'bang' and JESUS! This was gentle rolling, just a slow-motion . . . moment. The door swung open and Diandra was wearing a tiny robe, smelling musky. When she saw me, her face fell, but then she reset it.

— No Kenny? I was expecting Kenny.

— Sorry. He's busy.

She took the scripts, smiling bravely.

— You have got to be kidding with the 'he's busy'. Come in.

— I better get back.

— I said come in.

She was already storming down the hall, her robe revealing toned, caramel calves, brooking no argument. I scuttled after.

Magnolia, empty photo frames and news network umbrellas gathered in a stand in the hall. An atmosphere of unuttered sadness clung to the walls. I reached the living room and studied takeaway menus pinned to a cork board. She was rooting through drawers in another room.

— I'm gonna write that asshole a letter, and you're going to deliver it. Coffee, juice?

— I'm grand.

Her head popped around from another room and she was smiling again.

— That's cute. Do you smoke?

— I do.

— Well, Evan, I smoke too. So let's smoke. Wanna drink?

She was trying not to cry.

— I'm driving.

— Well, I'm not. Don't make me drink alone. Who's back there? Who's in the room with you?

— Umm, Kenny, and the editor, whose name I don't know.

— Stringy, blond hair?

— Yup.

— Bryan. Eww.

Diandra shuddered, then kicked the fridge door shut with a bare heel and screwed a bottle of Mexican beer open. When she threw the top in the sink and handed me the bottle, I took it and drank from it. She lit a Sherman, brown and stubby like a small cigar.

We clinked and she sat down, arranging her legs beneath her on an L-shaped sofa. I leaned on a slender-stemmed bar stool and sipped the beer, watching her write. After a few minutes of angry scrawling she looked up and laughed.

— You ever get dumped this bad?

— I'm single.

— But did you ever?

— I'm afraid single has been a permanent condition for me. More or less.

— So, what. You're post-sexual?

— I guess so.

We sat in approximation of two human beings at a natural comma in the conversation. I picked at the label on the bottle.

— So you're a plant?

— I'd like to think of myself more as an anemone.

She sighed and wrote a little more, then thought of something and looked up again.

— You're far too young for quitting, kid. You don't want to end up like Bryan.

— Bryan's an anemone?

— Although you may not prefer it, the term is bachelor.

— Ick.

— Yeah. And Bryan is a tired, sad old bachelor. And a total bastard. You with me?

We clinked bottles and drank. She flicked her ash into a glass ash tray and I thought of that desiccated fool in the edit suite alone at home, wanking into a sock. I did not want to be a bachelor. It took her half an hour and when she finished writing she licked the envelope, drummed it between the fingers of her spare hand, then resolved something and handed it to me. When I went to take it from her, she continued to hold it.

— Get in the game, kid. One way or another.

We looked at each other, deadlocked.

— You don't want to end up all sad and old, and alone.

— Is that the only option?

She smiled.

— Okay, you can go now.

She released the letter, restoring a breezy tone that I was pretty sure was for my sake, for when Kenny asked me how she was and how she had taken it.

Nobody noticed me arriving back, and the on-screen Diandras were perched on the very edge of a Forward-Slash employee's desk.

— 'Hey there. Working hard? Whatcha doing?'

— 'Oh, hi there, Diandra. I'm just working on the For-wardSlash homepage.'

Diandra turned to the camera.

— 'Homepage. That's a good term. That's the first thing you see when you visit a site on the Net, kind of the front door, the table of contents.'

As the editor punched keys Kenny began to mutter, on the phone.

— If we don't bump the ratings big time in sweeps week, we're in big trouble. Our numbers are horrifying . . . Still completely horrifying . . . . Sure, Charlie. They can indulge us and keep the show if there's moolah kicking around. But not for long. So no, dude. No IPO, no show. And no show, no dough . . . It's not today, buddy, that's all I know.

Kenny then sat up and hissed into the receiver.

— And I've got three kids going to college and a wife

with a taste for shoes. You've got what. A Labrador? Cry me a fucken' river.

He hung up and sat back.

— Fags and their dogs, man.

The editor must have caught my reflection in a monitor, and swivelled around, clearly delighted no longer to be the junior presence in the room.

— Top of the morning to ya!

I handed Kenny the letter. He sniffed the air.

— Did she give you a beer?

We finished at 5 a.m. and most of the offices were locked. It was a surprise when a door handle to one on the first floor finally yielded. We were to start again at 9, and I was looking for somewhere to sleep. I hit a light and scanned the area. Two sofas. On an oak sideboard, some framed photographs of people I didn't know, a woman in the bucket seat of a yellow Mustang presenting a tropical cocktail for the camera. A man in a Miami Dolphins shirt releasing a Styrofoam arrow from a toy bow. I put out the lights and lay down on the sofa. In the silence I could hear moaning. It sounded like it was coming from the office next door.

In the corridor I could hear it clearly for what it was – a person sobbing. I peered into an office and saw an Asian man in a stripy shirt, face down on the desk, cheek against the smooth wood, weeping and rocking on the castors of his office chair. I was overcome with such powerful déjà vu that for a few moments I didn't speak. His

hand moved over the wood, fingers searching for something to hold on to, then abruptly, he sat up and saw me.
I coughed then leaned into the office.

— Hey, are you okay? I heard . . .

He tried to disguise it.

— It's nothing. It's my contacts. They're stinging . . .

— Hey, why don't you go home and get some proper
rest? You can always come back tomorrow and finish
whatever it is you're doing.

He smiled as if I hadn't heard the news.

— Dude, there is no tomorrow.

The next morning Kenny was in his office, glued to the
OJ trial. When he saw me wander by blearily he came to
the door and barked,

— Hey, Dublin. Get in here right now.

I shut the door behind me.

— Why didn't you tell me about the crash?

— What crash?

He picked up a Post-it with a scrawl on it.

— I just got off the phone from a man who took my
registration after being hit late last night on Beach and
Fillmore. And considering I was in the control room at
the time and you had my car, I think it's fair to assume
you were driving. He gave a pretty good description
of you, right down to the accent.

— It wasn't a crash, per se.

— 'Per se'. Did you hit him?

— At like five miles per hour. I don't know how it happened.

— The car did it by itself?

I decided to admit it all.

— I've never driven before, Kenny. And it seems that
automatic cars move by themselves.

Kenny put his head in his hands.

— Do you even have a licence?

— No.

He looked up, wild-eyed.

— What the hell were you doing taking my car!

— It was my job. Everyone here is all 'can you drive,
can you drive', and I really wanted to be able to do
the right thing for you. You were busy, she needed the
scripts . . .

— So you decided to break the law? This guy is in
SFSU hospital as we speak, talking about a hip replace-
ment and you're telling me now that my insurance won't
even begin to cover this?

— I'm sorry. I'll pay for it myself.

— Do you have any idea about the cost of healthcare
in this country? You won't be able.

— I just . . . I didn't want you to think I was an idiot
for not knowing how to drive.

— And instead . . .

He didn't finish it.

— Oh, and Evan. You had a beer last night?

— Diandra offered it to me.

— And you said what-the-hey, and drank on the job, while you were driving my car?

I wanted to explain how hard it would have been for me to say no to Diandra. Then I wanted to remind him that he himself drove me home once when he was out of his mind. And then all these possible arguments drained out of me and I knew instinctively that all I had to do now was take my medicine.

— I should be reporting you to the cops.

— But, so, my job . . .

— Your job is done, Evan.

— Done done?

— Yeah. Done done.

The lawyers on telly continued to argue over OJ. Guilty, innocent, acquit, convict. But by now the verdict was in. Kenny turned up the volume.

It was the middle of the morning, and I found myself out on Battery, walking towards and then on into the Levi's staff canteen. Even when we weren't working together, the Royal Scam had continued to feed Fred and me individually. We must have saved thousands on lunch, and loading my denim tray with condiments, I spied the other founding member of the corduroy department sitting with Mickey over by the window. They had spent most of the morning loading desktop computers of wildly varying vintage and states of disrepair, laptops, printers and a few square miles of cabling. After eating they were bringing them to Fred's daughter's school on Potrero Hill.

I took my tray over and Fred pulled his towards him to accommodate me. Mickey looked up.

— Hey, Evan.

I sat down beside them, and we ate in silence – I didn't want to tell Mickey about what had happened. When we had finished, Fred pushed his tray to one side and stared out the window. Mickey picked at his teeth with the folded corner of a five dollar bill. They weren't speaking either. It was all strangely quiet. Finally, Mickey took up the reins.

— What's eating you?

— Just tired. How about you guys?

— We're okay.

— You okay, Fred? You're awful quiet.

Fred just smiled, still looking out the window. He seemed entranced by the scene outside though it was nothing special. A man ate a wrap. Another had fro-yo. A guy pushed a cart.

— Fred?

— It's all good, Evan. Don't sweat it.

A blond guy from ForwardSlash with a scrubbed red face and bright suspenders holding his pants far too high came over to our table and stood above us.

— Hey, you guys? What's going on? So, I heard you guys have a pretty awesome laptop in your lockup and I was talking to Dana in tech support about getting a laptop for me for the weekends, you know, for work, and he was saying that a new one would have to come out of the sales department budget. But we're pretty slammed as it is – waiting for the IPO, and what I was saying is that I should take the laptop you have. Like, the best one. So lemme grab your keys real quick?

He drummed his hands on the table. Fred spoke for the first time since I sat down.

— We can't do that.

— You've got the key, though, am I right? I mean you do have it . . .

— Every computer is loaded up and is being transported to charity this afternoon.

— To *charity*? Dude, it's a bunch of old computers, they're not worth shit. I actually need one.

I had to admire how no attempt was made to conceal his disgust at the notion of charity. Who in this town, awash in seed capital, split stock, venture funds and options, was not able to get whatever they wanted for themselves? And who here did anything but pity those people from a great distance? On one side there was enabling technology, and on the other, emasculating, pathetic charity. You want to help? Throw change in a bucket.

— Key?

The guy in the suspenders clicked his fingers, glancing around, his hand out, and when Fred did nothing, the crimson of his face rose into roughly the same Pantone range as his red braces. He looked at me, then Mickey, then back to Fred.

— Guy, this is for work. You want me to talk to Raj or

Tammy, or . . . Hardy? Do ya? You want me to pull rank? 'Cos, you know, from where I'm standing . . .

Fred stood up, his right hand shaking a little as he grabbed the knot of the man's tie, pulling him closer, until their noses brushed off each other.

— How about you go *fuck* yourself? Would that work?

Mickey stood up but Fred unhanded the man immediately, walking past and disappearing out the door. The guy straightened himself out and turned to me.

— Key?

— You heard the man. Fuck your self off, immediately.

He stalked off. In the distance, I watched him approach a security guard.

— What's up with Fred, Mickey? Is he okay?

Mickey attacked his dessert with a spoon, in his element.

— Daughter's pregnant. Keeping the baby. He's going nuts over it.

— His sixteen-year-old daughter?

— Yeah, kiddo. Shit happens.

He smiled with a mouthful of dessert. A huge security guard came over.

— Which department?

— Corduroy?

— Levi's corduroy line has been discontinued, sirs.

— Yeah, I know. I meant . . . 'Dockers'. We're in 'Dockers'.

Sensing the beginning of the end, Mickey began to

shovel my dessert in. The guard swept our trays away and held them above his shoulders like a sassy cocktail waitress, leaving us with just the cutlery and a small audience of diners. He jerked his head towards the exit.

— You're leaving.

— We are?

It was the only thing I could think of. The guard smiled, not unkindly.

— Please. Don't make me be that guy.

As we walked past the guard, Mickey whispered into his ear, mouth full of free cherry pie.

— You're making a big mistake.

Now that Mickey and Fred had gone back to work and left me on the street, I found myself wandering back to ForwardSlash and knocking on Tammy's door. She saw me and smiled.

— Yeah, I know what this is. I spoke to Kenny.

— The car?

— You've kind of screwed yourself on this one, Evan.

— I'm so sorry, Tammy. Is there any way I can have my old job back?

— I took Mickey on when you got busy with TV, and now he's in pole position. I can't fire him just 'cos you want to go back to maintenance. You know what I'm saying? And if I was to take you on as well, it would contravene the hiring freeze. But you're not back at square one. Do not think of it that way. You're at like square 1.5. We know you, we like you, we'll keep your resume on file . . .

Even as she continued I tuned out because the thing about the resume on file? I had heard it hundreds of times. We shook hands and I left, then I came back to the doorway because it was starting to sink in.

— Come on, Tammy. Mickey? He doesn't even know what convergence is!!

She was already refreshing her email on Eudora.

— Who the hell does?

You are what you drink, and at the far end of the warehouse floor Raj clutched a huge mocha in his paw and glared at a computer screen. Between his bomb-struck office and me was a room with twenty rows of twenty humming computers set on the old wooden tables, and in front of them, nebbish product testers held stopwatches and CD cases for 'Corel Draw!', slurping their own coffee variants. Each eyed me warily on my walk past and I imagined Raj controlling them via levers beneath his desk. 'Positive Education' by Slam blasted from a huge stereo outside his office. I caught his eye and he glared out. I pointed at me, then at the inside of the office and he beckoned me in impatiently, then threw his feet up on the desk and with finger guns bade me begin.

— I've changed my mind, Raj.

— About what?

— About it all. Honestly, I'm done with TV. I'd like to learn HTML. I want a proper job.

His face creased into a smile.

— They've got no positions in TV, is that what it is?

— No, I recognize what you were saying. Finally. I want to work here.

— What was I saying?

— About backing the right horse. Don't you remember?

— I'm sorry, man. Until we finally land the IPO, there's a hiring freeze. But I can give you this.

He got up and padded over to a shelf and came back with a yellow and black book called *HTML for Dummies*.

Then his phone rang and with his paw he signalled for me to leave.

Outside, the Asian guy who had been crying the night before was holding his stuff in a cardboard box, under the supervision of a man from human resources whose name I didn't know. These days you could no longer know everybody's name. Poking out of the guy's box was a Frisbee. He held his arm lightly and whispered in his ear.

— Let's keep it moving, bro. You're doing real good.

Then the Asian guy saw me and smiled, raising up his box a little as evidence.

— What did I tell you about no tomorrow?

Passing the Hayes Street projects that night, the bus shuddered to a halt, the wires at the back disconnected by two young black guys in 'Free OJ' T-shirts, who immediately ran back into the forecourt of the projects, yelling. By now everyone had heard the verdict and this time the driver didn't get off the bus to reconnect us. This time, he stayed right where he was and waited. When the two men got into the projects, they yelled something up the stairwell and people began to materialize on each of the balcony levels overlooking this block on which we were stranded, and began hurling milk cartons and flour bombs, then sticks, bottles and stones down at us.

The window to my left smashed and the petite white woman beside me screamed. It took a few minutes before the missiles were exhausted, then the kids on the balcony surveyed the broken glass, cowering passengers and the back-up of traffic waiting to climb Hayes, and cheered. The driver climbed down, ambled to the back of the bus and reconnected the wires, bowed to the crowd who applauded, then climbed back on board heavily and the bus shuddered into life.

— Next stop Steiner!

This was the cost of life in the city. We all wanted the ground upon which we stood to be secure, but every so often would feel a tremor and be reminded that it was in fact melting, sliding, a coastal shelf crumbling away beneath our feet.

OCTOBER 1995

The woman who took receipt of her new temp slave on Monday stank of anti-perspirant: the smear of a dry waxy stick barely masking a more pungent hum, of resignation. Janet was stern, with pointy spectacles, bandy legs and wide hips swaddled in pink towelling sweat pants; gold studs drilled through the lobes of her huge, protruding ears. She was the head of the file-pullers at the title company – Lord of the Files – and she didn't give a shit about no Internet. From that first day, before I had the chance to commit any transgression, she could barely bring herself to look at me, and who could blame her – I couldn't hide my disappointment either. Having lost my toe-hold at ForwardSlash, when I told Bettina Ho that there was no more work for me down in New Media gulch, I ignored the patronizing smirk.

— Is it time to get our head out of the clouds and go to work, Ethan? Hmm?

We walked through the low-ceilinged room on the third floor of an old office building and I shook the limp, chubby hand of a seventeen-year-old Guamanian.

— 'Sup.

Denny had a wispy moustache and brilliantined hair and wore a check shirt with only the top button done. A blue bandana peeked from the back pocket of low-slung Dickies, and though he had no limp, he carried a cane, the end of which had been sharpened to a point. Denny was Janet's foster son, and his guided tour began with a loud kick aimed at a huge metal cabinet. Clerks looked around in shock.

— That shit's the deeds. Microfiche. And over there? Papers for the copier. That gets empty, you gotta fill it up, otherwise when you copy shit, it don't come out.

Off we went around the desks of fifteen title clerks, Denny waving his cane in front of him.

— All these bitches here? They axe us for copies of titles, like property deeds. They bring they requests over an' leave them at our desk. We get one an' we look through the microfiche. We find the title they seekin', we pull it, and we print it. Feel me?

Denny thrust an elasticated bundle of microfiches into my hands; x-rays of documents.

— That right there? That's why we here. Show me.

Almost immediately he grabbed the bundle back, slumped in a chair in front of a blank back-lit screen and slung the fiche between two glass plates beneath it. He trapped it expertly, and with dull mechanical precision slid it under the microscope. There on screen beneath the odd hair and scratch mark, was the black and white outline of a death certificate, for some pre-technological ghost of yesteryear. Denny hit a button on a keyboard then sauntered across the office. At the Xerox machine, a paper copy of the death certificate was already cooling in a tray beneath it. Denny took it, smelled it then held it up as if it was a picture he had drawn.

— Boo-ya.

A huge pile of copy requests sat between his microfiche machine and mine. Whenever we reached the bottom of the pile, I could never stop myself wondering whether we would be allowed to leave, whether, miraculously, we might have finished our job. Then a clerk would come over with five hundred more requests, nonchalantly dumping them in front of us, and we would begin again. Sisyphus was a temp. Everywhere we walked on that office floor, with shelf after shelf of untidily stacked deeds – analogue, dusty, stained brown – I pictured the ghosts of temps perdu swinging from the rafters on ropes, still gripping their time cards for stamping. I wondered how many had been toured around on how many Mondays before me, what the final straw had been for them, and what it would be for me when it came, as it inevitably would.

As the days passed I tried to forget what had been lost on Chestnut, and tried to imagine some kind of a future. I took to listening to music, and work assumed a kind of rhythm that was all about submission. I shut down the restive part of my mind and coasted along on tiny pleasures, enjoying the snap of the fiche being caught beneath the glass window, the smooth rolling sound of glass travelling on tiny castors beneath the microscope, and the minuscule sense of independence that walking across an office floor listening to a song that I liked could offer. I removed my Discman headphones to scratch an ear.

— How d'you know about Rappin' 4-Tay?

Denny had heard the music leaking and was highly suspicious.

— I know him. He's from the Fillmore. Hey, do you like E-40?

— He from Vallejo, yo!

— I know that.

Denny made a kind of a clucking sound, then leaned over and whispered,

— Hey man, lemme ask you. Why you sitting with your legs crossed?

— Because it's comfortable. Why do you ask?

— 'Cos that's how fags sit. P-tschhhsss.

Those exasperated exhalations of air, the cane, the hair net. With all of these things Denny was saying that this was his world within their world, a tiny inviolable space within which he could dream about being someone else. In the big picture he was a temp slave, copying for six dollars an hour, but the trick was to ignore the big picture and focus instead on thousands of tiny pictures, stamped on transparency.

A few Fridays later, Milo greeted me on my stoop with a forty-ounce bottle of Olde English.

— Drink with me, man. I've been shitcanned.

Was he hoping to stay with me? It had been a couple of weeks since I had seen him. He was outraged, telling me the story of his dismissal from a furniture moving company.

— It was a two-man move and among the stuff we had to carry up five fucking flights was a grand piano! I mean come on. It sounds like the set-up to a joke. And about halfway up my back was breaking, and we were at the return and my half was kind of balancing on the handrail, and his half was kind of stuck into the wall, and it was like, I'm really really sorry, but I simply cannot carry it another inch. And the guy holding the other end is all 'Aren't you aware that lifting heavy objects is part of the job description for a furniture mover?' What else could I do? We couldn't move it up, and we couldn't move it down. It wasn't my fault. Just, it simply couldn't be done. The piano was too heavy.

Milo had walked out in the middle of the move, leaving the other guy holding the bottom end of the piano. He couldn't see an alternative.

— Moving furniture is really, really . . . hard.

Clearly he thought that after every move, they'd sit on crates unpacking bubble-wrapped crystal tumblers and listen to a nice lady talk about her divorce. And when they got done, she would ask him to stay for dinner and a bottle of wine, and then maybe blow him. He wasn't looking at the little picture. He was all big picture. Big picture and bad luck.

Having fought with Róisín about money, he was homeless again, and stayed with me that night, then pushed off on another romantic interlude with Caitlin the air hostess, and afterwards I didn't see him, Róisín, Casey or Asher for weeks, nor did I speak to anyone from home. It was Denny or no one, and because of our Discmans usually no one, and that was fine by me. I was heartily sick of company and in the evenings, I'd drink on my own in a bar on Post and Taylor that was decorated with stuffed owls. Inside had the white pepper smell of bad breath and a few lonely singles, stools apart.

A man in a suit wandered in and bought two ladies a drink and soon one was slapping him on the shoulder and saying, 'I'm bad to the bone!' over and over again, like a kid who gets a phrase caught in their head. The man kept buying drinks and then the laughter of lady drunks began: tinkling, hollow, not unlike the sound of crying.

— Barkeep? 'Nother Fat Tire, Skyy-Cran and a French 75. Amirite girls?

— Well, yeah, 'cos I'm bad and she's bad too!

— We is getting loaded.

— . . . bad to the bone!

I wished he'd just take them and go and leave us in peace. Later, I got talking to a guy who offered to smoke me out, and though I didn't like pot, I didn't see why not, and followed him out into a doorway, where I was reminded of Dead Dave. This time, with a grin, he produced a glass pipe fashioned out of a miniature bottle of whiskey. Somehow, a tiny hole had been scorched through the torso of the bottle, and as the guy filled it with two chalky white rocks I saw we weren't talking about pot at all. He sniffed.

— Yeah, friend. For reals. Are you sure?

— Course I'm fucking sure. Let me hit that.

I was sick of people making assumptions about me and I was pretty sure I could go all the way down. And smoking crack can make your mouth froth a little, but the ingenuity of the improvised pipe lingered for much longer than the feverish high or the gut-sickness.

After a few weeks, Denny introduced me to a new recruit, Lew. Through his uncommon tallness and his wardrobe, this new temp reminded me of Thurston Moore. He must have been six foot five, with a pudding-bowl haircut. Lew had arrived in the city five days before and exuded the overpowering musk of innocence, that which could only be scented by those who had begun to miss their own. He sat down beside me, across the table from Denny.

— And so, what's up with the boss? Ole big ears. Seems like she hates me, innyway.

— Have you met Denny? Denny, this is Lew. Lew, Denny is Janet's *foster son*.

— Sorry man. We just. You know. First day.

Already, he had been condemned in Denny's eyes, and therefore Janet's and those of California National Title. He leaned over.

— You smoke, hermano? Let's go smoke.

Outside, a single shaft of cold sunlight streamed between the skyscrapers, illuminating our stairwell and the sleeping quarters of a bum four floors below, who had been crashed out on a cardboard box and was now stirring under the glare. Lew gave me a cigarette.

— So yeah, I been here five days now. My ex-girl lives here. I followed her out and then we broke up so I'm like fuck it, I'ma stay here with or without you.

— Good for you.

— But the freaks, man, with their body art? And I got an ass grabbin' offa this one dude the other night. Straight up!!

— Now you're just boasting.

— You gotta girl, Evan?

— No.

Lew bashfully pulled his jumper sleeves over his hands.

— Hey, I didn't know he was her kid. Don't he look black?

— He's not black, he's from Guam. And he's her foster son.

— The fuck is Goo-am?

This was just tiresome. I threw my cigarette down into the stairwell, and though I hadn't meant to, when it landed on the back of the wind-burned tramp below, it barely cost me a thought. He swiped at it and it rolled off his back, onto the concrete beside him.

— Here, sort out your shit with Denny or don't sort it out. But either way, keep me out of it.

— Hey, we're just talking, ain't we? What's eating you?

— Nothing. Just . . . get on with your own life and I'll get on with mine.

The weather had turned serious again and billowing fog clouds raced across rooftops. Skin was damp and salty and it was wind-whipped along the alleys. When they flushed out the fish shops in Chinatown at the end of days, the water seeping into your socks was cold, but there was no point in trying to escape it. I could feel the circle closing, one full revolution. Our second winter was approaching, the advance inexorable, and nothing was new any more.

— Guy?

I woke up standing at the urinal in a bar. My forehead was numb from leaning against damp bathroom tiles. I pushed back from it and zipped up. The Maker's Mark clock above the sink behind me read 6.20 a.m. But which bar? What day? Where? The owner was behind, frowning at me, concerned. He must have been seventy, grey-haired, hawkish but not unkind. A dirty white apron and fat hairy forearms. He led me back into the bar, poured me a cup of coffee and insisted I drink it, offering me a pastry swirl of some kind.

— Eat. Eat a snail.

I didn't want it but I ate, and the sugar went to work. He watched me until I finished, and then the flashbacks began. A Daft Punk DJ set in Mission Rock. Then the EndUp, where someone pointed out that a cigarette I thought I was smoking didn't in fact exist. I shook my head free of the memory and gestured towards the taps, but the barman shook his head and smiled.

— Not today, kid. Get yourself on home.

Outside I lay on the bench in morning drizzle, drifting off. Gino and Carlo – North Beach, somehow.

On account of the silence in the office, we three temps were productive, so much so that one of us often had little to do. Denny took to joining us outside on the fire escape, not because he smoked but because the indolence of it all appealed to him on an instinctual level. He didn't want us to think that he was willing to do our work for us and now when we broke, we broke en groupe. This leading-astray of Denny clearly hadn't escaped the notice of Janet.

— Back to work!

In response to her screeches, Denny would always get up and push through the steel fire escape door. Janet knew the score. Three temps was one too many and her foster son's job was in jeopardy, and if he lost his job, wouldn't he be sitting at home using her electricity and grazing from her fridge? She must have let Denny know that if Lew and I both proved ourselves to be more competent than his ass, his grass would be mown. Thereafter, all tape swapping and chatting about hip hop dried up and Denny became a sullen, malevolent presence who never strayed from the desk and who pretended to work, glancing over to the stairwell. His cane disappeared, as did the hair net and the pimp-roll. Once, returning from the far side of the office I passed him by, and, dressed in a button-down and a pair of smart, plastic-y brogues that must have pinched both heels and self-esteem, he actually shoulder-barged me. We had been friends before Lew arrived and Denny was only being rude because he wasn't able to handle the complexity of this battle between me, his foster mother and Lew. But I continued talking to him, because I was sorry for him, sorry that he worked with his foster mom, sorry she was such a bitch, but much more than anything, sorry for myself.

We buzzed around the broken-down rental van exchanging cigarettes and cursing in the midnight snow, lifting up the bonnet hoping to know about engines, then slamming it back down when still we didn't. This was the parking lot of a strip mall some two hours from Squaw Valley and it was getting cold. In defiance of the needle rising into red and the acrid smell of burning, the other five passengers had taken turns hammering our minivan up the slopes towards Tahoe, until the accelerator simply stopped responding to the brute shoving of the driver's foot on a slight incline, just before this strip mall. We slowed to a halt about two hundred yards back, immediately after which the van filled with dense, plastic-smelling smoke.

After Starving Students, Milo's parents had lost their patience and cut him off, and the harsh imperatives of life without manzanita wood or a father's bankroll were beginning to impact him. Broke and jobless, he had stayed behind in the city to try and find a job, but not before he begged Róisín for a loan. When he was fighting with her he stayed with me and right now he was staying with me again because she had lent me money to come up on this trip but wouldn't give any to him. As he stalked the hallway of my apartment in a rage, watching me pack for my first ever snowboarding trip and eating a bowl of my cereal, his sense of entitlement was almost stunning to behold.

— She's paying for you? What the . . . *fuck* is up with that?

— She's *lending* me money to go – that's different. She thinks I need a holiday.

— Lending, paying, whatever. Why won't she 'lend' me any money?

— Maybe she thinks I'm good for it.

— I'm good for it! No. She's trying to punish me.

— Maybe it's not about you, Milo. Is that remotely possible?

He shook his head, disgusted at my naïveté.

— Don't be ridiculous. It's fucking women.

Up here in the white night, seven of us stood in front of a dimly illuminated bar, Róisín and her friend Orls from Dublin, and a bunch of others. Róisín grabbed the door handle and pushed into the warmth, sucking our peloton in behind her. Inside was gloomy and neon, the staff drunker than the customers, either dancing with them or arm wrestling in a booth or swaying at the pool table, jamming their fists into complimentary bowls of popcorn and singing along to Bonnie Raitt. Róisín had rented the van, from the only company that would do business with under-twenty-fives, and which took a 200-dollar deposit. Now she fed coins into the phone outside the ladies' and screamed down the line. She was waving her vodka and grapefruit about as she argued and I could tell she was getting nowhere.

— You keep saying that but I don't belong to Triple A!!!

The rental people were in bed and disinclined to get any mechanic up here until the next morning. All we could do was get drunk enough to wring a few hours of sleep from the tiny seats of the van. I kept to myself, drinking at the bar, but Orls sourced a couple of mechanics who were drunk enough to volunteer with our engine – only after the bar had shut. By the time 2.30 rolled around, ours had become the cause célèbre, every one of us was too drunk to drive and the barmaid sold us a case of beer to take outside for the workers. Lit by a weak lemon-rind moon and a street lamp, someone put a boom box on the roof of the van and people pranced about to 'Whatcha want?' as the mechanics fumbled drunkenly with the engine. Our breath was misty, but the night somehow warmer than earlier.

I stood at the edge of the incline and looked at the trucks shooting past on the highway below. I could hear raucous Irish voices, that up-and-down tone familiar and haunting. Róisín was on her own a little further down. She came over and stood beside me.

— I'm glad you came up, Ev. You're kind of quiet these days. Everything good?

— Everything good? Yes. Yeah. Everything fine.

— You know, I'm kind of worried about you.

— Nah. You should worry about Milo, not me. I'm grand.

— There's nothing wrong with Milo apart from he's a scabby fucker. I'm sick of worrying about him, but I am worried about you, properly. Seriously, Evan. You can't see how much you've changed.

— Hmm.

— You're kind of . . . somewhere else all the time . . . like, even when you're here. You know?

We looked at the snow on the hill.

— Róisín, can I ask you a question?

She paused then went to speak but didn't, and at that moment, I knew that she knew what I was trying to ask her, and regardless of how she would answer, I knew the truth about her and Sam. The first time I met him I remember thinking that if that man belongs to the other army and is not the elusive second member of mine, I give up. And now, on the side of the road, the gang all laughing behind me, I gave up.

— You slept with him.

She ground out her cigarette. A long, long sigh.

— Come on, Ev. What do you want to hear? That I rode his brains out? That we 'did it'? I mean, would that help you in some way?

— Yeah, it would actually.

She rubbed my arm.

— Okay, then let me ask you why that is, exactly?

I pulled away.

— Come on, Ev. Why do you care?

— I just do, all right? It matters to me.

With my toe I made a figure of eight in the hard dirty snow, but it was uneven and I tried to scrape it away. The more I scraped the more you could see black gravel underneath.

— Seriously. Is it a moral thing? Do you have a moral problem with it?

— Give me some credit here.

— What is it then?

— I don't know. I just . . . he's my friend.

She looked confused.

— Well, he's still your friend! He still talks about you, a lot.

— He talks about me because that's all you two have in common. Me. The 'friend'. Always the friend. The fucking . . . glue. The professional third wheel.

— Slow your roll, there. With you and Milo, I've always been the third wheel. You know that. But I never minded, because I like you. I always have. And I'm not talking about that drunken snog back in Tom and Sheila's. I'm talking about you as a friend. Because despite the fact that you went seriously weird and distant after that night, as if I had fucking . . . molested you, I still like you, Evan.

She turned to leave, then came back and I couldn't stop it coming.

— I'm just going to come out and ask it. Are you gay, Evan?

To hear it articulated, the hard word hanging there in the freezing air, sounded wrong. It just did. Despite everything, there was just no way it was right. When it finally evaporated with her breath I blew smoke over it.

— Just because I wasn't hot for you?

— It's got nothing to do with that! Come on.

— Fuck off, Róisín. Even to ask that shows a serious lack of imagination on your part.

She addressed the snow, trying to persevere.

— Okay, fine. You can lash out. But if you're unhappy – and I don't think you can deny that you are – and if you want to do something else, whatever you want to do, you can just do it. I'll be there for you. Your friends will be there for you.

— I'm not depressed if that's what you mean. Fuck's sake.

— Is it about work, then? Okay, so you lost your amazing job. Go get another one. I mean, what do you want? This is life, Evan. It's shit, sometimes. No one has a clue. We're all lost.

I heard the voices swell behind us. It was true, that. Nothing was remarkable in the way we thought. Nothing at all was remarkable. We were just these stupid atoms colliding into each other, wasting precious energy.

— If I knew what I wanted d'you think I'd be standing here in this parking lot with you?

She looked at me, her cheeks red as if I had slapped her, then turned and walked down the incline slipping on the icy bank. I heard an engine start, looked up and saw the gang whooping and hugging each other.

On Bring Your Daughter To Work Day, twelve-year-old girls trailed their parents around the offices of California National Title, each an echo of who these adults must have been in a different life, how they must have looked before disappointment threw an arm around them, leading them away from hope and whispering in their ear that now, the point of it all – the reason they were still alive – was to examine property deeds for life. Standing beside their progeny, every parent was degraded, a dog-eared facsimile of the ideal now flicking elastic bands or shyly clinging to their mother's skirts.

When I got back from Tahoe the night before, Casey and Asher had just returned from a mission to deep East Oakland, wearing downmarket jackets and hats, all excited like they'd robbed a bank. In fact, they had exchanged a thousand dollars for five hundred pills left under a barbecue in the backyard of this one Colombian guy, and were going to a party at an art space in 111 Minna. Milo was there too, trailing them around, very much wanting to be part of the whole deal, but penniless and kept on the periphery. The manner in which he watched the action unfolding around him reminded me of a pet dog on Christmas morning.

The party that night was being thrown by Om Records,

and Derrick Carter and Mark Farina were playing. We took some pills and went on down, Milo disappeared somewhere and I burrowed my way into the corner of a room full of happy faces. My mind sank into some hypnotic recess and when I came to it was 4 a.m. and the place was nearly empty, the atmosphere in each room charged with the malevolence of a proper come-down. Gone were the slinky boys in Kangol bucket hats and combats, the boyish girls in X-Girl T-shirts and tiny old school trainers. Now it was drum and bass and I was alone near a Crip-walking circle of topless guys. Sweat hung in the corners of the room, and the dancers whooped jockishly and strutted around wearing large silver chains with dollar bill signs swinging between sculpted pectoral muscles. It was over.

I woke up in a deep cloud of anxiety and in work, huge, daughterless Lew, Denny and I had been in each other's pockets all morning. I wanted to get away but it was pouring rain out and I didn't have enough money to go to a restaurant. We all sat in the staff kitchen, eating slender downtown burritos in silence. I don't know whether it was self-preservation or adaptation to his environment, but recently Lew had begun to get along with Denny. I would see them walking to lunch together, sharing a joke waiting for the elevator, and when they saw me they pretended not to and that suited me fine. So in the kitchen I pretended to read, cocking an ear to the big thaw.

— What's Goo-am like?

— Guam is hella fine, yo. The beaches . . . man.

— I wish I'da grown up near a beach. Don't you miss it?

— Course I miss it. But I can't go back.

— Why not?

— I ain't got family there no more. My daddy's in Vallejo.

— And your momma? Where's she at?

Denny put down his burrito and wiped his mouth with a napkin.

— Man, you like the popos. Don't never know when to quit.

A woman in her forties with short hair in a bob and a grey bolero jacket came into the room. Her name was Ally and I knew she was senior. I kept pretending to read and she opened the fridge and took out Tupperware, then glanced at my book. She turned back and performed a private inventory of the contents.

— What are you reading?

I showed her the cover and she raised her eyebrows. At exactly the moment that she mouthed the word *Lolita*, her twelve-year-old daughter materialized shyly at the door frame.

— Na-bokov. What a master.

— Don't know why you bother to read for.

Denny didn't look up when he said it, instead pretending to pick something from his teeth. I was sure he was speaking to me but even if he wasn't, the woman at the fridge could have ignored it. But it was clear that these two shared some kind of history, because she counted to five before responding to his comment, and in those seconds I wondered if she ever suspected him of stealing her lunch when it had in fact, on at least five occasions, been me. Or maybe she was getting ready to defend Nabokov and books and literature, protecting what she held dear from the rampaging Anschluss of culture by youth and hip hop, in all its misspelled, ebonic glory.

— He is reading, Denny, because he doesn't want to be photocopying death certificates for the rest of his life. Unlike some people I could care to mention.

When her daughter sniggered Denny noticed her for the first time. She was probably three years younger than him.

— I don't want to be doing that shit for the rest of my life neither.

— Well, you might want to think about reading something then.

When she closed the fridge door and went to the counter to get a knife, Lew jumped up and began to perform a mocking dance behind her, making the tongue-in-cheek fellatio gesture, glancing across at Denny for approval. Denny smirked and returned to his burrito, mumbling loud enough for Ally to hear.

— I can read, bitch.

She spun around, very nearly catching the tail-end of Lew's gyration.

— What did you just say?

Denny calmly put down his napkin, looked at Lew who was smiling, then looked at her.

— I said, you a bitch.

— How dare . . .

— . . . you a bitch I said, and you a trick-ass mother-fuckin' ho. How you like me now?

The plastic fork bent further and further in the white-grip of her hand, skin on her fingers drawing tauter and tauter. The fork then snapped, sending a shard of plastic whizzing through the air. Everyone followed that trajectory and as it landed, Ally flung her lunch in the sink and stormed out, her daughter in the slipstream. Lew went over to the sink and inspected it, picking up a lettuce leaf with his slender, freckled fingers.

— You could prolly still eat most of this . . .

Ally came charging back into the kitchen having summoned Janet, who had no trouble drawing from a deep well of general unhappiness. She scanned the room wildly, her crimson ears thermometers of rage.

— What in the hell is going on in here?

— I'll tell you what happened. Not only am I convinced that he has been stealing my lunch for the last couple of months (here Ally pointed at Denny), but he also just issued a stream of the foulest abuse. He (pointing at Lew) was making an obscene gesture behind my back (well done, daughter) while all of this was happening. And Rhiannon had to be here of course, to witness what basically amounts to a sexual assault of her own mother, in her own mother's place of work. Oh, my God . . .

Ally clapped a hand over her mouth.

— Okay, calm down. Let's start with him. What did *he* do?

Janet was pointing at me, her eyes narrowed to slits, but from behind her hands, Ally shook her head. I was reading Nabokov for Christ's sake. What could I possibly be guilty of, apart from extreme sensitivity? She wailed,

— He did nothing!!!

— Nothing?!

Janet couldn't conceal her disappointment.

— Janet, I ain't never stole no one's lunch!

Denny stood up uncertainly and was now pleading, his hands open in supplication. He knew this was serious, but Ally wasn't about to let him off the hook. She whipped her hands away from her face and we could see that she hadn't been crying at all.

— Of course you did, don't be absurd!

— I never!

Denny was a child again, lips quivering and genuine fear playing across his face. Nabokov knew the world of difference between children and adults, and this collapse of veneer restored all the vulnerability that with moustaches, canes and gangsters' posturing Denny sought so hard to conceal. So much more was at stake for him than anyone else. This was his world, and he was still a kid, unlike me.

I closed the book.

— He didn't steal your lunch. It was me. I have been stealing your lunch all this time.

As soon as I spoke, Janet's eyes lit up. Larceny! Perfect! But Ally wasn't remotely happy.

— No, you haven't. You're just taking the hit.

Just how much faith did she put in books and those who read them?

— I solemnly swear that I have been stealing food since the day I started. Onion bagels. Cran-apple juice. Your awesome salt beef sandwich that one time. Remember? Denny here is a good kid and I'm sure he's sorry for losing his temper, but Lew was giving him a very hard time just before you came in, weren't you, Lew?

Lew shook his head to say no but I glared at him, ordering him to agree.

— I think possibly, Denny took it out on you by accident, although I'm sure he didn't mean it. Isn't that right, Denny? Isn't that pretty much what happened here?

— I never meant nothing by it. I'm sorry, Miss.

We were sent back to work for the rest of the day. Denny was made to apologize profusely on further occasions, but he got to keep his job. So too did Lew, although I'm not entirely sure how. Perhaps the testimony of Ally's daughter was inadmissible on account of her being twelve, or perhaps Lew had done enough work with Denny to make the grade.

When I got back home that evening, the phone was ringing.

— I guess you know what this is.

— Ahh, Bettina! Is it about the liberation of food from the refrigerator at work?

— Are you making a joke about this, Ethan?

— The name is Evan. Please, even once, can you call me . . .

— Okay, let me just do this. You're not to go back to California National Title. Ever.

— They couldn't have told me that themselves?

— It's policy. They never tell the temp in case they freak out and go postal.

I had to admit, that logic was bullet-proof.

— So what next for us, Bettina?

And then she chuckled, for the first time genuinely humoured.

— No. We're through, Devon. Campus Connection will no longer be able to place you in temporary work. But we wish you the very best of luck going forward!

It transpired that I had photocopied death certificates for the last afternoon without knowing that mine was among them.

Lying on a street, head on the kerb, body in the road, between two cars. I heard a voice mumble. I opened my eyes and the light was blinding. The bastard sun was up and my blood beating away at the prison walls.

— Dude, are you okay?

A ridiculous enquiry. I shut my eyes again.

— Are you all right, Evan?

The voice knew me? I squinted and the outline of a head shifted slightly, blocking the sun from my eyes. Grey-brown hair, a furrowed brow shiny with perspiration. I pulled myself up to sitting and saw it was Fred. With a halo of sun behind him and in his general vigour, he looked messianic; Jesus on rollerblades. This was the Panhandle, and he had been circling the park on the cycle lane with his date, and wasn't smiling at the idea of me using the footpath as a pillow, like I thought he might have done. I hadn't seen him in months.

— You want us to call an ambulance?

He was bending over now, hands resting on his knees, squinting at me like he'd encountered an exotic frog in the grass. A drop of his sweat landed on my lip. I brought a hand to my face and it throbbed, as if it had been – I don't know what – attacked? Gravel was embedded in my cheek. His date frowned in concern.

— Did he get hit by a car?

My tongue worked its way across fissured lips. I wanted to say I can speak, I can hear you, but I couldn't speak after all. My throat was parched. No, no car crash. That was too much to hope for. I think I did this one myself. There had been quite a night the night before, one that started with the Sunset Boat Party and ended – or so I had thought – with retsina drained out of paper cups in a fast food restaurant on Polk by the name of 'Steve the Greek's'. There was a fight of some sort, a sickening meeting of jaw and sidewalk, but not here, if memory serves, somewhere down in the Fillmore, in a knock-first party above a laundromat that had blackjack tables and Chinese men smoking black tar.

I put my hands on the kerb behind me to raise myself up. I dragged my legs up under me, then dropped myself back into a sitting position, and with this move, the throbbing peaked and I retched violently, spattering yellow bile everywhere.

— Eww.

— Hold up there. Maybe you shouldn't move. Do you think something might be broken?

— Was it a hit and run?

— What's going on, buddy? Were you robbed?

I cradled my head, and the warmth of my palms against my temples sent such a jolt of nausea from my brain to my stomach that instantly I vomited again on my jeans, and with such force that my ass slipped from the kerb onto the road, banging my coccyx, landing me back in the gutter, covered in my own waste. And now, finally, I was well enough to speak.

— Go to hell, Fred. You know exactly what this is.

I came down to the ForwardSlash party not because I wanted to share in the unconfined joy of the IPO announcement but to see if, now that my time here was up and there was nothing left to play for, I would be able to tell Sam everything. When I ran into her recently on the 21 Hayes, Róisín asked me if I had heard from him recently, going on to mention that his wife had upped and left him not long before. When I got to Chestnut, I saw that he was serving food at the barbecue. Hundreds of people milled around, a good many of whom I'd never even clapped eyes on before. We wouldn't get a chance to talk until later and in the meantime there would be a whole lot of other conversations that I wasn't remotely interested in having, so I went down to the underground car park to sober up and stay out of the way. That's how I woke up in the back of the Land Rover, being driven somewhere. They say two things: that love is hell – which it most assuredly is – but also that all true romantic love is unrequited. And if that's the case, I was ready to kill the idea of romance stone dead, once and for all. I had no further use for it.

As the Land Rover moved up a hill then plunged down the other side, I made peace with the way my life had assumed its own momentum and was no longer in my hands. It was something of a relief. After being woken by Fred on Fell that afternoon, I struggled home, and on my front step encountered the bunched, keening form of Asher, who looked up at me with tear-filled eyes and a bottom lip that quavered like a child's.

— That motherfucker friend of yours! He stole my fucking records, man!!!

Asher was a skinny fellow, and when he launched himself forward at me with a weird punch/slap hybrid that somewhat awkwardly found my neck, it was funny until I fell back against a parked car and he reared up to hit me again. I backed away from him defensively, half on my hands and knees. I stood uncertainly and for a few minutes I had to move around him like we were sparring,

like a couple of drunks. I smelled of vomit, and could feel
passers-by watching as we circled each other.

— Wait, listen. What's going on? Can't we just talk? Tell
me what's up?

— Your . . . asshole . . . friend . . . last night . . .

As with smoking crack and sleeping rough, being a DJ
does nothing for your stamina and upper body strength,
and soon we were spent and Asher allowed me inside
the apartment to see for myself. Gone were the boxes of
CDs that Casey kept stacked in the hallway, leaving only
a heavy outline of dust. Gone too were thirty crates of
expensively accumulated vinyl from Asher's room: white
labels, dub plates, rarities, memories, a whole lifetime in
music. And from Casey's, another thirty-odd boxes. The
only four records that these two professional DJs now
owned in the entire world were the ones on the slipmats
of their decks.

— Couldn't it – and I'm just saying – couldn't it have
been a regular robber?

— Then why didn't they take the decks?

I didn't know how that incriminated Milo particularly,
as opposed to another dumb thief, and when I said so,
Casey's reply came instantly, and the way he said it told
me that as a result of my association and even if Milo
was ultimately proven innocent, within the walls of my
apartment I had been condemned.

— Dude, if you're a real criminal you know how to
fence electronics. Okay? You just know. And the four hundred pills we still had that he totally knew were hidden

in the *Maxinquaye* CD case? Gone, dude. Gone. So just drop it.

To my mind, what incriminated Milo more than anything else was his absence from the apartment, along with his belongings. If you wanted to proclaim your innocence you stuck around, if you weren't making a point – a particularly brutal and hurtful point. I prayed the doorbell would ring and it would turn out to have been nothing more than a food run, that Milo would be standing on the front step, holding barbecue from Brothers-in-Law or a burrito from Balazo with the tiny paper Mexican flag stuck in the top, restored to his old chirpy, robust self. But he never did come back in any form, and never now would do.

Everything was finished. Asher and Casey spent all afternoon at yard sales up and down the Haight, looking for their records, had apparently found a Daft Punk white label that was definitely theirs, and which was offered back to them for twenty-four dollars by a guy on Laguna who said he'd found it. Having woken up in a boozy sweat at 4 a.m. convinced that I had seen a lizard in my bed, I waited it out, shivering and stiff until the sun came up. I prayed that Milo would be sleeping on the futon in the hallway but he wasn't, so I took a shower and left quietly, and at the ATM on Belvedere I withdrew the 300-dollar maximum. I wanted to see if the CD boxes I had passed every morning in the hallway and every night before bed had resurfaced in Reckless or Amoeba

Records. Maybe I could make amends to Casey by buying as many of them back as possible.

When Amoeba finally opened I found fifty copies of Armand Van Helden's remix of 'Professional Widow' beside a bunch of Pussyfoot compilation CDs in the trip-hop aisle, and brought them all up to the counter. The seller was curt.

— We can't give 'em back to you because we can't verify that they're yours either. I'm sorry, brother, but that's the market. Buyer beware, hur hur.

— They were stolen from my apartment. I'm just looking for a description of the man who sold them to you. It's massively important.

— People come in here selling all the time. That's how we run the place.

— I need to know who stole them.

— You need to call the cops, friend. Not my problem.

— Come on, man. Help me out. He's my friend, this guy. Did he sell them to you?

— I'm not saying.

— Is he Irish? At least tell me that.

If he hadn't confirmed it to me there and then with a tiny nod, before moving away, Milo's continuing disappearance off the face of the earth in the days following certainly did. When I got back, Casey gave the CD boxes I had bought for him a cursory glance and threw them on his bed.

— You shouldn't have bothered. Work insurance.

That was that, so. I gave my notice to Asher and Casey and when I did, Casey clapped, with a saturnine smirk.

Back in the boot, the Land Rover was now stationary. Sam had left, and wanting to wait a decent amount of time, I had – of course – fallen asleep again. I peered out the window and it was dark. Rakes and a windsurf board. I was in a garage. An alarm light blinked on the dashboard. Wherever we were now, we were staying for the night. The windows were already fogging up with my body heat, and by morning it would be obvious that someone was in here, and even then I would have to find a way of getting out undetected. Already I could feel myself losing courage, so I crawled into the driver's seat, taking care not to sound the horn. I tried to see if the car alarm was on, but nothing gave a clue apart from the flashing light. I began to panic a little, then resolved to do something in this moment rather than fritter away the adrenalin in mere apprehension. I gripped the handle. One, two . . . a click, a beat, a squeak, and cooler air flooded in. No alarm.

I stepped out and peered around. As my pupils contracted, shelves of various tools revealed themselves all around. At my feet, a box of 'Activ8.com!' T-shirts from work. The outline of a staircase leading to a door, at the top of which was a bank of light switches. I crept towards the door. Sam could be sitting right beyond it. I took a breath, grabbed a hold of the handle, opened it and stepped forward into the dark. Inside, I stood perfectly still, hearing my own breath and heartbeat, becoming

conscious of my surroundings. Pictures, a prescription on
the fridge, a note clearly written by him to a gardener.
'Arturo. Weed killer!' I quietly opened a few cupboards
and when I spied a bottle of Maker's Mark, poured a nice
belt into a tumbler and drained it, gasping from the raw
heat. I felt it invade me, reinforcing the notion that being
here was okay, in a way, and after another glass I was
drawn magnetically up those stairs, towards the living,
breathing form that I knew to be up there. I crept along,
holding on to a banister, then passed the empty rooms on
either side of a long, narrow landing. I knew where the
Master was. I don't know how – I just knew.

The door was ajar. And there he was, my quarry, the
thief of me, breathing softly now, more of a whisper than
a snore. This was a large room. It would take about ten
steps to get all the way over to the bed, and between here
and there was a dressing table with some feminine effects.
I picked up a clear glass bottle, sprayed some of the per-
fume on my neck, and rubbed my wrists along. Sam was
sleeping on his wife's side and the other side was empty.
The bed was packed with pillows and a fresh, thick duvet.
I thought of my threadbare sleeping bag and was overcome with disgust. This was a proper bedroom, not a stale
repository of the disappointed, in the dark. I stepped
around to the far side of the bed, away from Sam's sleeping form. I hadn't yet glimpsed his face, buried as it was
in luxurious hills of Egyptian cotton.

I slipped off my shoes and socks, took off my trousers

and my shirt, and crawled into the bed beside him. He snored softly. I had made it. Here was the culmination of a lifetime of dreamed scenarios, in which the ending was always unwritten. A lifetime of running, chasing towers of vanishing smoke across my dreams until I woke, then chasing their animate image in my waking hours. It was possible to create a puzzle that you didn't have the smarts to solve, and for the life of me I couldn't figure out why I hadn't ever been interested in lying in bed with any man who wanted to lie in bed with me. Now, I owed myself this, because finally, I'd fused my dream life with a version of my real life. Isn't that a workable definition of heaven?

I remembered that day on the boat, how Lida jokingly referred to the extent of their bed as 'The Midwest'. As I moved across, Sam stirred and I froze, but then he backed towards me, taking my arm and wrapping it round his front. He inhaled the air, the scent.

— Baby. I knew you'd come back.

My hand rested on his stomach and through the pyjamas I could feel the undulation of breathing belly. Was he dreaming of a boat scudding across the water? His right arm was over mine, and I could feel his armpit hair at my own bare bicep, his hand resting on my arm. I sensed it tense a fraction as it fingered the hairs on my forearm, but it didn't matter now. After all the trauma and exertion of the last while, I had finally found a space into which I fitted, a place to be happy. And all I wanted to do was sleep, for once without dreaming. I was drifting off.

— What the FUCK!!!!!

Suddenly it got very bright in the room and automatically I got out of the bed, feeling so very weary. That was it, that was the glimpse, the revelation. That's all you get. Now it was gone, over for ever. Time to go.

— Jesus Christ. What is this? EVAN????

— I'm sorry I'm sorry. I don't know . . .

— You're in my house?!

My shoes were back on, and I stuffed my socks in my pocket.

— It's fine, it's okay, I'm going. I just had to . . .

— How did you get in here?

He was grabbing a robe and tying it around himself.

— Sam, sorry . . . I know you're married . . .

— What? It's not 'married' or 'single', Evan. It's . . . breaking and entering!!

— Okay, you don't like . . . I get it. I'm sorry.

— You terrified me! In my bed!!!

— I'm going . . .

I prayed he would forget this and searched his face. But through his bleary fury I saw that wouldn't ever happen, that he hardly knew me, that he was scared of me. The gentleness I so loved in him had coarsened through fear and it didn't matter any more if he loved me, because I no longer wanted him. I had to applaud myself on this latest bind.

— Bravo!

I jumped on, then over the bed, landed unsteadily, righted myself and marched out past Sam, who was pacing on the landing. I patted him on the shoulder like it had been nothing.

— I'm sorry, pal. You won't see me again. Don't call the cops, will ya?

— Wait. Evan. What's going on? Evan! Hold up. You're crying.

— Of course I'M FUCKING CRYING!

I wrenched my arm free of his grip and laughed, then tripped and fell four steps down.

— Evan, wait!!! Hang on!!!

I got up again and stumbled down the stairs before he reached me. I opened the front door and ran, my head filling with a shrill alarm sound that only began to recede once my lungs were burning and the salty sea wind slapped my face. Flames of wild fires were dancing on the beach and the sand whipped into my eyes. Clusters of people lingered in shadow, infernally lit, their laughter drowned by the crashing waves. I had reached the edge of the world, the furthest point away. From now to the end of time I could get on planes and fly all over, but no matter where I landed, no matter how distant the beach, the jungle, the granite façade, I would always be here, locked in myself. There is no point in looking for a way out and no point in wanting to be free, because out there, there is no other me.

EPILOGUE – JANUARY 1996

Unlike the first time round, when Róisín returned to San Francisco after Christmas, she knew to take a shuttle bus from SFO, and as they splashed through the intersections at night, on the radio Nina Simone was singing 'He's Got the Whole World in His Hands'. She looked around the shared ride, guilty for thinking it, but what an incredible downer the festive season had been, had always been in fact, and what a soaring relief to be back – almost home now. In front of her, a blonde in an American Airlines uniform. A trolley dolly, probably going to the Radisson. Behind her, these three Irish guys, fresh out of college, their hair in curtains, way too much aftershave, Beastie Boys T-shirts, lit with booze and jabbering excitedly.

Once a child learns that they get attention by crying, it's hard to stop them mewling all day, and when these three guys scanned the bus for smiles that would validate the joyful experience of just getting to be near them, they got one or two in return. Then, for the rest of the journey, without communicating it to each other, everything they said was for the benefit of everyone else, at least as much as it was for them. Reading the street signs they tried to outdo each other: 'Turk!', 'Eddy!', 'Polk!!!' – 'Polk' always got a laugh. One of them was flirting with the air hostess and Róisín had to laugh at that – he had no chance.

Having not seen him around the city during the months of November and December, Róisín was surprised to run into Evan at departures in SFO on the way back home for Christmas. It was one of those awkward situations where they stood in line and checked in together and everyone meant well. And just before they reached the top of the line she went out to smoke and when she came back in Evan had moved her bags up to the counter along with his because it would have been rude not to, and the man at the check-in desk found them seats beside one another on the plane because he made the assumption that they were together. For one of them to tell him that they didn't actually want that was to sound an openly hostile note to the other person, when at that point, that whole discourse was being conducted way beneath the surface. That's how Evan and Róisín boarded together and flew back to Dublin in neighbouring seats and glacial silence.

Really, their friendship had ended in Tahoe – on the side of the road to Tahoe, to be precise. All she had wanted to do was throw an arm out to a drowning man, but like so many people in her life, he didn't want to be saved. Boarding the plane they spoke about Milo, of course. He was either upstate now or in Sac or Santa Rosa, or maybe Santa Cruz. Neither of them had seen him in ages, Róisín since a fierce confrontation on her doorstep over some money that had gone missing. Of all people, Sheila Moreland had called her one night and tearfully asked her to help find him, but Róisín couldn't help her because she didn't know where to start looking. And when Evan told her about the records, she couldn't say that she didn't think Milo had stolen them, and she really felt for Evan then, because he loved Milo so much more than she ever did. But he wouldn't have accepted her sympathy because that might have let her back in, and Evan was a typical Cancer: all front.

Before popping two Valium on the plane and washing them down with plenty of gin, one thing Evan did offer was that this wasn't a Christmas trip home. He wasn't coming back.

— San Francisco is kind of played out, I reckon. I've got interviews set up with some content providers in Ireland, and with my West Coast experience, I'm way ahead of the curve.

Could he hear himself? Apparently, it was the opportunity presented by the Irish economy that had seduced him. Things were taking off at home, it was a money decision, a career move. Telling her about the gold rush in Dublin in a tone that invited no response, he sounded quite convincing. But could he possibly believe that? Before putting on his eye-mask he framed a rhetorical question for her to mull over as they flew over the Rockies, heading east.

— I mean, what's so special about California anyway?

After he settled into his conspicuous slumber, she

wanted to rip off his eye-mask and force him to admit that it was special and that he knew it was special – in truth, it was too special for him to make it there. But she couldn't allow the rising tide of anger to overwhelm her, because the way he had chosen to play it, it wasn't even about the truth any more. His argument about missing home was plausible and that was all that mattered to him. Plausible deniability. And why did she care anyway? Their race was run. As she watched the rerun of *Friends* on the communal screen a few rows ahead, she consoled herself with the notion that behind the mask, Evan's eyes might still have been open.

To be fair, by choosing to go home maybe he was playing it as it laid, because there was love in Ireland, a kind of love she couldn't say with total honesty had ever nourished her back home. Maybe he felt he couldn't gamble on finding that somewhere else. Standing in arrivals at Dublin airport, before she found her own mum, Róisín watched Evan hug his parents, and the way they hugged him, she could tell that they would never find the lie in his eyes because they weren't looking for it. And when they came over to where she was waiting for her parents and said goodbye and wished her a happy Christmas, Róisín knew from the way that Evan stood behind them and let them do the bidding, and the way he raised a weak peace sign by way of goodbye, she wouldn't ever be seeing him again.

Róisín's mum's hair was flame red in a way that surprised her. It was always red, but now much more so.

Maybe her memory had drained it of some brilliance, but after a certain point our wardrobe is frozen in time and Ellen Byrne was wearing a dress and knee-high boots as ever. For the first time in living memory, she was driving too, her husband in the passenger seat. Don Byrne had never let his wife drive before, but now everything was different. Maybe he was too nervous for the roads, and it was his nerves that got him in trouble in the first place. Or maybe her mum wanted to punish him. Maybe she wanted to convey something to her daughter, that she was doing her bit. Róisín hadn't wanted to go back to Ireland in the first place, but once the tearful summons had come over the phone, she didn't have much of a choice. Her dad needed her back, and that was that. Tickets were bought and paid for and posted over to her.

His new spot in the front passenger seat cast him in a boyish, chastened light, and Don was smaller than the last time she had seen him, slumped further down. The skin on his neck had puckered and deflated a little, he was grey around the temples, and his hands never stopped moving the whole way home, picking imaginary dust from his lap, counting the money in his billfold. Jangling keys. Winding the window. Turning down the radio, turning it up. It was kind of heartbreaking. By the time they crossed the toll bridge the car was quiet and they looked out at the bay.

Róisín never saw this view without thinking of when they took the ferry to England for a camping holiday in Pembroke and were standing on the deck at the front, looking out into the starry night. She wondered if upon seeing the bay her parents ever thought of that evening, when her older sister Annie was beside her listening to A-ha on her Walkman and her mum and dad on either side of them. It was dark, but the night was clear, and there were lights out on the water. Ferry boats, probably. Or maybe a trawler. It was more about what you couldn't see, really, the unbelievable size of the world. Her mum was wearing a head scarf, looking like something out of Graham Greene. She turned to her husband.

— I read this story once about two guys on deck, on a boat, on a Mediterranean cruise. They'd just stepped out to smoke their cigarettes after dinner on the first night, and were strangers to each other and to the ocean and just happened to be sharing the night air. One chap says to the other, 'God that's a lot of water.' You know, the cliché. And the other chap doesn't even look over, he just smokes some more and gazes out, and finally he says, tinily, 'Yeah. And that's only the top of it.' Isn't that great? I mean, do you ever wonder what's out there?

Her mum smiled and looked out to the water.

— It's just Wales, Ellen.

After her dad said that, all Róisín could remember was 'Hunting High and Low' leaking from Annie's orange foam headphones, and though they never spoke about it, in that moment she and her mum wondered separately how it was possible to see a view like this and want to reduce it to that, and whether it was possible to claim that perspective and ever be happy. Then, as if to answer, and even though he wasn't a drinker, Don stood away from the edge and went back down to the bar, to the fruit machines and truck drivers, the smell of diesel and sweat.

Róisín didn't love Milo but she liked him all right – he was fun and wild and not-her-father. In Dublin, the weeks after he left were dull and she couldn't summon the energy to look for a job. Despite what she'd tell other people when they asked her about life after graduation, and despite her ex-boyfriend's plans, Róisín hadn't really considered the prospect of emigration. Looking back, she might have been depressed, which might have gone some way towards explaining why, when her mother came into her bedroom crying and holding an empty bottle of Huzzar at two in the afternoon, she was in bed. When that sight presented itself at her bedroom door, she wanted to hide under the covers. She had been in The Globe and then The Kitchen and then Blazes the night before, but remembered nothing about a bottle of vodka – though that proved nothing much. As she held it up, Róisín's next thought was that her mum had just downed it, and she was so relieved when she finally spoke and sounded sober.

— I found this in the greenhouse. He's been drinking, Róisín.

— Christy?

Her mum laughed despite herself. Christy was their gardener and they already knew he drank – it was the very thing that defined him. Every year before Cheltenham, just as spring was poking its snout through the ground, he would disappear off the face of the earth and not reappear until June when the back garden was fecund and raucous.

— Christy's dead. I'm talking about Don . . . I mean your dad. He's been drinking. A lot.

— Is that . . . possible?

— The man's not a saint.

— But why would he hide it in the shed?

— Apparently he feels anxious . . .

Her mum was crying. Róisín debated whether she should get up and give her a hug or something.

— . . . anxious all the time. When I said he should think about seeing a doctor, he had a conniption. Will you talk to him?

— Has Annie?

— Annie's got two kids under two. He'll listen to you.

— What do you want me to say?

— He's your father. Can't you figure that out?

After her mum left the room, Róisín remembered the night before Evan and Milo left, when she called home for a lift, expecting her mum to answer, but her dad did. He sounded wide awake too, but when he picked her up she thought the phone call must have roused him from sleep because his eyes were ringed with red. She thought he probably hadn't told her he had been asleep because he didn't want her walking home. Milo had broken up with her and she was feeling kind of blue, plus she had worn the face off Evan, which was a really dumb move, so on the way home they didn't speak. They turned off the dual carriageway and bombed up the hill. Theirs was the kind of suburb where nothing much happened. Gardens were neat, it was off the main roads, speed bumps and round-abouts everywhere. They lived right on the far side of one of these little roundabouts, and approaching it that night, Róisín could see there weren't any cars coming on either side, which was just as well, because once he made it to the yield sign her dad just ploughed on through, mount-ing the island, the underside of the car scraping at grass and rocks and bushes, then crashing down with a bump and a screech on the far side and into their drive, narrowly avoiding the pillars on the right side. Once they'd skidded to a halt, they were quiet and he took the keys out of the ignition and kind of examined them in his hand.

— You know, I always wanted to do that. Go straight through.

At the time she laughed, because it was one of those rare occasions when her dad showed a bit of spark. Right then he reminded her of Milo and she wondered if it was true after all that girls marry their father. And she treasured the notion that he had a bit of something about him after all, and harboured only a tiny bit of resentment that he had been keeping it under wraps for all that time. But now she knew it wasn't 'spark'. He was drunk at the wheel.

Because her mum had asked her, they'd had a kind of summit on a drizzly Wednesday in the living room, one of those days where the fire won't take and the grey sky seems to graze your head and seep partly within it.

An arrangement of biscuits between them almost brought her to tears, and she could feel her mother hovering outside the room. The setting was just like those times when she was a bold child that needed a talking-to, but now he was chastened and she the adult, and despite all the worldliness she projected, she was unhappy about that. They had fought so hard down the years, about smoking and drinking, boys and men, and staying out late, and up until that moment she hadn't been remotely aware that she still wanted her dad to have control. There wasn't another way of putting it.

— Will you stop?

— I will.

— Can you? Can you just stop?

— Course I can. Don't worry. You're young.

She hugged him when he said that. And he did stop drinking right away, and without realizing before that she would, Róisín emptied her savings account, went into USIT and booked a flight, and only after that did she tell her parents that she was emigrating . . . to San Francisco. She had dispatched her duty but it wasn't her marriage. Talking to her, you'd never have guessed that the lie was that she needed to go away to grow up, and the truth much less heroic, that she went to America to remain a kid.

The first few months in San Francisco were awkward, because she was sure that Evan thought she was chasing him, which was emphatically not the case. He couldn't get past that stupid kiss back in the Morelands' house, and had a prurient fixation with the idea of relationships, if not the practical business of them. He couldn't believe or accept that they would be friends and it wasn't until he began to suspect that she had something going on with Sam that he stopped worrying about her chasing him, and seemed to invite it a little more. Only seemed, though. He was the crab.

Ahh, Sam. Lovely older Sam the Libra, with his beautiful brown eyes and the tasselled loafers and the ever-so-slightly cheesy come-ons. She had always had a thing for older men, and the first time they met, in that fairly dumpy bar down by Evan's work, he got her at a moment of weakness. Upon arriving in SFO, she called home to say she had landed safely and though no one said it, she could just tell that her dad was drunk, and she wanted to fly right back. When she finally found Evan in that bar he was too hammered to talk to, and she ended up talking to Sam, who was about the only remotely sober one there. And at the end of the night, when Evan agreed to take a lift from a guy he worked with, even though the guy was conspicuously hammered, there was no way she could get in the car with them. She couldn't do anything about the fact that Evan thought she was being pious, nothing without telling him the whole story of her dad, and she wasn't about to do that. Typical, though. Just when you get yourself far enough away, back the past always creeps, tapping at your conscience with an insidious new line of enquiry.

That night, Sam drove past her as she was waiting nervously for a cab on the streets of this strange new town, and he kindly offered her a lift. At that point she was woozy from jet-lag and looking for nothing more than a way to get home, but after you ride that first wave of exhaustion you find you can stay up for ever, and his car was warm and smelled good, and when he mentioned that he was married she agreed to let him stop for a night cap at a bar called Tosca in North Beach, kind of a martini bar. God, the innocence of one short year before. There's nothing like growing up in a country where divorce is illegal for giving you belief in the absolute sanctity of marriage. Sam was married, that was that, and she was just lonely. And she bent his ear about her dad's drink problem and he seemed to get it. And he politely took her number (Evan's number), and she took his, and that, she thought, was that.

Except that wasn't that at all. The next phone call from home came on the morning after the Folsom Street Fair. The previous day, Evan had introduced her as his girlfriend, so she had slept in his bed because she thought it might be fun, but it wasn't, really. Moments after he left for work, the phone rang, and somehow she knew to answer it before Evan's room-mate. It was her mum.

— He'd murder me if he knew I was talking to you about it. He feels guilty about getting you involved, all the way over there.

After she hung up, Róisín sat in the cold room with the clinging smell of smoke and knew that right then her mother was sitting in the kitchen with a kettle howling behind her and magpies in the garden picking at food that wasn't rightfully theirs, and that home wasn't fine at all. Though it pained her to admit it, she knew that her call home on Wednesday as arranged would have precisely no effect on her dad and his drinking, nor the one on three successive Sundays. She had pretended to be asleep while Evan was climbing over her and then dressing that morning, but even if he was still here, she knew he didn't have the tools to deal with this. Men like Sam were much less hung-up about whatever complications their own personal lives presented than the guys around her. Courting Evan's opinion about a man in denial was quite ridiculous. That was the day she fished out the number and called Sam.

That's how they began. Once she got her own place, on Sundays they'd come back to Masonic from Tosca in North Beach, where they liked to meet, and the message light would be blinking accusingly, and sometimes she would erase the message without even listening. Of course, the big call from her dad himself had to come the very first time Sam stayed over after sex. He even answered the phone. It was about two o'clock in the morning, which would have made it 10 a.m. at home. Róisín's first thought when Sam handed her the receiver, half-asleep and shrugging, was that someone had died. She held it, inhaled and only then did she put it to her ear.

— Róisín, it's your father. Who was that?

— No one. A friend. He's sleeping on the couch. That's how he got the phone.

Don Byrne gathered the collection plates at Mass, and one Saturday afternoon when Róisín was about ten, he brought the plates home from church without being asked and she watched him remove the grubby felt lining from the bottom of each and every one – fabric that dampened the sound of the coins dropping in. And while other fathers were smashing golf balls across suburban pastures, Don was washing felt squares in a bowl of lukewarm water with Woolite, then hanging each one out to dry, because he didn't trust a tumble dryer not to shrink them. After, he glued them back onto the original plates and returned them to the church for Mass, and insisted that because the congregation could smell the clean fabric on each plate, the takings would be greater than at any 6 o'clock before. He held his two fingers together and showed them to his watchful daughter with a smile.

— Cleanliness and Godliness.

Her mum was the glue that held the family together. She would tell Róisín how dad and Annie were, and she would tell her mum to say hi to them. But this was her dad now, and she waited on the line. He cleared his throat.

— Okay. Sorry to wake you. I'm going away this week. To . . . hospital. I'll be gone for a month or six weeks. I'm telling you in case you are looking for me. All right?

She could hear the Angelus in the background and shivered.

— Umm.

— This is a family matter. I would ask that you don't mention it to anyone. I know you have a big group of Irish friends over there and I know how things get around. But I don't want people discussing my affairs when it's really none of their business. D'you get me?

— Are you feeling okay?

— All the very best for now. Here's your sister.

The phone was passed and taken, then covered with a hand. There was murmured speech and a raised voice, then the receiver was uncovered and Róisín could hear a door slam, a long pause, then Annie spoke.

— Congratulations, chicken shit. We've been calling you for weeks.

Behind her breath Róisín heard a car start, and crunching out of gravel on the driveway.

— I tried, Annie. It was your go.

— My 'go'? He went to Gavin Sharkey and they've put him on a course of lithium for a week. A decreasing dose. Then he'll go to a residential centre in Galway for a month.

— Things have been very busy here . . .

— Spare me. I found him asleep in the driveway behind the recycling bin. Nearly under the fucking thing, yeah? He told me he'd lost his key and was looking for it. But the man had twigs in his hair. And then the first time I drove him to Dr Sharkey's, he walked around the back and then straight into the Eagle House in Dundrum. Mum called at eight that night saying the staff there had called to ask someone to collect him, because he was making a disturbance.

— Annie.

— I'm not done. The next time we went to Sharkey's, I had to walk him into the waiting room and sit with him until the nurse had him by the arm. And apparently, when the doctor mentioned that he might be clinically depressed and that he should think about seeing a psychiatrist, Dad nearly punched him.

— Annie, I . . .

— You know I have two kids, right? You know I'm a little busy right now?

After she hung up, Sam asked her if she was okay, but it was cursory, and because of that, she found that she didn't want to tell him any more about her family life.

That Christmas in Dublin, the afternoons unfurled in front of Róisín, Ellen and Don like a threat. Don wouldn't stand for use of the word 'rehab', and since he got out of 'hospital', everyone was desperately hoping to assume that the drinking chapter was closed and that everything would now be okay. Róisín was pretty sure that her mother never went down to the shed to check for bottles. When you live with an actor it's impossible to know the truth and nobody wanted to push it by looking for confirmation. Sometimes it's better to cling to the possibility that everything's fine. They passed each other in the hallway with polite smiles, and when they ate they listened to each other chewing and had to remind themselves that they all ate the same way and probably made exactly the same noises. It was still jail.

Towards the end of her trip home, sitting behind the wheel of the car at a stop light, Róisín glanced over to her dad in the passenger seat, when she knew he wasn't looking. They were going out for lunch at her mum's insistence. His hands smoothed the same trouser leg, over and over.

— Let's go to Humphries.

— I don't want to go to Humphries, Dad.

The lights turned green.

— You don't like Humphries? You used to like Humphries.

— I don't wanna go to Humphries.

— Okay, so where are you taking me then? Birchall's?

Birchall's was the first job Róisín had as a fifteen-year-old waitress. She still blushed when she heard the name. And it was a pub, in this town of a hundred thousand pubs and churches.

— We're not going to a pub.

— They only happen to be pubs, love. I'm thinking about them as places to eat.

— We're still not going to a pub.

— Grand, so where are we going?

— We're going to get a sandwich and maybe some soup.

— Okay, great. Where?

He stared straight ahead and they drove in silence for

a while, down past O'Dwyers and The Mill House by the church, then The Wishing Well and Goggins by the church, then The Purty Loft, The Breffni, and The Punch Bowl by the fucking church. Where could you go?

It was clear from the way she was driving that she was floundering, and he seemed to let her stew in the uncertainty of it, and then he began rubbing his knee. She glanced over.

— You okay?

— A little arthritis. It's the wet. Makes it hard to walk much.

This was ridiculous. It wasn't supposed to be about the destination, or the sandwich or the dumb soup she didn't want. It was supposed to be about them spending some time together, talking it out. His problems, hers. At the next set of lights they looked out at the bay. A ferry boat crawling towards the shellybank, along a pencil line of horizon. They would now be driving until an idea landed. Then she remembered. Hotels! Dublin was sprouting one every other week.

She had never been to this new place in the foothills of the mountains, and when they pulled in, Don pointed to the entrance.

— You wouldn't drop me over there? The knee's a little tender.

She let him off and drove underground, took a ticket and parked in a bay beside a pillar. She took an elevator which opened onto a lobby and she looked about. Deep carpet, the joint of the day under heat lamps. Wilting veg-

etables and a queue of retired with wooden trays. This was all new. On the far side of the line, her dad smiled brightly and waved her over, holding a menu. He studied the specials board intently and she took off her scarf.

— I'm getting a Diet Coke. Do you want a Coke, or . . .

He kind of glanced towards the bar, maybe looking for inspiration, raking his gaze, then he snapped back to her with a bright smile, the first in a very long time. Something caught in her throat. God, it was a delight to see, that.

— A Coke'll slake the thirst nicely. Thank you, love.

At the bar, a young blonde waitress from Eastern Europe opened the bottles, poured the Cokes and gave her change. As she did, she looked beyond Róisín to her dad and nearly said something, but didn't. Róisín brought the drinks back and they clinked and drank.

— Cheers.

They sat in silence for a moment, then Róisín saw the waitress coming over with a saucer of change and a receipt held beneath. She reached the table and set it down near Don.

— Your change.

Róisín spoke first.

— You already gave me my change.

— No. His change.

She looked at the pile of coins, then her dad. Suggesting the bars and the contentedness with a hotel, then the exaggerated rubbing of the knee. The warm smile and wave when she had come in. Vodka vodka vodka vodka on the receipt. As he swept the evidence off the table and held it in his fist, Don Byrne was actually trembling, and hissed at the waitress,

— I told you to keep that fucking change. Didn't I?

He stuffed it in his pocket, receipt and all.

Of course it's being close that causes all the problems. All that's needed here is some distance, a frame through which to view it all. If we dolly back to the far side of the room, it's just a couple sitting at a table in a new hotel in Dublin, two people who drink Cokes for their thirst and look a lot alike. From that distance you cannot tell that the man has passed through middle age and is now broken, and you can't see the pinch of fear in the young woman's eyes. From over here he looks younger and she's almost happy. Time and distance do their work, and given enough of either it could be Evan and his daughter sitting over there.

'He's Got the Whole World in His Hands'. A nursery rhyme, a tune so bald that you could easily dismiss it as doggerel and go to work on the dial. But Nina Simone's voice is a magic trick; simple like a hammer, tapping at your heart and probing for weakness until it finds the sweet spot and with one final knock, shatters the damn thing to pieces. On the shuttle, the young Irish guys behind Róisín began to sing along, a swaying parody of boy scout trips.

— No way. 'Nob Hill!!!'

Róisín had to laugh at that and when they saw her

laughing and noticed that just before she had been crying, one of them put his hands on her shoulder with a compassionate smile and made her sing a line.

— 'He's got everybody here in his hands, he's got you and me brother, in his hands . . . '

When she did that, the Japanese guy beside her sang a line too, as a joke. Then everyone was singing as they climbed the block, and even the driver began to hum as he gunned the engine, and she didn't know whether he choreographed it or just got lucky, but they crested the hill right as the song climaxed. The song ended, the bus landed and began to spin downhill, heading for the water, and silence settled between the passengers. For the briefest of moments they had left the ground, finally unfettered by gravity.

The author would like to acknowledge the support of

the Arts Council of Ireland,

and the advice and insight of

Paul Baggaley, Kris Doyle,

Cormac Kinsella & Jonathan Conway.